Mountain Refuge

Mountain Mutineers
Book 1

Elise Gedicke

Harry L. Gedicke
RIP Grandpa

Trigger Warning

This book contains reference to child abuse, violence, kidnapping, human trafficking, torture, and sexual abuse. Please be aware. Your mental health matters.

Cover design by: Elise Gedicke
Editor: Sarah DeLong
ISBN: 979-8-3306-1064-8

Chapter One

Adam

I was doing the right thing. I knew that down to the marrow of my bones. That fact, however, didn't make my situation any less terrifying. The scars on my back twinged with phantom pain as I took another fleeting glance in my rear-view mirror. Tufts of blonde hair and the rise and fall of little chests in innocent sleep reaffirmed my mantra that I *was* doing the right thing.

Why did the right thing have to be so goddamn hard?

It had been a stroke of luck I'd made it this far. I thought for sure I'd been caught at the train station. Going out into public, even a place as crowded as the transportation station, had been risky, but it had also been my only choice if I wanted to survive.

I was not made for being on the run. The constant terror, the paranoia, the inability to sleep for fear the moment you close your eyes and let down your guard will be the exact moment it all goes to hell... I needed help, but my options were limited when the people hunting me had such vast resources. I'd wracked my brain; I couldn't go to anyone who they could easily track me to, like my parents, my sister, or friends.

But I did have one friend that no one knew about. A friend whom I had not contacted in eighteen years.

Even eight years ago, receiving a snail mail postcard had been interesting. Bills came by email and my required apartment mailbox was just a physical manifestation of a spam folder. Receiving a postcard on one of the last days before my move and the start of a new job had been unexpected.

I never would have guessed that postcard would one day save my life.

I grew up a farm boy who had dreams of the big city. My best friend had grown up with dreams of a life without abuse, hunger, and constant lies. When I'd been accepted into NYU, I'd begged Corbin to go with me. I'd never lied to him and I'd never abused him, but the city was no place for him. Corbin, even at eighteen, had been tall, already six-six, but he'd been skinny and malnourished. I'd always shared my lunch with him, but his body still needed more. Then, a few days before I left for college, he'd been arrested. He'd finally ended the abuse. The law, however, did not agree with his methods and he'd gone to prison for manslaughter.

His last words to me were, "Go live your life. I'll send you a postcard."

And he had. I don't know when he got out. I'd thought about him a lot in the beginning but then college and life had taken my attention away from my incarcerated best friend. I'd moved on, I'm ashamed to say. I got my degree in Early Childhood Education. I later furthered my degree by receiving my masters with the help of my employer who funded my advancement.

I shuddered, though unsure if that had to do with my once naiveté or the bitter cold howling outside my borrowed car. I needed to call it *borrowed* because, until twelve days ago, I'd never broken the law before. I didn't need to add *auto-theft* to my resume.

Corbin's postcard had been nothing more than a phone number on one side and the picture of the ocean on the other. It had taken me two false tries before I realized that that phone number was in code. Our code, from when we were kids trying to hide messages and confessions from teachers, adults, and nosy kids. The code for the numbers was easier to remember because we'd been six when we'd created it, so the digits had been moved up only one number. Zero was one, one was two, two was three... My adult brain had not thought about the code in almost eighteen years, having long seen numbers for their actual value.

At the time of my move eight years ago, I'd been busy packing, organizing, and planning. The postcard had made its way into one of my favorite books, *A Tale of Two Cities*, where it was then forgotten until twelve days ago. Though I'd packed in such a rush that I hadn't brought any personal belongings, I'd grabbed the postcard. I had never called the number on it before ten days ago.

I remembered that first phone call perfectly:

It wasn't Corbin who answered when I called. It was a man named Jack with a business greeting of "Jack's. How can I help you?" I froze, unsure of what to say to that and fearful that I'd gotten the number wrong again. The written number had been for a Chinese restaurant in Lansing, Michigan. Had I messed up the code again?

But a small sob from behind me broke through my worries and I rushed to speak before being hung up on. "Corbin. I need to speak with Corbin."

There was a tense pause, and then the gruff voice said the one thing I never expected: my name. "Adam?"

I knew for a fact that I wasn't speaking to Corbin. Even if he'd changed his name, I'd know his voice. It had been eighteen years later, but I'd know it. The man on the other end of the line was not Corbin, which begged the question of how he knew my name.

And then the call got even weirder.

"Are you in trouble?" My silence must have been answer enough because his next question was, "Are you safe?"

That answer I knew. The smelly, cheap motel a mere two hundred miles outside the city was not safe. "No."

There was some rustling on the other end of the line and a weird mechanical click. "You're not in the city. What do you have on you that's yours? You're on a burner, which is good. I applaud you for not using the landline. I'm assuming you're stopped somewhere but, if you've been there longer than a day, I need you to pack up and leave. Right now."

Fear coursed through my veins. I'd been at the motel for almost two days. We were almost out of supplies, but I'd been terrified to leave the enclosed space. "Who are you?"

"A friend. Adam, I promise you, I'm a friend. Corbin bought the postcard from my store. He knew you'd call one day. Probably had hoped it wouldn't take this long, but at least you called."

A hiccup nearly broke through my lips. It wasn't manly; it was pitiful. But I was at my wits' end. I hadn't slept in over two days. Adrenaline and fear were keeping me awake. I was to the point where I was willing to accept help from anyone. "We need help."

It was the use of we that had prompted the next question. "Adult or child?"

My heart broke a little at my next answer. "Children."

There was a pause, some more rustling, and what I assumed had been typing. "Adam, do you have with you who I think you do? Because if so, we need to move fast. You're too close to the city. Far too close."

A tear escaped me. I'd never been a man's man, unafraid to show my emotions. I know what lies and the need to be macho got you. I'd never seen those men as men. I saw them as cowards. I was five-eleven, lean with only a few muscles. I was built for running, not fighting. Ironic, given my current situation. But what I wasn't was a coward. I'd done what I'd been dreaming of doing for the past three years. I'd done what I'd thought had been impossible.

But I wasn't safe yet. We weren't.

All I was able to get out was, "Yes".

A sigh came across the line, but it wasn't one of defeat. More like a silent expletive. "Get going. Head south."

Despite the order coming from a stranger, I jumped into action. I didn't know if I could trust him or who he was or how he knew Corbin, but he was correct. I'd been there too long. No one would be coming to save me, so I had to save myself.

"Toss anything of yours. ID, phone, tablet, anything that can be tracked. Cash only." I'd known that part because I'd seen enough dramas on TV to know it was a common 'on-the-run' mistake. I hadn't faulted him for reaffirming the need for anonymity. "This burner is only good for another day or so. Turn it off, take out the battery and SIM card. I doubt you have a Faraday bag with you so that's the next best thing. Even off, phones can be traced if you know what you're doing but not if you take out the SIM card and battery."

I got the feeling Jack was one of those people who knew what he was doing in unorthodox situations.

"Now this next part is very important. I know it might unnerve you, but you need to do it. At the next gas station, I need you to do something you're not going to like. Find a car that's parked in the dark, no lights, no cameras. Swap the license plates with yours. We'll ditch your car later. Did you hear what I said? Don't just take their plates. Swap them.

People rarely look at their own plates, but they'll notice if it's missing.

"Head south. Stop if you need to sleep. But keep going. Call me back in a few hours. I need to work on getting you new transportation, cash, and figure out the safest way to get you here."

"Here?" I picked up the two small bodies of the people I loved most in this world. They were my life, my reason for existing. I knew it as soon as I'd laid eyes on them at their births. I'd been put on this Earth to love, protect, and cherish these two small angels.

"Montana, Adam. I'm bringing you to Montana."

Several hours after that first phone call, I'd called Jack back. I couldn't go any further. It was too dangerous for me to keep driving. I was beyond exhausted. Every cop car I passed nearly gave me a heart attack. I was seeing shadows and monsters behind every turn.

But it hadn't been Jack who'd answered: it had been Corbin. I felt like I could finally take a breath. I'd been right to trust Jack. He hadn't been leading me into a trap. It had been eighteen years since I'd talked to my best friend, but there was no doubt in my mind that he still held that title.

Corbin gave me instructions to a train station in Pennsylvania. Not because we were catching a train but because of the crowds and pay-per-open lockers they offered. Jack had arranged—somehow that I was too tired to contemplate on but was sure my curious mind would later ask about—for a car to be dropped off at the train station. I was to ditch my car with its stolen license plate in the long-term parking lot.

Walking into that train station with a small hand in mine and a small body cradled against my chest had been terrifying. My paranoia was convinced that everyone was staring at us, that they *knew*, and someone was about to call the cops. The worst had been when two security officers had stopped me, but it was just to inform me that I'd dropped a baby sock. I'd shakily thanked them and continued on.

In the locker had been a backpack and a duffel bag. Between the two, there had been cash, car keys, burner phones, water bottles, protein bars, baby supplies, a *Barbie* doll, and changes of clothes for an infant, child, and adult.

Staring at the goods, I felt like I'd won the lottery.

Then I found myself driving west. Despite not getting much sleep, I'd felt renewed. I wasn't alone. I had people who were helping me. Corbin certainly hadn't been in Pennsylvania to leave those items in the locker. Someone else had to have been helping him help me.

The car that had been left for me had been an older looking *Ford* with car seats already strapped in the back. Its trunk was covered in bumper stickers. I wondered if that was so people would pay attention to the stickers and not the car or its occupants. After the instructions about swapping license plates, I had to wonder who was helping me. There were definitely some psychological tricks being used. My tired brain had pondered the notion of a group of renegade spies to a militia that did not follow any government rule. I may never know.

It had taken ten days. Ten long days of endless driving to throw off anyone on my trail. I'd found a bag of license plates in the trunk, which was terrifying in and of itself. Who were these people? Besides Jack and Corbin, I hadn't talked to anyone else. Every day I was to use a different burner to check in with them; they did not want the same SIM card to be traced in different areas. After that first day, it was always Jack who answered but he talked as if Corbin was just in the next room.

Once, Jack had made the off-handed comment that Corbin was "getting your rooms ready."

The minute I'd driven across the Montana state line, I'd breathed a sigh of relief. As if the state itself was a sanctuary that couldn't be breached. That feeling was foolish, but I'd needed it in that moment. A sense of safety.

My instructions were to head into Bozeman. I knew of the city, but I'd never been there. Born and raised in New Jersey and moving into New York City at eighteen, I'd never been out of the Tri-State area before ten days ago. I wondered briefly how Corbin had ended up in Montana, but my feelings of gratitude overpowered my curiosity. Once we were safe, I'd ask. I'd learn everything I'd missed in the last eighteen years.

After a much needed day of solid sleeping.

Once in Bozeman, I swapped cars again. This time for an all-terrain vehicle with high tires and four-wheel drive. Once again, car seats were included, so I didn't have to waste time getting them swapped over. We stopped at a diner to eat and stretch our legs. I felt so bad for the kids, being cooped up in the car for days on end. But I knew it was better for them to be upset now and on our way to safety than to dawdle.

Lydia had been amazing. She entertained her brother as best she could. She slept when he did and talked to me when I needed conversation to stay awake. She hadn't complained once. I wasn't sure how much her seven-year-old brain understood what had almost happened. She was not a stupid child. She'd heard and seen things no child or adult should, but seeing and understanding were two different things. I needed to have a long conversation with her once we got to wherever Corbin was sending us.

After we left the diner in our next vehicle, I made an impulsive decision. It was winter with snow on the ground. The kids needed fresh air, even if that air was a bit chilly. We stopped at a park. It had only been for an hour, but it had given Lydia a chance to run around, kick snow in every which direction, and to laugh. I hadn't heard her laugh in a very long time. It warmed my heart to hear it. She needed more of *this*, more time to be a kid. She needed freedom and safety.

I prayed that was where I was bringing us. I trusted Corbin, but I was putting a lot on faith. I hoped my credit didn't run out. A part of me knew we'd never be safe, not completely, but there was *safer* than our current circumstances.

Unfortunately, that stop had distracted me and cost us dearly in a way I wouldn't know until much later.

We drove out of Bozeman, past snow-covered fields, over bridges with frozen rivers, and higher into the mountains. There was a quaint little town called Whitefish that we drove through. I'd done a double take when I'd seen a sign over a corner shop that said *Jack's General Store*. Could it be a coincidence or was that our Jack? There were a lot of snowmobiles mixed with vehicles similar to the one I was driving parked on the sides of the street. The kids were worn out from our trip to the park, and I was grateful.

Corbin's instructions had been to follow the directions to the ski lodge. When I came to a fork on the mountain road where it said *Whitefish Ski Lodge* with an arrow pointing left, I was to turn right onto an unlit, unmarked road.

Which was how I ended up paused at this intersection, wondering if this was my literal and metaphorical crossroads.

I *was* doing the right thing. I had to be.

I'd come so far, done so much to get here, but turning right seemed daunting. There was a clear difference in the roads. The road to the left that led to the ski lodge was recently plowed. The snow currently coming down left a light dusting on the asphalt. The road to the right hadn't been plowed. At all. There were faint tire tracks that helped lead the way. With the setting sun, it was definitely the more eerie of the two paths.

But what choice did I have? I couldn't bring the kids to a ski lodge. I glanced behind me, down the mountain road. We'd arrived later than I had expected to. I could turn back, but to where? Maybe there was an inn in town that we could check into for the night? I hesitated at that thought. I didn't want to show our faces in town if this was where we were permanently going to be hiding out.

I looked to the right and prayed Corbin knew what he was doing. What could possibly be up the mountain that could help me and my kids? And yet, it was that thought that made my decision for us. Who would ever think to look for me, a city boy, up a Montana mountain?

I turned right.

Chapter Two

Adam

The vehicle handled the snow well. I'd grown up in northern New Jersey and lived my entire adult life in New York City. I knew how to handle a vehicle in snow, but, the higher we got, the thicker it became and, the darker it got, the worse my visibility became.

My fears slowly began to creep in again.

I was doing the right thing. Wasn't I? God, I hoped so.

The road became too hard to see, the tire tracks I'd been following were long covered. I was driving barely ten miles per hour. Enough to continue upwards and slow enough to hopefully see whatever was directly in front of me.

But after a near miss with a tree, I had to stop. I had no choice. This was no longer just snowing. This was a blizzard. And we were stuck. I couldn't risk taking the car any further without knowing where I was going. Jack had said to just keep driving and Corbin would find me.

What an idiot I was to listen. I looked out of the car into the white abyss and doubted all my life choices.

After putting the car in Park and activating the parking brake, I turned on one of the burner phones. It powered on but there was no signal. My head hit the headrest in frustration. Of course, there was no signal, because that was just my luck. So I could say I had tried all my options, I turned on the remainder of my burners to verify they did not have signal either.

I twisted in my seat to stare at the two joys in my life. I was terrified for them. I knew what would happen to me if I was caught. I knew what it had meant when I'd run with them. But these two innocents were everything to me. How could I live with myself, how could I call myself a man, a father, if I'd just stood there and done nothing? If I hadn't run, Lydia's fate would have been sealed.

Running then had been impulsive, but there'd been no time to follow our plan. There'd been no packing, no preparing. There'd been gunshots then grab, run, and go. Whatever had been previously packed in the diaper bag had been it. I'd grabbed a change of clothes for Lydia and myself, and the post-card. We'd jumped in my car, already fitted with car seats, thank God, and we'd gone. I hoped the ensuing chaos that had covered our escape would give us enough of a head start to avoid being followed. I'd dumped my wallet—minus the measly amount of cash I'd had on me—and my phone in a dumpster within the city. After a quick stop at a pharmacy to pick up my first burner phone and a coloring book for Lydia, we'd left.

The wind howled outside. It reminded me of wolves. I knew we were safe in the car. Animals wouldn't be out in this weather either. They were clearly smarter than I was, blindly following instructions from a man I hadn't seen or heard from in eighteen years. I could chastise myself all day, or night, long but that wouldn't save us. We were warm for now with the car running. We had protein bars, baby formula, and water. The kids were bundled up after our trip to the park. We'd be okay for a little while.

But once we ran out of gas, there'd be no more heat.

Without gas, we also couldn't move once the storm cleared. And who knew if the car would even be able to move once the storm cleared. Snow was coming down fast and hard. We'd soon be buried in it. Even if the snow stopped, I had no idea where we were or where to go from here. Corbin's instruction to keep going and he'd find us seemed so silly now. Why hadn't I asked for more information? Why hadn't I demanded he meet us in the town? Why hadn't I stopped at *Jack's General Store* and discovered if that Jack had been the Jack helping us?

Three hours later, the kids slept blissfully unaware that we were almost out of gas. My body shivered as if anticipating the cold we were about to face.

I crawled over the center console. Henry was sleeping the sleep of the exhausted infant. I prayed he kept sleeping. I prayed we weren't going to die here, buried in the snow and never found. I prayed I hadn't saved my kids only to lead them to a frozen death.

God hadn't been a part of my life since I'd left home. My very Catholic mother was only able to get me to Mass on the holidays, but I only went for her comfort, not for mine. Yet, I prayed. I was a good man, a good person. I loved my kids more than life itself. I needed to save them. I needed to be strong for them.

I watched like a condemned man as the gas gauge slowly crept past the E. I took Lydia, waking her slightly, and brought her to my lap. The kids would need my body heat. Henry's coat was on the floor. I grabbed it and laid it over his sleeping form.

Then I sat back and waited for the inevitable.

The pounding on the window scared me so badly that I jumped, waking Lydia completely. My heart thudded louder than a drum. We were in the middle of nowhere on a mountain in the middle of a blizzard. Had someone really just pounded on the window or had I imagined it? What if it had been a branch and a tree was about to fall on us?

The pounding happened again. This time, I saw movement outside my driver's frosted window. Lydia, quiet as a mouse, moved off my lap and back into her booster seat. I could see the caution and fear in her eyes. I squeezed her hand reassuringly.

Carefully, I moved myself back up to the driver's door. I knew opening the door would let out the heated air and let the cold in, but what choice did I have? What if the pounding was Corbin and he'd found us as promised?

I felt bad for doubting my best friend.

Making sure Lydia was as covered as possible, I opened my car door. It took some effort, as it was mostly frozen closed. I had to put all my weight into it to get it to budge. I could tell the person on the other side was pulling as well.

The frigid air wracked me. Despite my gloves, hat, and coat, I was beyond cold stepping out of the warmth of the car.

I could barely see. The wind, snow, and darkness prevented me from seeing more than a few feet in front of me. I closed the door so the kids were protected. We were almost out of gas. They didn't have that much heat left.

A figure stood in front of me, bundled up so completely that I couldn't make out a face or features. However, I knew he wasn't Corbin. Corbin was over six and a half feet tall. Unless he'd shrunk in prison, this guy wasn't him. The person in front of me was slightly taller than I was, but that might have been because he was in proper snow gear and I was hunched over against the winter storm. I cupped my gloved hands around my eyes to protect my face and to help me see better, but it didn't do much.

I didn't know who this person was but they were out in this blizzard too and it was obvious though that they were prepared far better than I was.

"Help us!" I pleaded, my voice a shout to be heard over the raging storm. My nose and ears hurt so badly that I feared frostbite, even though I'd only been standing out here a minute.

The man looked around me and into the car. His pounding on the window had knocked some snow loose and he could see inside a small gap. I didn't know if he could see Henry, but Lydia's blonde hair was very distinctive. The light was still on inside the car from when I'd opened the door.

The man stepped back. He took a backpack off his shoulders that I hadn't realized had been there. He pulled out what looked like a large rectangle of aluminum foil, but I knew better. It was a Mylar blanket for keeping in body heat. He handed it to me; I quickly donned it. It was big enough that I could carry the kids and still close it around us.

I feared for a moment that the man was just giving us the blanket and then leaving. But he'd been walking to a snowmobile I hadn't seen or heard. Thank God. We were getting out of here. I didn't know if the man was with mountain rescue, the police, or just a passerby, but in that moment I didn't care. I didn't know if the kids' door was frozen shut, but I knew mine worked. I quickly climbed back inside to get them ready.

Lydia said nothing as I climbed over the seats, the foil blanket crinkling as I went. She was already working on getting Henry out of his seat. I knew we couldn't take all of our stuff with us. The cash had come in a backpack, though, and I quickly transferred as much of Henry's baby supplies into it as I could fit. His needs were more important than mine or Lydia's at this moment. Feeling guilty about that thought, I threw Lydia's new *Barbie* into the bag too.

Once I saw she was bundled up, I instructed Lydia to climb into the passenger seat. She did without question. I leaned over and kissed her forehead. She was my good girl. I was so proud of her, I hardly had the words.

Henry woke as I picked him up. Unfortunately, his crying and needs would have to wait. I couldn't change or feed him right then. After I got his coat, hat, and boots on him, I handed him to Lydia. As I climbed into the driver's seat, I was careful I didn't hit them with the overstuffed backpack.

I opened the door and, by some miracle, the man was still there. He had brought the snowmobile closer to the car and was waiting by the driver's door. I stepped back out into the glacial winds. I wasn't even sure if it was still snowing at this point. The wind made it impossible to tell.

As soon as I was standing, I reached in and grabbed Henry from Lydia. I felt awful for ignoring his tears, but survival was more important than his current discomfort. I brought him out into the cold but, before I could cover him under the Mylar blanket, our rescuer took him from my hands. For a fleeting moment, I panicked. I couldn't let a stranger take him.

But then I saw what I'd previously missed. The man had unbundled his jacket. He had many layers on. He took a squirming and crying Henry and placed him against his chest. Then he zipped my son up inside his jacket. I feared Henry wouldn't be able to breathe under the heavy coat, but despite the layers I could still hear his cries. That brought me comfort.

Henry was protected.

Now I had to get Lydia. She handed me the backpack. Her eyes were resigned and held depths no seven-year-old should have. She understood this was a life-or-death situation and she was doing all she could to help me. My little angel.

I drew the Mylar blanket as close to my back as I could and put the backpack on. I hoped it would help keep the blanket more secure for the ride we were about to take.

I picked up my little girl. She clung to me of her own accord, allowing me to keep my hands free and draw the blanket around her completely.

"Is this everyone?" The muffled voice came from beside me. He had some sort of thick ski mask over his face and across his mouth. Over his eyes were snow goggles.

I nodded, not sure I could speak.

The man went to the snowmobile and straddled it. He indicated behind him. I had a hard time walking but was able to make my way over to the vehicle with Lydia. I was so cold, despite Lydia's heat and the blanket, but I needed to be strong for my kids. I needed them to survive.

I climbed onto the back of the vehicle.

"Get closer," I was instructed. It was so hard to hear him. I knew as soon as we started moving, I wouldn't be able to take any directions. "Squeeze her between us. Hold onto me as tight as you can."

"Th-th-the ba-baby?" I struggled to ask. I couldn't hear his cries anymore and still feared suffocation.

"He's fine!" was the answer I received.

Lydia curled her legs up between us and tucked her head under my chin. I brought myself as close to the man as I could with her protected. He had her back while I had her front. I took a second to tighten the blanket around her. Then I brought my arms around the man.

I didn't know how to tell him I was ready, so I tapped his torso where my right hand had landed. He must have felt it or just sensed we were as ready as we were going to get, because we suddenly lurched forward.

The wind was brutal as we started out. I could barely breathe with it blowing so hard into my face. I had to duck my head down into the man's back to protect myself. While I couldn't see where we were going, I hoped my tighter huddle protected Lydia more.

I lost track of time. I was concentrating so hard on making sure Lydia was protected from the harsh weather and that my grip on the man's coat was secure that I wasn't paying attention to how long we were driving. Eventually, though, we stopped.

I was slow to lift my head. My muscles were so tight and cold that it hurt to move. Light drew my attention, and I finally looked to my left to see a snow-covered cabin in the middle of a small clearing. We were surrounded by trees otherwise.

As I got myself off the snowmobile, I nearly fell. Lydia was still in my arms so I was grateful I didn't. The man shut off the engine and climbed off more gracefully than I had. He grabbed my arm and led me to the cabin. It had three steps for us to climb before leading us onto a small, covered porch. I was so grateful for shelter that I wasn't paying attention to the size or material of the cabin. However, the light that had caught my attention was coming from one of the frosted windows by the door. I didn't know how in the middle of nowhere there was electricity, but I was very grateful. Electricity hopefully meant heat.

I knew we were still on the mountain. I couldn't see during our drive here, but I knew we hadn't gone downhill. I wasn't sure if we had gone up either. At this moment though, I didn't care where we were on the mountain as long as my kids were safe and warm. I would figure out where we were and how to find Corbin later.

The man opened the front door and led us inside. Heat engulfed us. It felt so good, but also hurt as my body started to thaw. Frostbite was still a concern. I prayed my babies had been protected enough to prevent the cold from affecting them.

I couldn't get my arms to move. Thankfully, Lydia caught on to my predicament. She lowered her feet to the floor.

The man was unbundling his jacket, and I almost cried at the sight of Henry. My baby probably hadn't even noticed the cold. Lydia stepped forward and took Henry into her arms. We were dropping snow and melting ice all over the hardwood floor.

From the way the man let his outer coat fall to the floor, I guessed he didn't care. He continued to unbundle. I saw a flash of blonde hair but didn't pay attention to it.

As the cabin's warmth worked its magic, I was finally able to move my arms. Anxiety and the heat were making me very sleepy. I feared my eyes wouldn't open again with each blink. Gravity helped me drop the frozen backpack to the floor. The Mylar blanket went next.

The crackle of a fire drew my attention to a quaint living room. There was a single couch next to a large La-Z-Boy type chair. A square wooden table stood between them. A matching rectangular one sat in front of them on the only rug I could see. The stone fireplace was huge. My sleep deprived brain wondered if it was the fireplace or electric heat that warmed us. The winds howled behind me, once again reminding me of a pack of wolves.

My vision hazy, I barely saw the man lead Lydia, who was holding Henry, into a kitchen. I could hear the rattle of pots and pans, followed by the clicking of a gas lit stove. I wasn't sure what they were doing and needed to get myself unbundled to follow them.

I heard Henry's cries once more. It was time to feed him. His baby food and formula were in the backpack at my feet. I somehow got my gloves off and with shaking fingers got my jacket unzipped. Even as a New Yorker, I was not prepared for the weather raging outside.

I worked on getting my boots off too. I must've been more out of it than I realized because the outerwear from the man and Lydia were no longer on the floor. There was a coat rack to my left. I almost fell over as I slowly bent to pick my coat up. Thankfully, I was standing close enough to the front door to put a hand out and steady myself. After hanging it, I placed my boots next to the man's and Lydia's by the door.

Somehow I got my legs working enough to carry me into the kitchen. The man's back was to me as he stirred something on the stove top. I could make out blonde hair and a slim body, but locating my children was my priority. Lydia and Henry were sitting at a wooden kitchen table with matching chairs. There was a steaming cup of something in front of Lydia.

I think Lydia was speaking, but everything was muffled as if I had cotton balls stuffed in my ears.

I didn't realize I had been supporting my weight on the doorframe until my head clunked down against it. I was so tired, but we were in a stranger's house. We were protected by the storm, but I feared we'd only traded one dangerous situation for another. I couldn't sleep until I knew my kids were safe here.

A face appeared in front of my line of vision. Beautiful, vibrant blue eyes surrounded by dark lashes. Long blonde hair tied back in a braid. Full, red lips moved as if speaking but I couldn't hear what they were saying.

My eyes blinked and felt weighted as I tried to keep them open. Something hit my knees but I wasn't sure what.

Blackness crept into my vision, but I kept seeing that face. That beautiful, feminine face. I wondered who she was and why I was seeing her.

A sudden shriek of "Daddy!" finally reached my ears and then Lydia's face was also in my line of vision. Her little face, concerned and streaming tears, was right next to the woman's. The woman said something to Lydia, who stepped back.

It was then that I realized the shirt the woman was wearing. It was the same long sleeve tan shirt the man had been wearing as he stirred the pot at the stovetop.

Despite falling into unconsciousness, despite my fear for my children, despite the millions of worries I had, one realization hit me hard: our rescuer wasn't a man.

Our rescuer was a woman.

Chapter Three

Brooke

I caught the man before he hit the floor. Unfortunately, I wasn't in the right position to keep myself balanced and ended up on my butt with him sprawled across my legs. The girl—his daughter I cleverly deduced since she was calling him "Daddy"—kept a tight hold on the wailing baby in her arms while crying herself. She sobbed out constant questions about her dad, asking if he was okay and why he wouldn't wake up.

I looked at the girl from my position on the floor and felt out of my depth. I wasn't the gentlest of people, nor was I tactful. I gave those traits up a long time ago.

But I wasn't so heartless that I wanted to scare a kid. She was obviously already terrified. Based on her clothing, she was well taken care of. Maybe a little skinny for her age, but that might just be a growth spurt. The baby, on the other hand, was pissed. When I'd put him under my coat out in the woods, it had been the first time in years that I'd held an infant. I wasn't sure if it had felt good or bad, considering the dire circumstances I'd found the small family in.

I was shocked when I'd been driving home from Tommy's to see a red glow between the multitude of snowflakes. At first, I considered it was a reflection of a knocked down trespassing sign but soon threw that theory out the window. It had definitely been taillights, and they were off the main road. In fact, about thirty more feet and they would have collided with a tree. I didn't need to see through the snow to know that either—I knew these woods better than I knew myself.

With the car running, I'd assumed correctly that there were occupants inside. I just hadn't expected there to be kids. I'd assumed the car belonged to a tourist couple who got lost on their way back from the lodge or even trespassers who specifically wanted to journey further up the mountain for their own selfish reasons and got caught in the storm.

To my knowledge, Jack didn't have any special visitors on the mountain, so my suspicions hadn't been raised at the sight of the strange vehicle. We were always on high alert whenever there was a guest on our mountain.

Seeing that little girl in the backseat when I'd peeked through the window had been shocking. The dad, though... He had looked, well, *haggard*. He was clearly exhausted and worried for his children. Rightfully so, too, because this storm wasn't letting up any time soon.

That's why I'd been out there. I knew from past winter experience that a storm like this was only going to get worse. I wanted to make sure Tommy had enough supplies to last him the next few days.

We all looked out for Tommy. He looked like the creepy in-law no one wanted at the holiday party but was always invited out of family obligation. In reality, though, he was just a rundown old man who deserved peace and mountain air. He was cranky, but not malicious. I knew he was a veteran but no details beyond that. In his own way, he looked out for each of us up on the mountain. I probably wouldn't have survived my first winter without him.

When Tommy had broken his hip last summer, his fellow mountain dwellers and I took turns looking in on him. My property is the closest, so I check on him more than the others. Tommy probably wouldn't call me a neighbor or even a friend. In fact, he calls me a "nosy little girl" most of the time.

But I see the appreciation in his bright green eyes whenever I drop off extra food I'd canned, cured meats, and especially a pie if the berries were in season. Others did the occasional housework and maintenance for him or stocked his wood pile. Tommy would sit in his rocking chair on his porch with a shotgun in his hand, yelling for us to get off his land. But he was all talk, no bite—at least when it came to us. I had never feared for my life when visiting Tommy. In fact, I kind of thought of him like the grumpy grandfather I'd never had.

My snowmobile was still out, as was my emergency supply backpack I'd put in one of the saddlebags so I could carry passengers behind me. I needed to get them put away before they were completely buried. But first, I had to take care of my unexpected houseguests.

A snort escaped me. Hadn't thought I'd be hosting guests again so soon—and certainly not in the middle of a Montana winter storm.

It was difficult to get myself out from under the man's dead weight. He wasn't overweight or very muscular, but a hundred and eighty pounds was still a hundred and eighty pounds. I wasn't exactly built like a linebacker either.

From the quick glances I'd taken of him once he'd started unbundling his jacket and winter gear, the man was about my height, maybe two or three inches taller than my five-seven frame. It was hard to judge with how hunched over he'd been from the cold. He had sandy brown hair that either was growing out oddly or was in desperate need of a trim. His full beard looked just as unkempt as his tousled brown locks. I hadn't gotten a look at his eyes, but I imagined green or maybe brown. His daughter was a blonde with blue eyes, like me. I wondered briefly if she'd gotten that from her mother —as well as where that woman was and why she hadn't been in the car with them. Was she waiting for them back at the resort hotel?

Unfortunately, with this storm, I was not going to get answers to my questions until the man regained consciousness. No SOS message would make it through these winds and ice.

I laid the man gently on my wooden floor, stood, and turned to the crying children. I was not used to noise in my cabin, so this was going to take some patience I wasn't sure I possessed anymore. I wasn't what one would call a people-person. At least, not anymore.

I leaned forward to rest my hands on my knees. I hoped in lowering myself to the girl's eye level, it would make me seem more trustworthy. That was a thing parents did, right?

Doubt crept in but I hoped I kept it out of my voice. "So, um, your dad's fine." I hadn't really had a chance to look at the man; I was mainly trying to reassure the girl. Really hoped I wasn't lying. "I think he just fell asleep."

The girl clutched her brother closer to her. He looked big in her arms. I couldn't guess how old he was, but she was probably six or seven. Her crying paused, and she let out a small sob. "Are we safe here?"

I blinked. Though no longer on the force, my cop instincts rose at the odd question. From one perspective, it probably wasn't *that* odd a query, considering the conditions I'd found the family in. They had not been *safe* in that car in this storm. From another perspective, the one that knew the sort of people who seek refuge on my mountain, it was a necessary question.

Coming from a little girl though? I wasn't sure. The boat could tip in either direction given their circumstances.

Still, there was only one answer I could give and keep the

girl calm. I nodded, "Yes. I've lived many winters up here. We've got heat, food, and shelter. You're very safe." The girl didn't seem as reassured as I'd hoped by my answer. Maybe she wasn't a native to this area and this was her first time seeing snow. "So, um, are you hungry?"

She continued to stare at me for a minute, as if she was assessing me. It was kind of unnerving, coming from a girl so young. I briefly worried over what conclusions she came to about me. Finally, she loosened her hold on the baby a little. It was then that I realized how she was angling her body. Her feet and head were facing me but her upper body where she held the baby to her was turned away from me. As if she was putting her body between the baby and a threat. Seeing as I was the only other living soul around for miles, I could only conclude that perceived threat was me.

That also gave me pause. What six-year-old was ready to defend a baby in such a way? Why was it even an instinct to do so?

I glanced down at the dad. Did he hit the kids? I hadn't gotten that vibe from him. In fact, his reaction from when I took the baby from his arms at the car had given me an overprotective feeling about him. The girl's reaction to her dad's fainting was also one of concern and love. While I didn't tend to trust my instincts when it came to people anymore, I felt confident believing he wasn't an abusive father.

So who was the threat that the girl was used to protecting her brother from? At least, I assumed he was her brother. I couldn't see the baby's face to judge their features for similarities. Bottom line, it didn't matter.

I didn't want to step any closer to the girl—she was already on edge—so I squatted down in front of her. "You're safe, sweetie. My name's Brooke."

She looked a little more relaxed at that and even started to soothe the baby by rocking him. "I'm Lydia."

I nodded my appreciation of her offering me her name with a smile. "Nice to meet you, Lydia. That's a very pretty name." I glanced over my shoulder towards the front door. The dad had brought a backpack with him from their car. "Do you think there's supplies in that bag for your brother?"

She didn't correct the title, so I assumed I'd guessed right. With a nod, she said, "Daddy always makes sure he has diapers and food for Henry."

"Think you could go get it while I try to get your dad settled somewhere more comfortable?" I also wanted to look the man over for injuries but didn't want to tell the girl that for fear it would upset her again. If I found something, considering the condition and whether I had the supplies to treat it, I would figure out then what to tell her. "I'll heat up a bottle if he needs it and get us some food when I get back." I'd been reheating soup on the stovetop when the man had first entered the kitchen, but I'd moved it off the burner and to the side when I'd noticed him starting to sag. Good thing too, or that'd be one more mess I'd have to deal with.

And to think, I'd been anticipating curling up by the fire and reading tonight while waiting out the storm. Silly me for not having seen this coming.

Assignment given, the girl leapt into action. With her attention preoccupied, I did a quick assessment of the father to make sure there were no obvious broken bones or open wounds that would prevent me from moving him. Thankfully, I found none. Deciding the couch was closer, plus nearer to the fireplace, I rounded his shoulders, hooked my arms under his pits, and started to drag him.

Geez, the guy was heavier than he looked. While I was not anti-feminist in any way, nor did I hate my gender or have any designs on switching genders, there were times when the reality of my situation was that my life would be easier if I was built like a man. Despite this being my ninth year living up on my beloved mountain, I was not buff. I worked but didn't work out. My upper body strength just wasn't what it would be if I was a man living this lifestyle. Most of the others on the mountain, all others being men by the way, were huge. The work and lifestyle of living a mountain life was not easy. While it kept me fit, I still had a bit of flab that just wouldn't go away. The men, on the other hand, didn't have a single ounce of fat between them. Lucky bastards.

So while I had the strength to get the unconscious man across my living room's wooden floor and eventually was able to boost him up onto the couch, it certainly would have been easier if I had the strength and height to just lift him and place him on the couch.

Satisfied with the man's position on the couch, I took a deep breath and congratulated myself on a job well done. He hadn't awoken screaming in pain as I maneuvered his body around, so I was leaning towards exhaustion as his reason for collapsing and not injury. To complete my self-pat on the back, I mentally say the mantra I often use while doing mountain work: *a penis was not required to complete this task.*

I chuckled silently to myself.

Even though he hadn't made a sound while I moved him, I knew I needed to give him a more thorough check for injuries.

I glanced towards the kitchen. My open floor plan meant I could see clearly into the kitchen from the living room without having to strain my neck or move. Since I didn't have a high-chair, the girl had the baby sitting in her lap at the table. She was spoon feeding him from a small jar. I didn't have baby sized spoons so I'm assuming she was using one that they had had in their backpack.

I didn't have baby clothes or toys either so I really hoped that bag was a Mary Poppins style where it was bigger than it looked.

I looked down at my patient. He really did look exhausted. There were dark circles under his eyes. His forehead, cheeks, and nose were red with windburn. He looked gaunt, like he had lost weight quickly and not in a healthy way. I had him lying on his back with a pillow under his head. Thankfully, his boots were already off. He had a long sleeve fleece shirt on with jeans.

That last bit caught and held my attention as I realized for the first time that they weren't dark colored pants but soaked through blue jeans. Shit. In this weather, jeans were not the appropriate attire. The Mylar blanket would not keep his internal body temperature from dropping if his jeans were frozen and soaked through.

I needed to get those jeans off of him. As far as I could tell, his shirt was dry. Really hoped the guy was wearing underwear or I was about to get any eyeful.

The baby suddenly made a giggling sound, breaking my train of thought. Shit, the kids. I didn't know what type of family they were, if the dad was comfortable with his young daughter seeing him half-naked. As the only conscious adult in the room, I made the decision because I was not comfortable with it.

I grabbed a thick blanket off the back of my lounge chair. I took the guy's socks off first. I felt his feet. They were cold but not freezing. That was a good sign. He must have been wearing good winter boots. The outer extremities lost heat faster than internal organs did, but it didn't mean the guy was out of the woods yet.

I snorted at my pun and quickly got back to work.

I took one more look into the kitchen to make sure Lydia was still occupied. I think she mentioned the baby's name, but damn if I could remember it. Unbuttoning and unzipping the guy's jeans, I was relieved to find he was wearing a pair of boxer briefs. Not that I should have been paying attention to such things while the guy was unconscious, but they were black and did nothing to hide the fact that the guy had something to be proud of in his pants.

It was a struggle to get the jeans off with him just lying there unable to help. I checked multiple times on the kids as well as made sure he hadn't woken up yet. I wasn't sure if I wanted him to wake up so I could get some answers and he could help me get his pants off or if I preferred he stayed out so he didn't wake up to find a strange woman taking off his pants.

Then again, not sure if guys would freak out about something like that. If the roles were reversed, I certainly would if I woke to find a strange man was taking my pants off, but women had different things to worry about in a situation like that.

I chastised myself for once more going off topic and worked harder to get his jeans off faster. His legs were damp but not overly cold to the touch. Again, this was good. He hadn't been exposed that long. The snowmobile ride from his car to my cabin had only been about fifteen minutes, but, in these conditions, fifteen minutes could be a very long time.

I covered him with a blanket and then went into my bathroom. It made me realize the girl hadn't asked to use it. Was she afraid to or maybe didn't want to leave her brother long enough to use it? I'd inquire when I got back to the kitchen.

I grabbed a bath towel and went back to the couch. I made sure the guy's legs, arms, pits, hair, and torso were dry. No need for him to get a cold or pneumonia with no medical attention accessible. Mind, I generally didn't go see one myself. I was in great health with no conditions that needed regular attention. I checked my breasts monthly, got my period regularly, and wasn't on any medications. During the winter, going into town was doable in an emergency but not something I did or relied on doing. There was no point. I spent my spring, summer, and fall months preparing for the four to five months I'd be stranded on the mountain during the winter. It was only recently that I started prepping extra for Tommy.

I canned my own fruits and vegetables, hunted and cured my own meat, and kept my own garden. I had access to a fresh water source on my land I used during the warmer months and used melted snow for my water source during the winter. I was self-sustaining. It took a lot of learning and many, many mistakes to get to where I am today, but it was all worth it. I got my private, quiet, and peaceful lifestyle. Did I get lonely sometimes? Sure, but it passed. Generally, with a trip to town where I am reminded of how petty and loud people could be.

I didn't go into Whitefish often. When I did, it was usually for something I wasn't able to grow, hunt, or make on my own up here. The last time I went was to get extra parts for my hot water heater just in case something happened to it over the winter.

In my previous life, I hadn't been very mechanical. Hell, I remember joking once that the only thing I knew about cars was which pedal was for the gas and which was the brake. Back then, I never would have imagined that I could or would ever learn every part of my truck, snowmobile, and four-wheeler so I could maintain them myself. While my truck was parked in town due to there being no direct road to my cabin, I rarely needed it or used it. In fact, I think the last time I did use it was going on six months ago when I'd gotten lumber for Dalton to build Tommy a ramp over his stairs while he'd been in his wheelchair following his hip surgery.

My life here was so different than I ever pictured or imagined for myself. But it was also what I needed when my life had gone belly up ten years ago. I never would have chosen this life for myself and yet I also wouldn't trade it. I needed my cabin; I needed my peace. I worked every day to make sure I had food and shelter. The little money I spent was generally earned back when I brought Jack extra bear, deer, bobcat, and/or coyote jerky. He bagged it and sold it in his store during tourist seasons. I also made soaps from the animal fats and added spices to make different scents to also sell at *Jack's*. Occasionally, when I bagged a male deer and his antlers were full-grown, I sold the antlers to my neighbors for them to make their furniture or weapons with. They also hunted, so it wasn't often that they asked for extra parts I might have.

While I was proficient in gun usage, hunting, tracking, and treating my own meat were new skills I had to learn. I used to look down on hunters, thinking the sport was inhumane. But it only took me one winter up here to realize there was a difference between hunting for food and using all the parts I could rather than hunting for trophies or bragging rights. I would never hang a deer head on my wall, but I would use the hide to make blankets. The bear-skin rug in my living room was one of the firsts that I'd made on my own. The bear had come too close to my cabin and I'd had to shoot to defend my meat-stores. When at all possible, I did try to let bears be. They tended to be more of a nuisance than dangerous. It was coyotes and bobcats that were the real dangers. They weren't as easily deterred as bears were. Plus, bears were usually too big for me to handle on my own.

Tucking the blanket around the man, I decided to let him sleep. I was not a doctor, but I couldn't find anything wrong with him other than signs of exhaustion and being cold. Keeping him by the fire and letting him rest were the best I could come up with for now. If he woke up and there was something more serious going on, I'd figure out what to do then.

His jeans were an obvious sign that he was not from this

area or used to this type of weather. I searched his jeans when I'd taken them off for a wallet or ID but there'd been nothing in his pockets except a very worn postcard of the beach. Random and not helpful.

I journeyed into the kitchen to see how the kids were faring. I still needed to move my snowmobile, bring in my bag, and check my gas levels. The generator had plenty of fuel, especially if I only used the fires to keep us heated. Many times, on stormy nights like this, I slept in front of the fireplace in my living room so I didn't have to keep a fire going in two different rooms. I always had a fire going in the living room, as it was my most frequently used room. I only kept the kitchen and bedroom lit during extreme cold waves. Tomorrow, depending on the conditions, I should be able to dust off my solar panels to conserve the generator. Regardless, I had a feeling this was about to be a long night.

Chapter Four

Adam

Sunlight woke me. My head was pounding, so opening my eyes to the brightness was difficult. It took several blinks to get my vision to focus. I was staring up at a vaulted wood ceiling, though I had no idea why. The beam across the center had lights built into it, but they weren't on. No, it was the light streaming in from the window that had roused me.

My head was foggy, and I wasn't entirely sure I was awake. After all, my bedroom in the mansion was painted white on the ceiling. Certainly wasn't wooden or vaulted. I wondered briefly if I'd had too much to drink. I wasn't a drinker, but I liked the occasional beer. I hadn't overindulged since my college days. But after the shit I'd seen and experienced recently, I might have given in to the temptation to escape for the night.

My brain, though muddled, immediately rejected that conclusion. I wouldn't risk not being able to be there for my kids.

I sat up quickly, my heart pounding. "My kids!"

"Easy," a gentle voice said from behind me. "You're safe. The kids are safe."

I spun where I sat, a thick blanket tangling in my legs. A woman knelt by a large stone fireplace. It looked like she was in the process of adding more wood to the flames. She was beautiful...and somewhat familiar, I realized. She had long blonde hair, braided down the back of her neck.

Since I had a seven-year-old, I tended to relate that look to Elsa from *Frozen*. If she had red, frizzy hair, it would have been Merida. While I tried to keep the children engaged outside of video entertainment, I did allow the occasional movie. My little angel used to love *Disney* princesses. Not so much anymore. Her innocent outlook on life had been stolen from her, and she no longer dreamed of fairytales and happily-ever-afters.

I looked around but I didn't see my angels anywhere.

"They're in the kitchen," the woman told me. She handed me a glass of water. "The baby's been a food monster since you guys arrived. We're almost through your stock of baby food." Her face scrunched up in a way that, if the situation was different and I wasn't so confused, I would have thought cute. Maybe even alluring. "Unfortunately, we're almost out of diapers too. I was grateful when Lydia had pulled out such a big stack from your backpack. But damn, that kid can poop! I've already had to wash his onesies, so he has clean spare clothes."

I wanted to comment, since I knew firsthand how much Henry could eat and poop, but my brain was caught on the fact that I was almost out of diapers. How long had I been out? I looked to the window, as if it could tell me what day of the week it was. All I knew was that it was daylight.

I remembered the journey here. My confusion was clearing the longer I was awake. I knew the decisions and choices I'd made. I also remembered my mistakes. The biggest one being turning right at the intersection and blindly following Corbin's instructions to drive until he found me. Clearly, he hadn't found me.

But this woman had.

I remembered our blizzard rescue on the back of her snow-mobile. I remembered assuming she was a man, and then my shock as I passed out that she was in fact a woman. Did she live up here with her husband? I don't recall seeing another man before I passed out but that didn't mean he wasn't here.

"Who are you?" I felt that was the most sensible question to ask. While I couldn't see the kids, and I desperately wanted to, I could hear them. Lydia was singing to Henry. The fact that she was singing Taylor Swift's *Love Story* to her infant brother was a little weird, but it reassured me she was happy and safe. Lydia didn't sing otherwise. When she felt threatened, she went scarily quiet.

It was the terrible reality of our lives that I knew that fact about my daughter. I once again chastised myself for not being able to protect her better. I was a teacher, not a warrior.

"My name is Brooke. This is my cabin. You're on Big Mountain near the town of Whitefish, Montana. I'm assuming you guys are staying at the ski resort and you got lost in the storm? It was very lucky I came upon you when I did. It snowed all night and into the day."

Thank you was on the tip of my tongue, but the lack of snowfall outside caught my attention. "Into the day? What time is it?"

She pointed a thumb out the frosted window. "That's west. You slept through last night and today. I was trying to figure out if I should wake you so you could eat or go to the bathroom, but Lydia told me you hadn't slept in a long while so I figured I'd let you be." She paused. "What's your name? Lydia just calls you 'Daddy', but I doubt you want me to call you that."

Her eyes widened as if she hadn't realized the implication behind her words until after she'd said it. My eyebrows shot up. I'd never had an age-play kink or any desire to be called 'Daddy' by an adult, but I had to admit I did like the way her cheeks flushed over her slip.

To save her embarrassment, I didn't draw attention to her unintentional innuendo. "Adam."

I had told Lydia I'd planned on us using fake names but we'd never settled on what names. Though her favorite for Henry was "Poopy St. Smelly Pants". Since this woman, Brooke, already knew Lydia's and likely Henry's, I figured she might as well learn mine. After all, we wouldn't be staying here once I figured some things out. Knowing our names shouldn't hurt. I just hoped Lydia hadn't given away our surnames. "And thank you. For saving us, I mean. And taking care of the kids while I slept. I shouldn't have fallen asleep like that."

It really was careless of me. What if something had happened? What if, despite the blizzard and mountain terrain, we'd been followed? What if we'd been found while I'd been snoozing? That was a dangerous mistake, and I couldn't make it again. I had to keep my kids safe.

I wasn't even sure how to find Corbin now. The burners Jack had given us were left in the car in my hurry to pack. I knew electronics and cold didn't mix, so I wondered if they were even usable now.

I thought of the *Jack's General Store* that we'd passed on our way through Whitefish. Maybe I could get there and figure out if that was the same Jack. He'd mentioned Corbin had bought the postcard in his store. It wasn't until I saw the snow outside and the trees surrounding the cabin that I wondered why Corbin would buy a beach scene postcard to send from a mountain town in Montana.

"Are you hungry?" Brooke asked. She walked past me, and my eyes fell on her round ass. She had some hips on her, that was for sure. I'd never been a man to prefer one body type over another, but I certainly liked the way those round hips worked on her. She was wearing black leggings, tall gray wool socks, and an oversized pink sweatshirt. I could see the straps of either a bra or tank top on her left shoulder where the large neckline hung low. She had lightly tanned skin. It was the kind you could tell came naturally, not from a bottle.

The oversized shirt made me remember my wonder if there was a man in her life. It was probably his. But as I looked around, taking in the cabin, I didn't see a man's touch. Not a jacket by the door, not boots on the rack. The décor seemed functional more than decorative, but it was also distinctly feminine.

I stood up, untangling the blanket from around my legs, and noticed for the first time that I wasn't wearing pants. I looked down at my bare legs in confusion. I didn't recall taking off my pants before I'd passed out. Which begged the question who did take them off. A glance around told me they weren't nearby.

"Shit," I heard softly. I looked up in time to see Brooke turn quickly around to give me her back. "Sorry, I forgot about that. I mean, not that I forgot I took off your pants. I did. I mean, I had to. I mean, your jeans were soaked through and you shouldn't have had that cold clothing against you in this weather. Even with the fire going, you could have gotten sick and done some serious damage to your body. I mean, not to your... Well, I mean, it could have been to your... But that wasn't what I was looking at! I didn't look, I swear! I just wanted to make sure you were comfortable. But, um... Your pants are in the bathroom. I washed them and dried them. Well, the air dried them. I don't have a dryer. Just a small washer. It's just me so I don't need full machines, plus they take up too much space and energy."

She stopped babbling, dropping her face down into her hands. For the first time in what felt like forever, I felt a smile tug on my face. God, how long had it been since I'd had a reason to smile outside of my children? It had certainly been years since a woman had made me smile so. As ungentlemanly of me as it might be, I found her floundering to be extremely alluring.

In quick motions, she stood straight and squared her shoulders. "I'll go get you your pants."

I picked up the blanket and wrapped it around me like a toga. College had made me an expert on how to tie a sheet around me like that. I was still wearing my underwear but clearly Brooke would have been uncomfortable if I walked around without covering myself up more. Was that because her husband could walk in any minute?

No, my gut told me. I didn't think there was someone else here. I didn't see pictures on the walls or a wedding picture on the mantel above the fireplace. Actually, the fact that the walls were mostly bare of pictures was interesting. No family photos or even one of a dog or vacation. The only picture was one of a sunset behind a mountain ridge.

As soon as I walked barefoot into the kitchen, Lydia looked up from where she had Henry perched on a chair. It took me a moment to figure out what he was sitting in. It looked like someone had taken a plastic bucket, drilled holes into it for his legs to fit through the sides, and strapped it to a wooden kitchen chair for a makeshift highchair. The fact that Henry was held in by bungee cords brought another smile to my face.

I didn't know how I knew but this had Brooke written all over it. Upon closer inspection, I noticed there was caulking around the edges of the bucket where Henry's legs stuck through.

"Daddy!" Lydia ran over to me.

Keeping one eye on Henry, I caught her up in my arms and swung her around. She clutched me as hard as she could, burying her face in my shoulder. My little angel. She'd been so strong. I shushed her as I felt her start to shake. I finger-combed my hand through her hair, noticing it had been recently washed. She was also wearing the spare outfit I'd had in the backpack for her. Most of the clothes inside had been Henry's but I knew there'd been a spare set of shoes, undies, shirt, and pants for Lydia.

I walked her across the floor, nearing where Henry was bouncing in his makeshift seat. One-handed, I undid the bungee cords keeping him in and lifted him out by his diapered bottom. Henry, all of six months, giggled and baby-cheered at seeing me. He gripped my too-long hair in one fist, his other hand going to my overgrown beard near my mouth. I play bit his hand, making sure to cover my teeth with my lips as I nibbled. He giggled some more, which was the best sound in the world.

There were no words for how I felt in this moment. The terror we'd been facing over the past couple of weeks, over the past couple of years for Lydia and me, was overwhelming. To have this moment of peace, this feeling of security given by this cabin, mountain, and snow, was beyond words. It was everything to have my children happy and healthy. Safe. Whole. Mine.

I sat down on the floor, crossing my legs in front of me. I rested Lydia's butt on my right leg, keeping a tight grip on Henry with my left arm. I closed my eyes, breathing my children in. The greatest gifts in the world to me were these two kids. I was beyond proud to call myself their father. They were worth every sleepless night, every law broken, every risk taken. They were my whole world. I needed them like I needed air to breathe. If anything happened to them, I would be destroyed.

As a teen, even a young adult, I'd pictured myself as a father...someday. It was the clichéd dream of finding a wife, buying a house, getting a dog, and then having two kids. Never would have imagined my kids being born under the circumstances they had been, or the trials I'd gone through to claim them.

I was their father. At the end of the day, that was all that mattered. It was my job to protect them. I'd been doing a crappy job of that over the past two days, first with getting caught in the snowstorm and then sleeping for over a day.

Lydia's knee collided with my belly, and I realized for the first time that my bladder was also awake. Damn, I didn't want to move from this spot.

Movement out of the corner of my eye drew my attention to Brooke. She stood awkwardly in the doorway, almost exactly where I'd been standing when I'd collapsed. She held my jeans in her hands, staring at the floor like it had the secret to life etched in it.

"Thank you," I said softly. She looked up, shocked that I'd spoken. Her eyes widened when she saw my eyes on her, as if she hadn't been expecting to be acknowledged. I gestured downward to the little angels in my arms. "You looked out for them when I couldn't. I owe you everything."

She shook her head immediately. "You don't owe me anything. I did what anyone would do coming across your car like that."

The fact that I knew that wasn't true, that most of the populace was too selfish to step forward and help a group of strangers, was sad. I'd reached out to Corbin in my desperation to keep my kids safe. He and his friend, Jack, were oddities to help me so selflessly. Brooke, even more so.

It took me a moment to realize Lydia's shaking had ceased and her breathing had evened out. She was asleep. My little angel, I had to wonder how much she'd slept while I'd been passed out on the couch. With me out of commission, she would have felt it was her responsibility to guard and care for Henry. She likely hadn't slept while I'd been sleeping.

I kissed the top of her head. Then looked back at Brooke. "She's asleep."

Brooke nodded. "She paced most of the night. She barely set Henry down even though I'd made him a little crib out of a plastic bin and blankets."

My eyes flew to the highchair. "Crafty."

Her cheeks reddened, and I found it adorable. Damn, what was wrong with me. My kids were on my lap. I could not get an erection right now. And yet, that little blush made my blood pump faster.

I looked around, mainly to get my eyes off of her, and that cute dusting of freckles across her button nose and cheeks, but also to contemplate my predicament. I was sitting cross legged on the floor with a blanket toga around my body and my children asleep against me. I also needed to take a piss like, well, like I hadn't gone in two days. Some personal hygiene attention was also needed. I couldn't remember the last time I'd showered. Body wipes were good for the kids or quick gas station bathroom hair washes for Lydia. But I hadn't washed or shaved in a long time.

I was suddenly embarrassed. Here I was having a cartoon heart throb moment staring at Brooke while I no doubt stank with BO, and who knew what else, looking like a hobo. Not exactly a turn on for her. I didn't embarrass easily, nor did I consider myself a vain man, but I suddenly needed to get to that bathroom *now*. I did not want her seeing me like this longer than she had to.

And why was I even thinking about that? I had to concentrate on my kids, on finding Corbin, on figuring out our next steps. I should not be thinking about how great her long legs looked in those leggings or how I really wished that oversized shirt revealed more about her shape underneath and yet found the mystery oddly alluring. Peeling off that shirt would be like opening a gift on Christmas, the anticipation—

Fuck. I stopped that train of thought before it went any further. I really could not get an erection right now.

"Um," I cleared my throat, "I could really use some time in the bathroom. Do you think you could…?" I gestured to my sleeping kids. I was prepared to take them into the bathroom with me so they wouldn't be a bother to her, but I needed help standing with them. I was not what one would call graceful or athletic.

Brooke came forward, draping my jeans over the back of one of the kitchen chairs. For being just her living here, which was the assumption I was going off of, I wondered why there were four chairs around her kitchen table. I could understand one or two, being just her and maybe a guest, but why four? Maybe I was wrong, and it wasn't just her living here?

Bending down, she took Lydia from me. The perpetual psychology student in me pondered if there was a reason she chose Lydia over Henry. Did it have to do with their ages or gender? Was she uncomfortable around infants? Maybe she felt sorry for Lydia after what I'd put her through the past couple of days?

Regardless, one less child freed a hand to allow me to stand. I went to reach for Lydia so I could take her into the bathroom with me, but Brooke took a step back and shook her head.

"I'll put her on the couch. Follow me, and I can show you what I made for Henry. Hopefully it's safe enough for him. I wasn't sure but I'm also limited on supplies in the house during the storm. My tool shed is out back and difficult to reach in the snow right now. Plus, I didn't want to leave the kids alone that long to fight through the snow to get there."

She started walking away, not meeting my eyes. Had she seen the lust in them? I hope I hadn't made her uncomfortable. I really did owe her for giving us food and shelter. The thought of food made my stomach grumble, but I really had to take a piss before I could eat or drink anything.

A shower would be nice too. My hunger could wait. I was used to putting off eating by now. Nerves and a need to make sure my kids had enough to eat first had kept me from consuming much over the past two weeks. If I'd been asleep one plus days then this was day fourteen since we'd run. Exactly two weeks since that awful day.

I followed Brooke back into the living room. Her cabin was quaint. Probably only had one bedroom and one bath. There was a loft that I hadn't realized before looking out over the living room. I wondered if that was her bedroom. I didn't see stairs though, which made me ponder if the cabin was bigger than it looked. I don't recall what the house looked like from when we'd arrived. I'd been out of it and hadn't been noticing much at that point. When the snow died down some, I'd like to take a walk around the cabin to see the outside.

I watched Brooke lay Lydia on the couch where I'd woken up. Since I had the blanket still around my waist, she reached over the back of the couch for a lighter throw. It looked home-made, maybe knitted. Had Brooke made it? Maybe her mother?

The thought of family made me doubt yet again if Brooke lived here alone. If she did, more power to her. I didn't know what it took to live on a mountain, but I'm sure it took more guts and brains than I had. But it also made me wonder *why* she was alone. Brooke was beautiful, strong, and independent. She could be living it up in the city or being the small town's golden girl. Why was she living in a cabin in the middle of the woods on a mountain? Clearly the snow secluded her. I wasn't sure where the electricity that was lighting the cabin was coming from, but she had to have a source other than electrical lines. What about water and plumbing? She had to be self-sufficient in a place like this. And, again, I wanted to know why.

Brooke gestured me over to a plastic tub by the fireplace. It wasn't so close that it would be overly hot for Henry. "I wasn't sure what was safe for him. Obviously, there's no lid." She gave off a nervous giggle at her own joke. I found myself fighting a smile again. "I put this blanket down to cushion the bottom. He didn't look old enough to climb out but I was hoping it was tall enough to keep him from standing. It's not the greatest crib but, unfortunately, it's all I have." She sent me a fleeting look and then faced forward again. "I wasn't exactly expecting a baby to be sleeping here."

I reached forward, touching her arm. Henry was out, probably not having slept that well over the past couple of days. Babies picked up on moods, and if Lydia was scared or nervous, he likely had been too. I kept him secured to my chest with my left arm.

Brooke jumped. I wrenched back my hand. Shit, I shouldn't have touched her without her permission. I chastised myself, calling myself all sorts of stupid. I knew better. I really did. I never touched without asking first. Consent was important to me.

But before I could open my mouth to apologize, she did.

I blinked, confused. "What are you apologizing for? I'm the one who touched you without asking if it was okay."

Brooke turned to face me. I really wanted to say *finally*, but the torn look in her bright blue eyes gave me pause on my excitement that she was looking at me. "I'm not used to people. I generally only go into town once every month or two. I don't usually talk much either, yet I seemed to have found myself babbling whenever I try to talk to you. You probably think I'm this weirdo lady who lives out in the middle of nowhere and are doubtful I can or should watch your kids. But I swear, I can. I mean, not long term. That would be silly. But for the thirty minutes you need in the bathroom, sure."

She stopped talking to take a deep breath. I thought she was done and opened my mouth to speak, and once more she cut me off. Her eyes went really wide. "Not that you only have thirty minutes to use the bathroom. Use it for however long you need. I'm not timing you." Then she slapped a hand over her mouth, muffling her voice. "I'm going to stop talking now."

I didn't fight my smile this time. "Brooke, I don't think you're a weirdo, nor do I think you can't watch the kids. I just didn't want to be a further burden to you and figured I'd take them into the bathroom with me to give you some peace."

Her hand slowly lowered from her mouth. "Oh."

"Can I touch you?"

That cute blush crept over her cheeks again. "Yeah. I mean, yes. Um, where?"

Unable to stop smiling, I leaned forward and placed a kiss on her cheek. She was shorter than my five-eleven height by four or so inches, which was nice that I didn't have to duck too much to reach her. "Thank you for taking care of us. I really do need to get to the bathroom though."

She nodded, silently stepping out of the way of the makeshift crib. "Down the hall on the left."

I didn't plan on leaving Henry in a plastic bin overnight or long term, but it was fine for the minutes I needed in the bathroom. He didn't even stir as I lowered him down. I touched Lydia's hair on my way past her. She was snoring slightly, which she did when she was overly tired. My little angel.

I needed to be stronger for her, for both of them. She should be a child in her own right, not co-parenting her baby brother with me. I needed to put less on her and work on giving Lydia her own freedom and fun.

Brooke's voice followed me down the hallway. "You look

like you have the weight of the world on your shoulders. Take it from someone who knows, up here in the mountains, that weight becomes a lot less."

I didn't respond verbally, only nodded my head in thanks. She had no idea how much weight was truly on my shoulders. And I didn't want to drag her down with me or lay my problems on her. As soon as possible, I needed to figure out how to find Corbin and get out of here.

Chapter Five

Brooke

Why couldn't I keep my mouth shut around this guy? From the moment he'd opened his deep brown eyes, it felt like my brain was mush. I couldn't function and seemed to have turned into a babbling idiot. Lord, what he must think about me. I truly hope I never found out. I'd thought I'd left my ego behind when I'd moved up the mountain. I was wrong because I didn't think my psyche could handle him telling me I was a fool or not worthy.

Worthy of what, I wondered. Adam was a stranger. He probably had a wife waiting for him and the kids at some hotel, terrified when they hadn't come off the mountain. Mind, he wasn't wearing a ring or had a tan line from having once worn a ring. I glanced down at my left hand, grateful yet again that my tan line had faded. I didn't need the daily reminder, despite the lack of jewelry, of the biggest mistake of my life.

And Adam didn't feel like a tourist. I'd been doubting that assumption since I had made it, but it was the only logical explanation for why he and his kids were up on the mountain road. No one journeyed up that road unless they lived here or it was by accident, and those who lived here used four-wheelers or a snowmobile depending on the weather. When Jack had special visitors join us on the mountain for a time, there was a specific way we got them to their destination—and telling that visitor to drive onto the mountain themselves wasn't it.

Cars, even a *Jeep* like the one Adam had been driving, would not make it very far up the mountain before they ran out of room. In fact, Tommy's place was really the only one that could house a vehicle. I cringed at the thought of Adam having arrived at Tommy's uninvited and in the middle of a storm. I doubted Tommy would have welcomed him inside or even heard him out long enough to realize he had kids with him.

So, if Adam wasn't a lost tourist and he wasn't one of Jack's visitors, what was he doing on the mountain?

Since coming to the mountain nine years ago, I prided myself on staying out of other people's business. They kept out of my way and I kept out of theirs. I did not believe Adam to be dangerous. Really, I *could* just provide him and his kids a safe haven for another couple of days. Then I could dig out the snowmobile to journey out to his car to see if there was any damage done or if it was possible to dig it out and get him back down the mountain. More than likely, I'd have to take him down on the snowmobile though.

I *could* do that, but I wasn't going to.

Even if Adam wasn't a tourist, that didn't mean someone wasn't waiting for him and his kids. What if there was an active search party trying to find them? The Whitefish police department wasn't big. Last I heard, there was the sheriff, his deputy, and a part-time patrolman. The town was a safe one and a big police presence wasn't necessary. Jack told me during high tourist times, some of the townspeople were deputized if they needed extra help. I'd met the sheriff when I'd first arrived at Whitefish. To be honest, when I went to town, I kept to myself and didn't listen to any gossip. I have no idea if the man I met, whose name I had forgotten, was even still the sheriff.

There was no cell reception on the mountain. Spotty though it may be, one could get reception from Tommy's place because there was a tower not too far from his property that butted up to the resort. However, when I'd first moved up here, I'd learned that, while my fellow mountain dwellers were reclusive and antisocial, they did look out for one another. Jack had gotten me a HAM radio so I could communicate with him or the others if I came across a problem. Other than my first winter here, and the time I'd fallen off the roof cleaning the solar panels, I hadn't had to call anyone for an emergency situation. Most of my communications were requests for Tommy or my own check-ins with the others after a bad storm.

Jack had one in his store. He lived above it in a small apartment so, even if he was upstairs, he'd hear the beep or soon see the message indicator. He was sort of the fairy godfather to all of us. He lived in town but he looked out—or up—for us. I think he was more nervous than I was when I'd first arrived and revealed that I was moving up the mountain. He didn't doubt me because I was a woman—at least, I don't think that was it. He was concerned because I'd moved in late August, and there'd barely been any time for me to prepare for the harsh winter months ahead.

Corbin rarely answered his radio. Jack was really the only one who could get him to respond, and that was usually with bribes of food or beer next time he was in town. I didn't know much about him, though I saw him occasionally on a hunt or at Tommy's. He was sweet and protective. He was a big guy, probably the biggest if I lined the other mountain men up beside him, but I'd never feared him. There was something in his eyes that was haunting him. I'd never gotten up the nerve to ask him about his life. Each of us was on this mountain for our own reasons and it was our business to share if we chose. I certainly hadn't told anyone my reasons.

Dalton was on the other side of my property from Tommy. He was also a veteran and had a prosthetic leg. When I'd first met him, I figured that the fake leg slowed him down, but honestly, unless he was wearing shorts, you'd never guess he was an amputee. He generally was the first to start the round of check-ins after a storm, as well as the first to volunteer to come help fix any damage. I thought he was hitting on me once, but he'd assured me he'd given up on love long ago and just wanted to be friends. If I was making pies, I always made sure to make extra in case I ran into Corbin or Dalton at Tommy's.

Walter was even further up the mountain than I'd ever journeyed. I'd only met him once in the nine years that I'd been living here and probably couldn't pick him out of a lineup. However, I would know his voice anywhere. Sometimes, when the loneliness got too much I think, Walter would get on the radio and sing. When his amazing bass voice came across the channel, I would lay down on the couch, close my eyes, and just listen. Some nights in the summer, I'd open my windows, look up at the stars, and bask in the vastness while his deep notes remind me that I'm not as alone as I sometimes feel.

And then there was Huck. I honestly didn't know where Huck's property was in relation to mine. I'd never met the man. From what I understand from Jack, he'd never come down off the mountain since he arrived some twenty years ago. When we did our rounds of check-ins, all we ever got from Huck was a series of clicks. I'd never learned Morse code, but Jack claimed he understood. I feared the day when Huck didn't check-in and wondered how we would ever find him in person.

My radio was up in the loft. I loved my loft because of the giant windows that looked out onto the mountain. There was a slight drop about twenty yards from the back of the cabin. On days like today when the snow covered everything, even in the spring or the fall when the leaves were changing, and especially at sunrises and sunsets, I would sit up in my loft for hours. Just watching nature at its finest. My knitting and sewing equipment were up there too. When I had a new hide or knit pattern I was working on, that's where I did it.

The loft wasn't very big, only about eight by twelve, and I could keep an eye on the children from there.

I picked up my hand-mic and hit the code for our channel. Technically anyone in the world could listen in but it was rare to hear a stranger's voice. There weren't that many HAM radios left in use. At least, in this technological age, I doubted there was. I didn't know actual statistics.

"Calling Charlie-Foxtrot-Two-Two-Niner-Charlie, over."

I peeked over the rail to see that Lydia had rolled onto her side, facing the back of the couch. Henry was still laying on his stomach but his butt had risen further up in the air. I had no idea why baby butts were so adorable, given the deposits they left behind, but I smiled when I saw the position he'd moved himself into.

"Calling Charlie-Foxtrot-Two-Two-Niner-Charlie, over."

If Jack didn't pick up after my third hail, I'd hit the key to leave a message on the channel. He wouldn't know which one of us was reaching out but he'd know someone had tried.

Then the speaker crackled. *"Brooke, is that you?"*

I keyed my mic. "It's me, Jack. How are you?"

"Good. We're snowed in and the locals are loving it. There's a snowball war happening on Main Street as we speak."

While I could imagine the scene he described, it didn't hold my interest. "Has there been any missing person reports?" A long pause came across. I checked my channel and waited. "Jack?"

"Why do you ask?"

I found that reply odd. Jack was usually very forthcoming with information. He wasn't one to answer a question with a question. I opened my mouth to answer—and paused. What if there was another reason Adam and those kids were on the mountain? What if it had nothing to do with bad directions, a family vacation, or skiing? Lydia's first question rang through my mind again. *Are we safe here?* I could see clearly the memory of the way her little body was turned, as if to protect her brother. What if Adam hadn't been lost? What if he'd been running *to* someone or something? There wasn't much up here on the mountain but if someone was trying to get lost, this would be the place to do it.

So what were the odds that Adam would choose to come to the same mountain where people were often hidden? But if Adam was one of Jack's, why hadn't Jack told me? I hadn't gotten involved in his side business until recently. Jack mainly used me for when a female wasn't comfortable being around one of the men.

What was different about Adam? Why the secrecy?

"Brooke, did I lose you?"

"No," I answered quickly. "Um, I found tire tracks on my way back from Tommy's on Tuesday just as the snow was hitting hard. Made me wonder if a tourist got caught up in it."

I was generally not a liar. In fact, I despised liars and how they believed they could spin any tale to get away with something. But until I knew what Adam was doing on the mountain, I didn't want to say anything that would draw suspicion on me or lead someone to my doorstep. Not that they could reach my doorstep without me knowing they were coming, but with the kids here, I didn't want any surprises.

Never thought I'd be the overprotective mother-type but looking down at those innocent kids... I couldn't risk it. No chances. Jack's radio was in his store. Unless he was closed, anyone inside right now could hear our conversation.

"No one is missing as far as I know."

That meant no one had reported Adam and the kids as missing. Not a wife, not the ski resort owner. So where had they come from? People don't just appear on the mountain as if by magic.

The shower turned off below me. As much as I wanted to let Adam have his privacy, I needed answers. They were strangers living in my home after all. I needed to know I wasn't harboring criminals.

A snort escaped me as I imagined baby Henry dressed up in an old fashioned black and white striped prisoner's uniform onesie. While my concern was real, I couldn't help but find that image adorable.

Huh, maybe there was a maternal bone in my body after all. Who knew?

"Thanks," I said, wanting to cover the silence. "Have you heard from the others?"

If Jack realized I was changing the subject, he didn't say anything. I was glad for that. With as much as I hated liars, it was a good thing I was a crappy one. I blushed too easily and got flustered. Who could remember all those stories anyway? It was too much pressure. Though sometimes I wished I could get away with a little white lie without the entire world pointing out that I was a crap liar. Maybe because we were over the radio and not face to face, Jack didn't notice.

"Most checked in earlier. Haven't heard from Tommy or Walter."

I hoped they were okay. I'd seen Tommy on Tuesday and he was in for the storm. I didn't like him there alone at his age, especially after his injury, but there was no way we were ever going to get him to move out of his home or allow someone else to move in with him. If Walter was in trouble, I had no idea how to even start helping him. I knew where his land was but not where his house was on it. Maybe next time I was in town, I should ask Jack to print me off a map of each of their lands so I knew where to go if they needed me. Mind, given that we all loved our privacy and all of us were armed, it probably wouldn't be a good idea to ever show up uninvited or unannounced.

"If you need me to go to Tommy's, let me know. I'd rather do it in the daylight."

"Old man's probably ignoring me after last time. I suggested contacting family to see if they would come and help him. I think he destroyed his radio after that. Kept threatening to do so if I pushed, and of course I pushed."

I snorted. Of course, Jack did. We were like his little lost ducklings and he was our mama duck.

"Might not be a bad idea to contact them anyway. He needs more help every time I visit, and he's starting to notice I've upped my visits recently."

"You're a sweetheart for looking out for him. I know he appreciates it, even through his cursing. But I'd never break his confidence, no matter how much I think he needs help. He's out there for a reason, same as the rest of you. I don't know all of his story, but I do know that there's a reason he hasn't spoken to his family in over forty years."

Forty years. I couldn't imagine it. When I visit Jack's store, he lets me use his desktop to check my email. I had renounced communicative technology when I'd moved out here. I don't own a computer, a phone, or a tablet. All my books come from the library or a secondhand store. I don't even have a TV or a DVD player since streaming would be impossible out here. However, in order to prevent my mother from siccing the FBI on my trail, I send her emails to let her know I am okay. I also gave Jack my username and password since my mother was the only person with that email address so he could send her a message from me when I couldn't get down off the mountain. On her birthday, thankfully a summer date, I would call her from Jack's landline.

I hadn't spoken to my dad or brother in almost nine years. My sister, once my best friend, was no longer considered a member of my family tree.

My mother had mentioned visiting. Other than the state of Montana, she didn't know where I was. If my mother took the initiative, she could trace Jack's number to his store, but that still wouldn't tell her where I was exactly.

I was beyond frustrated and fed up with my family. They were clearly as done with me as I was with them or my mother would have mentioned at least one of their names in her emails or our annual phone call. Yet, I never asked and she'd never offered.

It made me wonder. In forty years, would my family even remember I was alive? If something happened to my mother, would anyone even bother to tell me?

I was estranged from my family, but at least I still had communication with one of them. To not talk to anyone in forty years... That was difficult to grasp. What had happened to Tommy? Was it something he had done or they had done? Did it have to do with him being a Korean War veteran?

Realizing I'd been quiet for a while, I keyed my mic. "Forty years. Hard to imagine."

"I worry in forty years you'll be the same, kitten. I hope whatever drove you up to that mountain doesn't keep you there indefinitely."

Except I knew it had. I was never leaving this mountain. I loved my mountain. I loved my life and, most importantly, who I was on this mountain. I couldn't imagine anything ever bringing me permanently off this mountain.

"It's not so bad up here. It's down there that I can't stand."

Jack's laugh came across loud. *"I got customers, sweetheart. Thank you for checking in and I'll keep my ear out for any lost tourists."*

"Thanks," I said. "Over and out."

"Over and out," came back to me.

I turned off my mic but kept the volume up on the speaker. If Tommy or Walter came across the channel, I wanted to hear it.

A throat cleared behind me. I spun around, still not used to having another human being in my cabin. In fact, Adam and his family were my first and only guests. Dalton or Corbin stopped by occasionally to check on me in person but they'd never been inside my cabin or I in theirs. It was a silent agreement that inside was sacred grounds. We'd sit on the porch or the stairs. Even around the fire-pit I had out back. But they'd never stepped foot inside.

Adam being here was...different. But somehow not intrusive. Before two days ago when I'd invited them inside, I never would have contemplated having guests.

"Sorry to scare you."

I gave him a reassuring smile. He was still standing on the stairs, as if waiting for an invitation to the loft. He looked...good. Like really. Not that he didn't look good before, but he'd clearly been ragged before. Exhaustion and the bitter cold could do that to a person. Right now, though, his hair was dark from the shower, towel tossed and hanging low behind his ears. His full beard looked washed and a little puffier. He wore his jeans but had a different shirt on. He must have had another shirt with him in that bag, or it had been under his long sleeve fleece. I hoped it was a clean shirt, which would give me time to wash his long sleeve one.

Adam was lean. He wasn't bulky-muscular like I was used

to from the men on the mountain. He had a defined figure though, and I liked the way he held his shoulders back. Stress still weighed heavily on him. The shower had done him wonders, but I could still see it in his eyes.

Maybe that was what had given me pause when I'd been talking to Jack. Beyond Lydia's initial reaction to me, Adam's obvious exhaustion had been different than the exhaustion of a man on vacation with his family. His exhaustion was one of fear. I could tell upon him waking that he'd been ashamed he'd fallen asleep. Not because he'd left his children with a stranger in her cabin in the middle of the woods, which was an unusual scenario in and of itself, but because he hadn't been there for them. Why? To watch and care for them? Or was it something more? Was it because he hadn't been there to protect them?

Protect them from what?

What could a man and two small children be running from that they would end up on a mountain? A tourist was looking less and less like a possibility.

"Who were you talking to?"

His question came across as casual curious, but I could tell it was more. He was afraid. His eyes kept flickering to the sleeping kids as if he needed to know where they were so he could grab them and run.

What if all of this was in my head? My instincts had been wrong before. So wrong, in fact, that when my life had blown up, I'd been so blinded-sided I'd moved myself to a remote cabin on a Montana mountain to never have to face that humiliation or heartbreak again.

And yet, I could see his fear. It flowed off of him in waves. He was a father who would do anything to protect his children. That took such strength, in my opinion. He needed to know they were safe here. I'm not even sure if he knew where *here* was, and maybe that was a good thing. If he was lost, could anyone still find him? If they were even looking for him?

"A friend," I said vaguely. It was my house and my radio after all. As much as he needed reassurance, I did too. "I think it's time we talked while the kids are still sleeping."

I didn't miss his wince. "I don't know what you're talking about."

"I'm talking about what or who you are running from. I'm talking about why a little girl feels the need to constantly guard her baby brother while her father is sleeping the sleep of the dead from over-exhaustion. I'm talking about why you are up here on this mountain, stranded in a snowstorm." When he remained silent, gaze still fixated on the kids, I let out a long sigh. "Look, I don't let strangers into my home. Obviously, your situation demanded immediate action and I'd had nowhere else to take you, but I hope you understand that this is my home. I don't come here for vacation. I don't live here casually. I live here to get away from people and their problems. I don't mind helping you out while you're stuck here, I really don't. Those kids are beyond adorable and I've found I've enjoyed having them around more than I thought I would.

"But I need answers. I need to know who I let into my home. Because you're no lost tourist."

"How do you know I'm not?" Adam challenged. He still wouldn't look at me though. "I took a wrong turn and that's all."

"And I call bullshit." I wasn't trying to be harsh, yet I needed him to understand my perspective. Now that he was awake, it was hitting me hard that I'd let a strange man into my home and I lived in the middle of nowhere with no next-door neighbors to hear me scream. Did I believe Adam would do anything in front of his children? No. Yet, I still needed to take precautions. "Adam, there were no reported lost tourists. Believe me, this time of year with these storms, they check. The resort hotel is very thorough to make sure no one is left stranded and the inn in town is the same. If you had a reservation—and trust me that's the only way you're getting into that resort—and you hadn't checked in, they would have reported you to the sheriff. Since there was no search party for you or your car, that leads me to wonder how or why you were on this mountain."

It took a long moment, but Adam finally looked at me. The sorrow in those eyes was heart wrenching. I was starting to doubt my conclusions—after all, it had been a lot of years since I'd been a detective—when he nodded slowly. "I can't tell you much. In fact, I'm not even sure I should be telling you anything at all. But you helped us and are keeping us safe. I owe you something."

I gestured for him to come up. I was sitting in a chair similar to the ones in my kitchen in front of a small table that held my radio. The loveseat that was the only other piece of furniture in the loft faced the opposite direction from me. I stood, picked up my chair, and moved it around to the other side of the loveseat. I wasn't about to sit next to him for this. I wanted to see his face.

I let him take the chair. First, because the couch was more comfortable and it was my couch. Also because I figured he'd want to be able to look over the rail and still see the sleeping kids.

Adam sat, looking as forlorn as a schoolboy being sent to the principal's office. He rubbed his hands up and down his legs nervously. "I can't tell you much but I can tell you I was instructed to come to this mountain. My best friend told me to take the turn away from the resort and to keep going, that he'd find me. Unfortunately, we were caught in that snowstorm and never made it, or he never made it. I'm not sure which."

My face scrunched. His best friend? Who would be crazy enough to tell a guy to take his kids up a dangerous mountain in the best of weather? Mind, our storms tend to have a mind of their own and we don't always know when they are going to hit or how long they are going to last. Our winters are very unpredictable. So why would someone send a man and two children up the mountain knowing that? Unless they *didn't* know that. What if there was a stranger on my mountain? What if there were others out here that I didn't know about? The only reason I knew of some of them was from Jack. We weren't exactly what you would call a sociable group.

There was also the possibility that he was lying. His story certainly was vague.

"Why not send you into town? Why the mountain?"

Adam bit his tongue on that one. So either he was lying or the town hadn't been an option for him.

I scoffed. Look at me, trying to play detective again. Wasn't as if my 'detective instincts' had worked out that well for me the last time I'd needed them anyway. My head started to throb. Finally, I said, "Fine. What can you tell me?"

"Not much. It's obvious we need your help and I'm sorry I can't tell you why but I can offer you money."

That statement shocked me and, to my surprise, offended me. Did he think my silence could be bought? Out here, who would I tell anyway?

"I don't want your money. I just need to know if I'm harboring fugitives or if trouble is going to come knocking on my land once the snow clears."

Adam shook his head quickly. "I'm not a criminal," but something in his eyes told me he was lying. Or, at least, not telling the full truth. Could someone be half a criminal? "And we'll be long gone before the snow clears."

Instant doubt broke through my train of thought, making me forget the criminal aspect for the time being. "And how do you expect to do that, mister? Are you familiar enough with this mountain to trek through it in the dead of winter with an infant and a kid in tow? Your car is likely buried deep and, unless you know where you are right now, you're not finding it. In fact, do you even know where you are to know which direction to turn when you leave the cabin?"

Adam's face flushed. He stood up in frustration. "Look, I didn't mean to bring this to you. I know I owe you. If you won't take my money then let me help out around the house while we're here. I need to call my friend. Do you have a phone?"

I gestured behind me at the radio. "You just saw me use it."

His confusion only grew into further frustration when he saw I was talking about my radio and not an actual phone. "Really? You don't have a cell phone or anything I can use to make a phone call?"

I shook my head. "Reception doesn't work out here. The radio is the only reliable way of communication."

"Shit," I heard him mutter. He ran his hand down his face, tugging slightly on his beard like he wasn't used to having it. I wondered how old the beard was. I liked the look of him with it, but then, I'd always preferred a beard to bare skin. "How long will the snow last?"

"Well, let's see, today is Thursday so... April?"

He looked at me with a start, and then burst into laughter. It took me only a second to follow behind him. I hadn't meant it as a joke, more like a sarcastic comment, but it had broken the tension that had been building between us. I liked the sound of his laugh. It was full bodied, and it made his eyes sparkle. I wondered when the last time he laughed was.

Adam shook his head, looking up at the ceiling. With his arms on his hips, he looked taller than he was, his chest wider. It was only then that I realized his feet were bare. I'd need to get him a pair of wool socks for around the house and could only hope mine fit him.

"I guess I had that coming. Truthfully, I'm completely out of my depth here. I have two little people who are counting on me and I have no idea what I am doing. I have no idea how to help them or protect them. Hell, I've spent over a day here and have only been awake for an hour of it."

I couldn't congratulate myself about reading him right regarding his shame for falling asleep. Wasn't like he'd had a choice. The man had literally collapsed from exhaustion. He needed to cut himself some slack.

"Your children are safe, Adam. The snow would have covered our tracks here. Even if someone found your car, and that's a big if given where I found you off the road, they wouldn't automatically find you here. So you have time. We're expecting snow again tonight. Not as much but it'll still come. Anyone out there looking for you won't get far. So take a breath and realize you're safe for now."

A shudder went through him. He let out a long breath, as if he'd been holding it for a while. Slowly, he sat down again. His gaze was straight ahead, but not on me. He was staring out over the loft rail again. "We haven't been safe in a long time, so thank you."

Despite my uncertainty before, I knew in my gut this man was not a criminal, but it was obvious he was running from something or someone.

Maybe my little mountain paradise could be his sanctuary as well.

Chapter Six

Adam

I wanted to tell her. I wanted to unload all my problems. Not to give them to her, but to purge them from my system. I needed to be free as much as I needed my kids to be protected.

But this was not my home. We would need to leave here one day—clearly not any day soon with this snow—but still one day. When we did, I could not leave my problems with her. I had to take them and solve them on my own. Telling her, if she was ever found out to have helped me, would only put her in further danger. If someone ever did come to her door to question her about us, all she could say is that she helped out a father and his two kids when they were stranded in the snow and she'd never seen them again. With no information, they should have no reason to harm her.

I flinched. Just because they didn't have a reason, didn't mean they wouldn't. Christ, had I just signed Brooke's death certificate by accepting her help? Would it have been better if I'd refused her help at the car?

I looked down into the living room, saw my sleeping son with his little butt up in the air, saw my sleeping daughter with far too many worries for a child her age, and knew I'd made the right decision. Even with the possible consequences, I'd had to protect my children. We would have died out in that blizzard.

Yet, how could I call myself a man or even a respectable human being, knowing the danger my very presence was bringing to her doorstep if we were ever found out? How could I pay Brooke back for her kindness in that way?

Was it better to tell her everything so she could be prepared?

No, my brain immediately answered for me. If she knew everything, she'd likely call the police herself. I needed to keep my kids safe for as long as possible. And if Brooke's predictions of the forecast were true, we would be stuck here a little bit longer.

"I hope you know how grateful I am." There were no words to repay her. "But I can't tell you the truth. It would put you in danger. Please know that you are safe with me, I would never hurt you, but I need a safe place for my kids. I can't take them out in this weather. Please allow us to stay."

I hated the pleading in my voice, but I would get on my hands and knees if it reassured her enough to let us stay.

Brooke snapped her fingers in front of my face to bring my attention back to her. I found her eyes too intriguing. I wanted to stare into them for far too long, which was one of the reasons I kept looking away from her. I didn't want her to think I was a creep by constantly staring at her.

"You leaving was never an option." Then she added, "Well, not unless you admitted to being a serial killer. But then you'd have been kicked out and I was keeping those kids."

I cracked a smile. "Not a serial killer."

"Good to know." She smiled back. "Look, you don't need to tell me your life's story. I just find it very...*dangerous*," she said pointedly, like she'd intended to say another word and switched at the last second, "that your friend would send you to this mountain. The people up here aren't known for being friendly and welcoming."

Guilt coursed through me for having blindly put my kids in such danger. "Well, it wasn't actually him who said it. It was more of a friend of a friend situation."

Brooke looked confused. "A friend of a friend?"

I could feel myself start to sweat and knew I'd never last in a real interrogation. "I'm not exactly an expert on evasive maneuvers or hiding. I needed help. I guess I trusted someone I shouldn't have or misunderstood a direction. I can't see how me ending up stranded on the mountain in the middle of a snowstorm was their plan after all the effort and money it took them to get us here."

Brooke contemplated that for a moment. "What's your friend's name or the friend of your friend?"

I hesitated. The way she asked it, almost like she didn't believe me, was what gave me pause. She'd already admitted to living out here secluded from society. It didn't sound like she got out much. Mind, she'd been out on her snowmobile the day she'd found us stranded in the car. She'd also been talking to someone on the radio.

Would she even know Corbin's name? If I told her Corbin's name and someone came looking for us, she would be able to tell them where we went. Then again, I wasn't even sure Corbin was here. Maybe he'd gotten us to the mountain with the intention to only meet up with us and then was taking us to a different final safe house.

Though what could be safer than a secluded mountain in the middle of nowhere in a snowstorm? Brooke was hopefully right that our tracks had been covered up in the snow and no one could find us here even if they found our abandoned car.

The possible stolen abandoned car. Shit. What if the cops

found it and ran the plates? What if they found the bag of license plates, our burners, and the rest of our supplies in the car? How would I contact Jack or Corbin then?

"Look if you don't tell me, I can't help you when the snow clears. I can get you back to town but that's it. I can't point you in a direction to go."

Maybe that was safer. If she didn't know which direction we'd gone in then she couldn't tell anyone which way we went.

Christ, I was going to develop an ulcer if I kept this level of stress up. How did people survive this? Was this what witness protection felt like? Except those witnesses had the police to help hide you instead of hunting you.

"Fine." Brooke stood up, clearly annoyed.

I didn't blame her for that, because this wasn't her problem. How could I lay this on her? Yet, if I didn't, I didn't know what my next steps were. How did I keep her *and* my kids safe? If there was a choice between keeping her or keeping my kids safe...? Geez. In reality, I knew my choice was my kids. It would always be my kids. But to intentionally put her in danger?

I shook my head. I couldn't do that either.

But how did I protect my kids when I didn't know where to go from here? We'd have to leave this cabin in a few days, maybe a week. Brooke was right that I didn't know which direction to leave in. I didn't even know where I was.

I looked up in time to see her at the top of the stairs about to head down.

I had a sudden image of her walking out of my life. I wasn't in love with her, that was a stupid notion, but I was attracted to her and I liked her. She was brave and it was adorable how she babbled when she was nervous. She was selfless enough to help out strangers and had opened her home to us.

This feeling of consternation went deep.

I was once more at those crossroads. Left or right. Talk or

stay silent. I had this irrational fear that if I let her walk down those stairs, I would regret it. What did that even mean? Why would that even matter? I was leaving in a few days. Brooke was not coming with us and we were not staying here.

So why could I not let her walk down those stairs? It felt like my heart had dropped into my stomach and I couldn't breathe. Irrational, possibly dangerous, but I needed to talk. I needed to choose a path. I couldn't do this on my own. I'd trusted Jack and Corbin, and it had landed me stranded in the middle of a snowstorm on the side of a mountain.

Brooke had been the one to rescue us. I had no desire to put her in danger, but I needed her help. At the very least, a direction to point me in.

"Corbin," I said just as her foot hit the first stair. She stopped. "My friend. His name is Corbin."

Brooke turned back around. I couldn't tell the expression on her face, but it wasn't doubt. Maybe shock, curiosity.

She stepped back up onto the loft. Then walked over to her radio without saying a word to me. She flipped a switch, pressed a button, and grabbed the microphone.

"Calling Omega-Delta-Four-Six-Two-Two-Tango. Pick up the mic, I know you're listening. You're going to want to hear this, over."

I came around the loveseat. I didn't bring her desk chair with me, too preoccupied with wondering what she was doing.

Brooke put the microphone closer to her mouth as if she was going to click it again when a voice I knew well came over the speaker. *"Brooke, babe, are you okay?"*

Babe? I wasn't sure why the endearment bothered me, but I had a sudden urge to hit my best friend. Were they dating?

Then it hit me: she knew Corbin! Elation filled me, and I could have flown with relief.

Brooke keyed the microphone. "I have someone here who wants to talk to you."

"*What?*" His confusion was clear, but I didn't hear jealousy or worry in his tone.

She handed me the microphone and moved out of my way. I stepped closer so the cord didn't pull tightly. There was only one button on the side, so it wasn't difficult to figure out how to use it.

I pressed the button. "Corbin."

A pause then, "*Adam? Holy shit!*" I went to talk again, but he kept going. "*I've been trying to reach you. None of the burners connected through. When you missed your last check-in, I feared the worst, but Jack assured me you weren't caught and I trust him. I kept hoping you'd call. We wanted to tell you about the storm, to wait to come. When I hadn't heard from you, I hoped you'd bunkered down in a motel somewhere to wait it out.*"

Yeah, that would have been smart. If I'd known about the storm. I hadn't realized I'd missed a check-in, but, then again, I was pretty out of it by the end of our journey to the mountain. I'd been so focused on arriving that it was entirely possible I'd missed a check-in.

Then I remembered our stop in the park. I'd never called Jack that day. I was planning on it after we picked up the *Jeep*, but then I'd decided to let the kids have some fresh air at the park. As a result, I'd forgotten to call.

"Shit. I never called that day. The kids were so restless so I let them play at a park in Bozeman. We made it onto the mountain just as the snowstorm hit."

"*Oh fuck! The kids! Are they okay?*"

"Yeah, man. They're fine, I'm fine. Brooke found us and rescued us."

"*Brooke, babe, if you're listening, thank you. I owe you.*"

I leaned to the side so she could talk if she wanted to, but she shook her head. Then she indicated to downstairs and the kids. I took that to mean she was going down to give me some privacy. "Thank you," I told her before turning back to the mic and speaker. It would have been better to see him in person, but this was second best. I keyed the microphone. "We've been at Brooke's house for two days."

"*Hold on, man, let me scramble the channel so hopefully we can talk without being overheard. Jack, if you're listening, turn off your speaker.*" The radio made a whirling sound, almost reminding me of the AOL dial tone from my childhood, giving me some serious flashbacks from the 90s, and then beeped twice. Corbin's voice came back over. "*Okay, we should be good now.*"

"Scramble the radio? Shit, man, when did you get so techie?"

Corbin laughed, which was great to hear. He hadn't had much to laugh about in his childhood. "*I literally hit one button. Be grateful I knew how to do that. Me and technology still aren't friends.*"

Before we got into the heavy stuff, I had to ask. "How are you, Cor? Really? It's been eighteen years and I'm so grateful that you helped me out. I just need to know how you're doing. Are you okay after...everything?"

Corbin had been convicted of manslaughter. In my opinion, unlawfully. It had been self-defense but because his father had been a cop, well, the judge had taken one look at tall, scrawny Corbin and found him guilty. The underpaid, overworked public defender hadn't even stood a chance.

"*It wasn't easy,*" he said with a sigh. "*I don't like to dwell on it. I'll fill you in on how I ended up here when I see you. This place is amazing, Adam. It saved my life and I know it can save yours too. I have never regretted my decision to come here.*"

I was almost afraid to ask. After her husband's death and

Corbin's sentencing, his mom had moved away. As far as I knew, my mom had lost contact with her years ago. "And...what about your mom?"

There was a pause and then a feminine voice came across the speaker. *"Hello, Adam."*

My mind almost blew. Holy shit! "Mrs. Mullaney? Holy... I mean, it's so good to hear from you. I can't believe you're here." Then I paused. "You guys are here, right? I mean, you're on this mountain too?"

A feminine laugh. It made me realize that I don't think I'd ever heard his mom laugh before. Ever. *"Yes, we're on the mountain too. My Corbin found me after he was released and brought me here to live with him."*

I was so happy to hear that. Corbin and Mrs. Mullaney both deserved peace after what her husband and his father had put them through and then how justice had failed them. Corbin had killed his father. That was never a question. He'd admitted it when the cops had come to the house. What no one seemed to take into account was that Corbin had walked in on Mr. Mullaney beating Mrs. Mullaney with his belt. Corbin, enraged and terrified for his mom, had pushed Mr. Mullaney away from her. He'd tripped, hit his head on a glass coffee table. The glass had shattered, and a piece had pierced his heart. But what had condemned Corbin as a murderer was picking up another piece and stabbing his father nine times in the back as he'd laid there already dying.

At least he had only gotten ten years. Manslaughter was generally a lot longer. His age had been the one thing going for him. He'd only just turned eighteen the week before and the public defender had gotten him tried as a minor instead of an adult given the history of abuse.

Corbin's voice came over next. *"We can catch up on us later. Tell me about the kids. Are they okay?"*

"Better than okay," I said with confidence. "I was in bad shape when we arrived. I was exhausted and cold from keeping the kids protected from the storm. I passed out soon after we'd arrived. Brooke kept the kids calm, fed them, and watched over them while I slept."

That still grated on me, but I needed to give Brooke credit where credit was due.

"*She's amazing,*" Corbin said with admiration. "*She helps out one of the old mountain men next to her. If she hadn't been doing regular check-ins on him, he might have died last year when he fell and broke his hip. She found him, got ahold of Jack, and got him down the mountain so the paramedics could meet them.*"

Wow. My Brooke was a regular heroine. The pride I felt in that moment was suddenly bombarded by shock. What the fuck was that? *My* Brooke? She wasn't *my* anything. In fact, based on the *babe* endearments Corbin had called her, she might be *his* Brooke.

"Yeah, she's been great." I didn't like how my voice cracked. Christ, I felt like a teen with his first crush. I cleared my throat. "She said it's supposed to storm again. I take it that it's not safe enough to travel to you now."

I wasn't sure if I was grateful or frustrated by his negative answer. I shouldn't want to stay here. "*Definitely not. I've got baby supplies and toys here for the kids, but I wouldn't risk bringing them out in this. If needed I can bring supplies down to you, but my recommendation is to leave them there. You're already safe and holed up. Let's keep you where you are a bit longer. I need to update Jack and make sure you're in the clear. Can you tell me where you left your car so we can dump it?*"

My fear that it had been stolen resurfaced, but I didn't comment. "Honestly, I have no idea. Brooke mentioned we were off the main road, but I couldn't even begin to tell you where.

I'm just so grateful she found us and was able to bring us here. Corbin, my kids could have died out there."

A low expletive could be heard before, "*I know, man. I'm so sorry about that. It wasn't supposed to go down that way. I've been really worried. Brooke's amazing like that though. You're in really good hands with her. And if you're lucky she'll cook you some of her venison stew.*"

"Venison?" I repeated, wanting to make sure I'd heard him correctly. I wasn't so city that I didn't know that venison meant deer.

"*Welcome to Montana,*" he laughed.

I shook my head. Deer was not a meat regularly available in NYC. "Thanks, man. I feel the welcome." I was terrified to ask, but I had to know. "Has there been anything from the city? While we were driving, Jack kept saying we weren't being followed but there were times when I would swear we were. Cor, how do you know we are safe here?"

"*It's as safe as we can make you.*" It wasn't much of an assurance, but it was more than we'd had since we'd run. "*Look, I'm not happy about us losing contact all these years but in this instance, it's actually helped you. No one will ever guess that you're here with me. Why would they? Beyond that, even if they guessed you are with me, no one knows where I am. My land isn't under my name. I have no utilities or bills in my name. The mountain is the safest place I can imagine for you and the kids to disappear. Plus, between me, the others up here, and Jack down in town, we have eyes and ears everywhere. No one steps foot on this mountain without us knowing.*"

I breathed out a sigh of relief at that. "I don't want to endanger you either."

"*I'm not in any danger and protecting you and those kids would be worth any trouble. You did the right thing, Adam. I know it's tough right now but you got them out of there. I don't know your full story but I do know that.*" He paused for a second then added, "*Listen, I'll check in with you guys tomorrow. Let me know if you're running low on any supplies. I won't bring Mom out in this, but I can manage to get stuff down to you if necessary.*"

The word *down* caught my attention. That meant he was higher up the mountain than we already were. I wasn't sure if I was comfortable with that. Were the kids safe out here? There was no medical attention or pharmacies nearby. What if we ran out of diapers and formula? I vaguely recalled Brooke saying when I'd first woken up that we were almost out of baby food.

"I'll take an inventory and get back to you. I don't want you coming out in this either if it's that dangerous."

"*Don't worry about it, man. I'm used to it. I can get down and back up the mountain just fine, rain, snow, or shine.*"

While I was thrilled Corbin seemed to have found his place in life, I still didn't want to risk his life if we could survive with what we had. Problem was, I didn't know what we had. "Thanks, man. I'll let you know. What time are you going to call tomorrow?"

"*During storms, Brooke tends to leave her volume on in case anyone else hails through. Conversations aren't possible, but the occasional SOS can break through. Depending on what this storm decides to do, I'll try around nine if that won't bother the kids.*"

I didn't know where the kids or I would be sleeping, so I didn't know if the volume being on the speaker would bother us. Based on what I'd seen of Brooke's cabin, she only had one bedroom and the one bathroom. No need for guest rooms when you don't host guests.

"Thanks. Talk to you tomorrow." I didn't know how to hang up, other than to just stop pressing the talk button.

"*You're supposed to say 'over and out', dummy.*"

I snorted. It had been many years since anyone had called me a dummy. "Over and out, jackass."

His laugh came across. *"Over and out, asshole."* There was a click on the radio. I didn't touch it otherwise, not wanting to mess up any of Brooke's settings.

Eighteen years, and it was like no time had passed at all. God, I loved that man. He was the brother I never had. I loved my sister, but it was Corbin I'd been closest to. The fact that we could talk like this, that he'd dropped everything to help me despite the time between our last conversation, only proved that fact. Brothers for life.

It worried me for a moment that I was bringing my problems to Mrs. Mullaney. I didn't want her mixed up in any of this. But it would be great to see her again, and she would be wonderful with the children.

I'd taken a leap in trusting Brooke and it had paid off. Corbin was on this mountain, and now he knew I was too. Soon, we'd be together again and I couldn't wait to see my brother.

Chapter Seven

Brooke

How did I not know that Corbin had his mother living up there with him? Mind, I don't think I'd ever asked if he was married or had anyone living with him. He hadn't said either. I wondered if anyone else had partners or parents living with them. I had made the assumption we were all alone in our own little slices of heaven.

While eavesdropping had not been my intention, my cabin's open floor plan made voices echo from the loft more than I ever realized when it was just me. I was also willing to admit that I made no efforts *not* to eavesdrop. As capable as I was in defending myself, I was alone in the very literal middle of nowhere with a strange man. I trusted Corbin—as much as any of us who dwelled on this mountain trusted each other anyway —but there was something *peculiar* about Adam's situation that had my hackles standing on end.

I wandered into the kitchen as I heard Adam's footsteps descend down the stairs. My cabin only had one hallway, which led to my bedroom, the bathroom, and the stairs to the loft. There was little storage space in the cabin because I didn't need it. My pantry was probably the size of my bedroom to help house my winter supplies. My meat stores were outside, kept frozen by solar panels on the roof. Any jerky I made was housed inside, not needing to be kept frozen. After my first winter here, I had invested in a meat grinder so I could make ground meat and patties. Well worth the money for the variety. In addition to learning how to make jerky, I also learned how to make different types of bacon.

I canned all my fruits and vegetables that I didn't eat right away. I had a veggie garden at the back of my cabin that I kept during the spring, summer, and fall. Most of the fruits I picked grew naturally around and on my land. My favorite was huckleberry, but blackberries were more abundant. I made sure to pick any that grew too near to the house so they didn't draw bears and prey animals close to home. Learned that one the hard way about five years ago.

My pantry also housed rice, flour, sugar, and baking spices. While I grew most things myself, there were some things that didn't grow well in this area or were too difficult for me to make on my own. I bought those from Jack at his store and had learned tricks on how to keep them from spoiling.

A good part of the warmer months was spent prepping meals for the winter. I would make stews, roasts, soups, pies, lasagnas, and a variety of other meals, then I would dehydrate them so I didn't have to freeze them. Dehydrated meals also took up less storage space. Add hot or cold water, maybe some spice later, and *voilà!* Dinner is served.

I always make too much food for the winter. First of all, one never knew if winter would last longer than normal. Sometimes, even if it wasn't actively snowing, it was still too dangerous to journey down to town. Ice was a big concern in these parts, not just packed snow. Also, it didn't make sense not to. It was better to be over prepared than under prepared.

But I prepped for one mouth to feed. I now had three and a

half mouths to feed. Henry was going through the baby food Adam had brought with them very quickly. I wasn't sure if that was normal for a baby to eat so much or if Lydia had been over-feeding him. Maybe I should have stopped her from giving him some of those meals. But how did one tell a child not to feed their baby brother when they were clearly hungry?

Nope, couldn't do it. While I didn't know how long Adam and the kids would be with me, it would still dip into my stores faster than I had anticipated. I had plenty, but I might have to do some calculations if they were here longer than a week. I'd have to watch my gas and water levels too. I generally could go a week before needing to refill my water tanks, but with three and a half people showering, eating, drinking, using the toilet, washing their hands... My water stores were going to go down a lot faster.

They shouldn't be here longer than a week, I predicted. Not that I wanted them gone, but if their plan was to meet up with Corbin, it didn't make any sense to delay once it was safe for the kids to travel.

Having heard bits of their conversation, I understood now why Adam was on the mountain in the middle of a storm. Corbin, and it sounded like Jack too, had lost communication with Adam. It had been their intention to tell him to wait to reach the mountain but they couldn't reach him to relay the message. I felt better knowing that fact. Adam being stuck in that storm had been a freak accident. No one had put Adam in specific danger and Adam had not been reckless in his need to get onto the mountain.

What I didn't understand was why Jack would keep it a secret that Adam and the kids were coming. As far as I knew, he'd always told us when one of his special guests was coming to the mountain before. We helped look out for them and offered supplies when needed.

The terminology Corbin had used was telling. Somewhat, anyway. He hadn't said that Adam and the kids had left or even mentioned a leisure vacation exit. No, Corbin had said that Adam had gotten the kids *out of there*. Out of where? He'd also used the word *caught*. As in captured and taken against his will?

What if Adam *was* married? What if his wife or someone else in their family was abusive to him and/or the children? That would explain his running, but not why he needed to come all the way to a Montana mountain to escape. Abusive spouses could be cruel and manipulative, especially when kids were involved. But he must have family who could have helped him? Parents, siblings...?

Except when my life had fallen apart, my family hadn't lifted a finger to help me. Even my mother, who claimed to love all her children equally, had chosen a side, and it wasn't mine. Maybe his family hadn't supported him either.

I hated that for him and those kids. No child should have to live life in a constant state of fear.

I knew Adam hadn't eaten since he'd woken up. Other than using the bathroom, I didn't think he'd taken care of himself at all. His concentration was all on his children. I needed to watch him to make sure he was taking care of himself too. There was no reason he shouldn't be getting a full night's sleep and three full meals a day up here. Maybe his time on the mountain could help him gain back the weight he'd clearly lost recently.

At the stovetop, I put a pot on the burner with a dehydrated soup mix and then added water to bring to boil. I chose soup for his meal because he hadn't eaten in over a day. If I gave him something thicker or heavier, it might upset his stomach. Noticing the shredded coyote meat in the pot, I had the absent thought of *what if he's vegetarian?* If so, Adam was not going to survive out here long.

It took a lot of carbs and energy to survive a Montana

winter. Protein was important, and the best source of protein in these parts was game. I certainly didn't have any shrimp in my stores. I did keep a lot of vegetables and fruits on hand, but most of my prepared meals had both meat and veggies in them.

By the time Adam had finished checking on his children, the soup had finished boiling and was now simmering on the stovetop. I reached into one of my cabinets for a soup cup. Most of my utensils, drink-ware, and dinnerware were bought at the thrift store in town. Since it was just me—usually—I only had a couple of sets. I didn't use paper or plastic to preserve the environment and to keep my trash levels down.

Generally, I only accumulated a small amount of trash, which I would dump when I went to town. There wasn't much about my way of living that left trash behind. Mind, now that I had a baby in the house who was going through diapers like they were a rare commodity, I had more trash in the past day than I had in the past year.

I gestured for Adam to sit at my table and brought him over the steaming cup. "I gave you more broth in that cup to get something easy into your stomach. If you can keep that down, we'll get you some chunky bits in your next cup."

He gave me a grateful smile. "Thank you." He cupped the warm mug between his hands but didn't move to take a sip. "I take it you heard."

After going to the fridge to pour a glass of lemonade, I sat down opposite him. Most of the time, I drank water. I filtered it from my stores and kept it in the fridge in a pitcher. However, I did have dehydrated milk, lemonade powder, and iced tea powder. When I asked Lydia what she'd wanted to drink this morning, her eyes had lit up at the mention of lemonade. Rather than making her just a glass, I made up an entire pitcher for her.

"Sorry, voices echo in here more than I realized."

Adam snorted. "I guess when you live alone and the only

person you talk to is yourself, that's not something you would pick up on." Then he flinched. "Sorry. Was that insensitive to say? I wasn't trying to knock your lifestyle. In fact, I admire it. It must take guts to live out here all alone."

I shook my head, trying to reassure him. "It wasn't. It's just a statement of fact. I do live out here alone."

He hesitated, then asked, "Why?"

I studied him for a moment. Despite feeling comfortable around him, we were strangers. I knew his kids better than I knew him. "That's a story for another time."

As in never, I added to myself. Adam had enough serious problems that he didn't need to hear my sob story.

He looked down at his steaming mug. "Didn't mean to pry."

"You weren't."

Silence fell between us. I took a sip of lemonade, he took a sip of broth. I didn't know what to say next. I hadn't had to force small-talk in a lot of years.

"Corbin suggested we stay here longer. He doesn't think it's safe to travel with the kids right now. I don't want to overstay our welcome—"

"I was already planning on you staying about a week. With this next storm, it'll be a few days before we'll be able to dig ourselves out of here."

"Thanks." He took a bigger sip. "Deer?"

"Coyote."

He nodded once. "That's a new one."

I cracked a smile. "Wait until you try squirrel."

Adam actually looked curious. "Does it taste like chicken?"

"Better in my opinion."

Again, he nodded. "I look forward to it. Though if Lydia asks, everything is chicken. I don't need her accusing me of serving her Bambi and his woodland friends."

"Definitely don't want to scar the kid."

He winced and I wondered what went through his mind just then. He cleared his throat. "I need to take inventory of the kids' supplies. I don't know what we have left. I don't know where the car is to try to get what we left behind there. Corbin said he had supplies at his place in anticipation of our arrival. Despite the weather, he claims he can get it to us if we need it."

Unfortunately, I think there were only a few diapers left. Lydia had changed Henry again just before Adam had woken up. "We could definitely use the supplies."

"Is it safe for him to come out in this? I get not wanting to take the kids out, but what about him?"

"He's a mountain man," I said in lieu of an explanation.

"And you're a mountain woman. Would you go out in this?"

He was looking at me like he was trying to read my soul. His eyes were so intense, they darkened. I liked how the black of his pupils blended in flawlessly with the deep brown of his eyes. His sandy beard twitched slightly and it made me realize that, even though he'd been staring at me, he'd noticed me staring right back.

I blinked, shaking my head to clear it. I sat up straighter. I hadn't intended to lean forward towards him. My body had just done it.

"If I needed to, I could. In fact, if my neighbor doesn't answer his hails by the end of today, I might just have to in the morning."

Concern crossed his face. "I don't want you putting yourself in danger."

"My lifestyle is dangerous but this is the life I chose, the life I love. I know what I'm doing." I wasn't sure how I felt about his concern. It was sweet and not entirely unwanted, but it also brought on strange feelings in the pit of my stomach. Feelings I hadn't had in almost a decade.

"How old are you?" I asked to change the subject.

"Thirty-six," he replied. "Am I allowed to ask you the same?"

I fought the urge to roll my eyes. I knew my hard lifestyle aged me more but I wasn't ashamed of my looks or the years I'd lived up here. "Thirty-five."

"Really?" Adam tilted his head to the side, studying me. "This isn't a pickup line but I would have guessed younger."

Now I knew he was lying. "I don't have access to anti-aging skin-care products up here." Even if I did, I wouldn't use them. Too many chemicals.

"You don't need them." Having finished his cup, Adam stood to walk to the stove. He refilled his soup and took his seat again. "How long have you been living up here? Were you born here?"

"Nine years and no."

His eyes narrowed when I didn't elaborate. "We're going to be stuck here a week together. The least we can do is get to know each other."

"Oh really?" I leaned forward again. "And where are *you* from?"

Adam clamped his mouth shut. After a long pause, he conceded. "Touché." I sat back. "How about this?" he continued. "We can talk about our lives without specific details."

I was intrigued but not sure how that would work. "Like?"

"Like if we mention the name of a friend or relative, we use fake names or just the title. Mom, dad, sister, uncle... And we use fake locations too."

"How does this get us to get to know each other better?" I was surprised he wanted to get to know me at all. After all, would we even see each other after he left in a week?

"We can still talk and learn, but it keeps the specifics a secret."

And you couldn't tell a secret you didn't know. What was

the saying? The only way to keep a secret between two people is if one of them is dead.

I didn't like lies but was this even lying? It was storytelling, maybe. I'd still get to learn about him. Eventually, my curiosity won out. "All right."

Before Adam could respond, a baby cry echoed through the house. He looked over his shoulder at his son, then looked back at me with a smirk. "Raincheck."

I watched him go, wondering yet again why it was so important to me that I learn about him. He was a stranger. Even if I did learn all there was to know about him in a week, it didn't change the fact that he was leaving.

Chapter Eight

Adam

As much as I wished to continue the conversation I had started with Brooke, I was also grateful for the interruption. Had I gone insane? Why had I suggested learning about each other like that? Yes, we were stuck in a cabin together for the next week-ish, but that didn't mean we had to offer up details about our lives.

But the opportunity to get to know her, even a little bit more, was too great to pass up. Brooke felt important. She lived on the same mountain Corbin had moved the kids and me to. Maybe when we left in a week, it didn't have to be goodbye.

What if we couldn't stay on the mountain though? Just because we hadn't been found yet didn't mean we were never going to be found. What about the kids? Could I keep them on this mountain? School wasn't a concern. I'd been homeschooling Lydia her entire life and planned to do the same with Henry. But they needed socialization. They needed to be around other kids. To run and play and be free. Could I raise them on a mountain in a cabin, maybe no bigger than Brooke's, with Corbin and his mother?

As I bent to pick up Henry from his makeshift crib, I could

feel my fears that had abated at Corbin's voice over the radio returning in full force.

There were too many unknowns.

Lydia was awoken by Henry's cries. I knew how tired she was and wanted her to rest, but I also knew that if she slept now, she'd be up all night. It was best to get her up, fed, and keep her entertained at least until eight in the hopes she'd sleep through the night.

"Good morning, my angel." I bent to kiss her forehead.

"Hi, Daddy." She stretched her little arms up in the air. "Are you okay?"

My heart expanded at her sweetness. "I am very okay. Thank you for being my big girl and taking care of your brother while I was sick."

She looked bashful, not meeting my eyes. "I was scared. You said not to trust anyone, but I had to trust Brooke. I had no choice!"

"Shh," I calmed her, stroking her hair. "You did the right thing, Angel. You were right to trust Brooke."

She still looked unsure. "Really?"

"Yes, Angel. In fact, with the weather outside, Brooke has invited us to stay a little longer. Then we're going to meet up with Uncle Corbin."

Lydia had never been introduced to extended family before. She was excited to meet someone I'd claimed to be her uncle. I wondered how I would explain Mrs. Mullaney. My little girl was short on female attention and I wondered if she would view Mrs. Mullaney in a maternal way.

"Come on. Let's get you up." I moved the throw off of her, keeping a tight grip on a squirming Henry. "Potty and then we'll head into the kitchen for some lunch. Brooke made us some soup."

I did not offer up the detail that it was made with coyote meat.

The rest of the day was spent organizing the supplies we had left. Brooke went outside to check her water stores. I didn't know what that meant or what she would do if they were low. I supposed this was stuff I was going to have to learn if we were going to be living on the mountain for the time being. Maybe I'd ask her to show me the next time she went out.

Brooke went through her available food to determine what was baby appropriate. She didn't have a purée machine or a blender. Mashed potatoes, sweet potatoes, mashed corn, and the like should be easy enough to make with what she had. I didn't know what baby supplies Corbin was able to bring down, but I figured that would last us a while. I had enough formula left in the tub to get him through two more weeks.

Diapers were another story. We were going to be out of those likely sooner than Corbin could get here. Thankfully, Brooke found some towels she was willing to sacrifice to the cause and cut them into the shape we needed to be a secure diaper. Safety pins were also located. I was sure there were other ways to make reusable diapers but we had to work with what we had. Brooke adjusted her predictions of her water stores with the added laundry that was going to be needed.

I had forgotten Lydia's coloring book and crayons in the car when I'd packed in our rush to escape the storm. Brooke got her a notebook and a pen. We spent the afternoon working on math problems while Henry had some tummy time. I wished I had a mobile or something visual to entertain him with.

I could tell Lydia wasn't paying attention in her studies as much as she usually did. She was still tired, but she also kept glancing at the door like she expected it to be broken down at any minute. I needed to get some privacy from Brooke to have an overdue conversation with her. Lydia was old enough to understand the severity of the situation we'd found ourselves in. I wished she didn't. I wished she was too young to remember any of this like Henry was.

I didn't want to wait the week until we were at Corbin's to have the conversation either. After dinner, which was an unknown meat roast with veggies, I took the kids into the bathroom to have a bath. I was very grateful Brooke's shower was a tub. Brooke followed us to take the kids' clothes. She said she would wash them while I kept them occupied. I smiled my gratitude to her. She smiled back, almost nervously.

Today had been...nice. For the first time, I had a sense of what it would be like to have a partner in raising the kids. I'd never had that. The support felt intoxicating. To not always have to be *on*. To not have to have an eye on each child on opposite sides of the room. To be able to leave the room to have a moment of privacy in the bathroom without worrying the kids were out of my sight.

I turned away from the door, closing my two naked children in with me. My train of thought was approaching dangerous territory. Even if Brooke and I did learn more about each other, even if I was attracted to her, she could never be a permanent part of our lives. For the rest of our lives, the kids and I would be in hiding. Brooke would never be a part of that. It was selfish to even contemplate.

I liked her. A lot. She was funny, tough, sweet... She didn't cringe or flinch when holding a diaper full of exploded baby poop. She was a great cook and I admired how she had carved out a piece of this mountain as her own. While the prospect of living on a mountain had never occurred to me before, I knew people did it. I probably stereotyped them as crazy men or doomsday preppers. It never crossed my mind that a woman would choose to live this lifestyle.

But it suited her. Brooke was confident in everything she did.

Once I got a low level of water in the tub, I guided Lydia in and then sat Henry down next to her. He immediately started giggling, splashing his chubby little legs and hands around. I kept a hand on his back to support him while handing a loofah to Lydia. She was reaching that age where she didn't need her dad to bathe her. I knew this playtime with her was limited and was grateful she enjoyed playing with her brother in the water. I didn't see any harm in letting her have this time, even if some parents would look down on me, a dad, for having my seven-year-old daughter naked in the bathtub.

I looked at this as extra time for her to be a kid. Maybe even giving her back time that she'd lost to be a kid.

As the water started to get cold, I knew our playtime was coming to an end. I needed to take advantage of this time to talk to Lydia without Brooke overhearing us.

"Angel?"

She looked up at me, her blonde hair soaked and a giant smile on her face. I hated to take that away by reminding her of our situation. "Yes, Daddy?"

I loved it when she called me that. It was the best title in the world. "You know I will keep you and your brother safe, right?"

She nodded, the trust in her eyes evident. She had such faith in me. I prayed I never destroyed that in her.

"I know I was sick yesterday and that scared you. I'm sorry I left you the responsibility of taking care of your brother. But I'm better now. I want you to relax and let me take care of you again."

Her face scrunched up. "What if you get sick again?"

That was a good question, but hopefully not one she would ever have to worry about. "Uncle Corbin is going to bring us to his home. We're not going to be here very long. If something ever does happen to me, Uncle Corbin will keep you and your brother safe."

"You mean if the bad man finds us?" Her voice was so low that I barely heard it. If I hadn't been paying attention to her face, I may not have heard her with Henry's splashing.

"Yes, Angel. If the bad man finds us, I will do everything I can to protect you. If I can't or if I'm taken away, Uncle Corbin will keep you safe. I promise."

"What about Brooke?"

I was surprised by the question. "Brooke won't be with us much longer. She's sweet enough to let us stay with her while we wait out the storm, but she won't be with us when we go to Uncle Corbin's." Her little face scrunched up. "What are you thinking, Angel?"

"I want Brooke to be my friend."

Ah, and she'd already had to leave friends behind. "Maybe we can visit with her after we leave." I knew I shouldn't have said it, I didn't even know if Brooke wanted contact with us once we were gone. She might be glad to wipe her hands of us.

Lydia nodded her little blonde head. "I will ask her."

I gave her an indulgent smile. "Of course, Angel. It can't hurt to ask."

She looked over at Henry. "Daddy?"

"Yes, Angel?"

"Would it keep Henry safe if I went back?"

My heart sank into my stomach. For a moment, I was back in that horrible room on that horrible day. Bile rose at her words. I couldn't imagine it. I couldn't fathom it.

I needed to keep a hand on Henry in the water, but I used my other to turn Lydia fully towards me. "Angel, you listen to me very carefully. *Never*, and I mean *never*, say that again. It won't save me and it won't save Henry."

Tears welled in her eyes. "But it's me he wants."

I sealed my lips closed, trying to keep the rising bile down. She wasn't a stupid girl. Of course, she'd figured that out. I needed to calm myself so I didn't scare her. Or maybe scaring her was the right course so she never even contemplated sacrificing herself again.

I took a deep breath and let it out slowly. She was looking down at her hands in her lap. "Angel, look at me please. I'm not mad." She looked up, tears falling from her beautiful blue eyes. "Lydia, my angel, my wonderful and special girl, I love you more than anything. Henry and you are my everything. So trust me when I tell you that you cannot stop fighting, you cannot stop running. If he finds us, you take Henry and you run. Uncle Corbin or I will find you. Never, *ever*, let yourself be caught."

She was shaking by the time I finished my plea. I hated to see her scared but she also needed to understand. Sacrificing herself would not save me or Henry. Reality was, Henry was probably the safest one out of all of us.

Lydia threw her arms around my neck, soaking me with her hug. I couldn't have cared less. I wrapped my arm around her little back and held her to me as tight as possible. Henry started to tip over, but I caught him by his arm.

My little family. There was nothing I wouldn't do to keep them safe.

Chapter Nine

Brooke

The kids were finally asleep. I'd barely lasted the day. I had no idea how exhausting parenting was, and I wasn't even the parent who was with them or bathed them or took them to the bathroom. Geez, how did Adam do it? No wonder he'd passed out from exhaustion when he'd arrived. I was ready to collapse after half a day.

Tonight was their third night staying with me, Adam's second while conscious. The snowfall last night had been heavier than I'd anticipated. Due to ice, Corbin had been unable to bring down the baby supplies safely on a snowmobile and he lived too far away to have made it on foot. When we spoke with him on the radio, we agreed we could survive a bit longer with what we had. Therefore, it was decided to wait an extra day for the snow to settle before Corbin would try to come down. Current plan was that he should arrive by early afternoon tomorrow.

After a whispered argument so the kids didn't pick up on it, Adam had conceded to my insistence that he and the kids take my bedroom during their stay. They needed the space, and I was perfectly comfortable falling asleep by the fire in my lounge chair. Adam felt like he was kicking me out of my room and it had taken the better part of last night's dinner to convince him otherwise.

Last night, Adam had gone to bed when the kids had. He'd still been tired and he wanted to be close to his kids after their near-death experience. To him, it must have seemed like it had only just happened. I understood it, but I was also disappointed he hadn't come out to spend time with me once the kids were asleep.

He either felt his own disappointment about that or he'd picked up on mine, because he'd apologized for falling asleep so early when he'd gotten up this morning. I'd brushed it off, claiming it was no big deal, but I was touched by the sentiment.

Tonight, before he'd taken the kids to bed, he specifically stated that he'd be back out once they were down. My heart—my stupid, stupid heart—had leapt in anticipation. When Adam came out of the bedroom, I was sitting on the couch with my legs curled up under me. I had a book open on my lap, but I honestly wasn't reading it. I had been too distracted listening to Adam's voice from the bedroom as he told Lydia and Henry a story about a rabbit that was looking for his lost carrot. I didn't know if he'd made it up or if it was from memory of one of their children's books. Either way, it had kept my attention despite the genre.

Adam let out a long sigh as he collapsed on the other side of the couch. His head was resting against the back and his eyes were closed. I had the strangest urge to run my fingers through his beard. Was it coarse or fine...? My fingers tingled with the need to find out.

I clenched my hands into fists. Shit, what was wrong with me? All day it had felt like we were dancing around each other. Our eyes would meet, hold, and then one of us would move. Circling, always circling. He would reach over my head to grab a glass from the cabinet. I would reach over his shoulder to adjust the settings on the radio. Never touching, but always near. It was like static along my skin, and I was just waiting for the inevitable shock.

Which was so stupid. Corbin would be here tomorrow with supplies. We would make a plan then as to when it was safest for Adam to bring the kids out of the cabin. He was leaving. Doubtful tomorrow, but maybe the day after or the day after that. What if this was all we had? One, maybe two nights, together?

Shit, fuck. I needed to switch my thoughts to a safe mood-killing topic. The only one I could think of on short notice was the children. "So I had an interesting chat with Lydia this afternoon while you were getting Henry's bottle ready."

He peaked one eye open, smirked, and then closed it again. "Did she ask you if you'd be her friend?"

"Actually, she asked if I would be yours."

His eyes flew open and he sat up in a quick motion. His dark eyes burned bright as they bore into mine. Okay, so maybe this topic hadn't been as mood-killer as I'd intended. "Why would she say that?"

I swallowed hard. "Apparently, you could use someone to play with."

He didn't say anything at first. It was almost like he was trying to read any alternate meanings in my words. While I hadn't intended there to be, as I was just repeating Lydia's words, we both knew otherwise.

The air between us became very heavy. I felt like my heart was beating a million miles per hour. It had been almost ten years since I'd been intimate with a man. I was no stranger to pleasure, but it was all self-administered. Yet, temptation sat across from me on my couch.

I'd never had a one-night stand in my life. I'd only ever been with one man. He'd been the love of my life and I'd had no interest in pursuing other relationships after I lost him. I had never imagined, especially with my living conditions, that there would ever be another man.

And yet...here one sat.

I knew deep down that it was more than just the opportunity. There had been other chances for me to have engaged in a no-strings-attached arrangement. No one had affected me like Adam was now.

It was the *man*, not the opportunity. I'd never before thought fatherhood to be a turn on, but I'd been wrong. The way Adam was with his kids, how attentive and caring... It was like an aphrodisiac. Never thought watching a man change a diaper would get my motor running. Mind, thinking about it like that was a little weird. In the moment, though, it had been anything but.

When I finally found my voice, even I could hear the huskiness in it. "I know we said no details before but I have to know this. Just a yes or no: are you married?"

My heart nearly burst from my chest when he shook his head. "No. You?"

I shook my head. "No," and did not elaborate.

His eyes never left mine. "I want to kiss you."

"I want you to kiss me." He inched his way forward, a smooth slide across the couch. My heart started beating faster. I stupidly opened my mouth. "But I'm not sure you should."

He stopped. His leg was so close to touching mine. If we both leaned just a little towards the other, our lips would meet. God, I wanted to feel his beard tickling my skin.

"Why not?"

"I don't do casual and I don't do relationships."

He didn't look disappointed. More intrigued by my answer. "Not sure there's anything in between that."

I swallowed, kicking myself for having spoken at all. I *wanted* his kiss. "I know."

He studied me for a long moment. "What do you want to do then?"

I had to close my eyes. I needed to break the intense connection we were starting to form. I couldn't think with his deep gaze boring into mine like that. "I don't know."

"We're strangers." It seemed interesting that he would point out that obvious fact. I opened my eyes so I could read his expression. "But you don't feel like a stranger."

He didn't either. Being with him felt like reuniting with an old friend I hadn't seen in a very long time. "What if we play twenty questions?"

The fire popped behind me, but neither of us looked its way.

"No details?" I wasn't sure if it was a question or a reminder.

I nodded. "No details."

He hesitated before agreeing. "I don't want you to be a stranger. Once we are able to safely move to Corbin's, we'll be out of your house, but I don't want that to mean we'll be out of your life."

"I don't want it to mean that either."

"Do you want to go first?"

I did have a burning question to ask but I wasn't sure how he would answer it without giving away details. "Where is the kids' mother?"

"Going for gold, I see." Adam let out a sigh and scooted back a little. He wasn't back where he'd started, only provided some much-needed space between us. "Mothers," he finally said. "They're half-siblings." I fought to keep my face blank; I never would have guessed that. With their blonde hair, blue eyes, and fair skin, they looked extremely similar. Additionally, I did not like the implication that Adam had been so sexually reckless with the women he slept with. "I don't know where Lydia's mother is. She left after her birth and I never saw her again. Henry's died in childbirth."

"I'm so sorry." It didn't sound like he had an emotional attachment to either woman, but they still had to mean something to him as the mothers of his kids. Adam didn't seem so heartless as to not care.

He shrugged. "Thanks." Then a smile appeared on his face. "My turn. How do you restock a water supply?"

A laugh escaped me. "You have only twenty questions and that's the one you ask me?"

"Does that count as one of *your* questions?"

I mock glared at him. "No, it's not." He was still grinning. "I have two tanks out back that provide me with water. During the winter, it's easy to refill them because I just have to shovel snow into them. The heaters melt the snow and the filters take out anything mixed in with it. During the summer, I have a river not too far from my cabin. I take a portable tank down and fill it up from the fresh water source."

"Sounds like a lot of work."

I shrugged. "It is, but worth it to be able to live up here. There's no city or well water available out here."

"What about electricity and sewer?"

"Is that your next question?"

It was his turn to glare. "Yes."

"Only eighteen left for you." I pointed over my shoulder at the fireplace. "Electricity is mostly done by solar panels. I have to take them down during storms like this or run a generator during the day. Candles generally save me electric needs at night, though I have been leaving the lights on at night for the kids. During the winter, my fireplaces keep this place warm. The one in my bedroom is smaller but still effective. That's why I pushed for you and the kids to take my bedroom. It's really not an inconvenience for me, because I love to sleep out here next to this fireplace. Plus, if I keep all the doors open, it's only the kitchen that gets a bit brisk. I have the wood stove if I need to warm that one up too.

"As for plumbing, just like with the water, the town doesn't bring pipes up this far. I'm not on any grid map. The only reason the ski resort has the amenities it does is because they bring in a lot of tourist money. As you know, I have a flushing toilet, bathroom and kitchen sinks, a washing machine, and the bathtub. I have two tanks out back for gray and black water. The gray water comes from the sinks and bathtub. It gets treated and recycled back into my water stores. The black water goes into a compost tank that I turn into fertilizer. Most of my trash goes there too: peels, seeds, spoiled food... It's all recycled into fertilizer for my garden."

He watched me so intently as I spoke. I wondered if I'd lost him or if he now thought my lifestyle to be gross. Not many people would admit to fertilizing their garden with their own waste. It wasn't until he spoke that I felt like I could breathe easier.

"Wow. That is amazing. I can't believe the effort you take to live up here. I mean, it's inspiring and intimidating all at the same time. When do you take a day off? Your work literally is doing everything you need to stay alive up here. Wait, do you work otherwise? Do you have a job?"

I shook my head. "I've already answered two of your questions. You'll need to save yours until after I've asked my next one."

He conceded with a bow of his head. "My mistake. Go ahead."

Except I didn't know what to ask him. No, that wasn't true. I didn't know which to ask him *first*! There were so many things I wanted to know. I started with, "How do you know Corbin?"

Adam paused. I wondered if he was trying to get his answer straight or to come up with false names. "Corbin's story is his own. I don't know what you know about his history and I don't want to say anything out of turn. Simplest answer is that we grew up together. We met in kindergarten and have been best friends ever since. He's more of a brother to me really, even though he's not blood."

I understood that completely. "Sometimes blood isn't everything. Blood can bond you or destroy you."

"Very true," he nodded. "Unfortunately, we lost touch for a very long time. Longer than I care to admit. I can throw out every excuse there is, life got in the way, I was busy with the kids... But the truth is that I was afraid to contact him. I wasn't sure if he blamed me for leaving him behind. I went off to college and he...didn't."

There was definitely more to that story but since it also mixed in with Corbin's I let it drop. "It's good you got in contact with him again."

"No doubt. He didn't even hesitate. As soon as he learned we were in trouble, he didn't even question the last eighteen years. He just dropped everything to help us get here."

"Sounds like a true friend." I was trying not to be jealous, but it was hard. He had what I hadn't had when I'd needed it most.

"My turn."

I was grateful for the change in topic. My line of thinking was making me feel morose.

I knew what his question was already and didn't need him to repeat it. "I don't have a job. At least, not in the way you're thinking. I don't clock in or work nine to five. It doesn't take much money to live out here once I got myself set up. I got the land for a steal. My cabin, stores, and tanks cost a pretty penny, but they were necessary to live out here. I had recently come into some money, and I also had a trust fund I'd never touched from my maternal grandmother. It wasn't much, not like millions or anything, but it was enough to buy me this place and still have a little left in savings.

"I grow or hunt most of my food. My amenities are natural resources. I don't have a phone or cable. I buy propane and gasoline in town when needed but even that is in small amounts. When I find myself running low on cash, I sell my jerky, jams, or furs to Jack down at the general store. He gives me a commission off of anything he sells of mine. Honestly, I think he gives me too much commission but he's never allowed me to give anything back."

"It's so hard to believe in this day and age that you can survive without any regular bills or a paycheck."

I nodded. "It took a lot of research before I came out here. I thought I'd done enough to prepare myself, but I was in for a lot of lessons those first couple of years. I made a lot of mistakes and spent money I didn't need. Once I picked up on specific things, it cut my spending down to almost nothing."

"Do you get bored with no TV or internet?"

I didn't count that as one of his questions. "Most of the time, I am so tired from working all day that I don't have time to think about it. I read a lot but, even during the winter when I'm stuck up here, there's always housework or things to do." I tipped my head at him in curiosity. "Have you or the kids been bored without the internet or a TV?"

He seemed startled by the question and then shook his head. "Actually, no. I wish I had some workbooks or coloring books for Lydia. Some sensory simulators for Henry. But I haven't once reached for a phone or had the urge to check on something online."

I grinned. He just proved my point. "It's this mountain. It's magical in its own way. There are no distractions up here, no noise. It's like nature is its own form of entertainment. Some days I sit up in the loft and just stare out the window. It always surprises me how much time has passed once I come back to reality."

"I guess time would have a different meaning up here. In the city, it's *go-go-go* no matter the time of day. And everyone is so concerned with getting somewhere by nine o'clock on the dot."

I nodded, while keeping quiet that he'd just revealed he'd come from a city. "I don't even put a watch on anymore. I judge time based on the sun or the moon, because exact time doesn't matter up here. If it wasn't for my occasional trip into town, I probably wouldn't even pay attention to the date and month."

Adam leaned his head against the back of the couch but didn't take his eyes off me. "That seems like an amazing freedom. I'm envious."

"Well, you're up here now too," I reminded him. "You'll soon get the hang of our way of life."

I was expecting him to smile again. Instead, his expression fell. "I came here out of necessity. I wasn't even sure what to expect when I was told to take the mountain road. Hell, I think a part of me was expecting a private resort or something less known than the ski resort. I certainly wasn't expecting...*this*," he gestured around my cabin. "Or you."

I gave him a small smile.

"But the truth is, I'm not mechanical. I've never chopped wood in my life. I don't cook. My version of cooking is a pile of takeout menus in my drawer. Yesterday, I saw you restock a water tank. You have served us meals of unknown animals that you killed and processed yourself. And frankly I don't want to know what that roast at dinner was. I'm happy just knowing it was delicious. You also drove a snowmobile in the middle of a snowstorm in complete darkness. Brooke, you're a total badass."

I felt myself blush at his praise. He shrugged self-deprecatingly. "I don't know if this life is for me. It was forced upon us and I'll do my best if this is what my kids need, but I'm not a mountain man. I can't lift boulders onto my shoulders or wrestle with bears." Then he said like it was a shameful addition to what he perceived as his shortcomings, "I'm just a teacher."

I'd begun to feel disheartened when he'd started talking about how much this lifestyle wasn't for him. At his admission to his occupation, I felt intrigued. "You're a teacher? What grade?"

"I taught second grade for a few years until a private opportunity presented itself." His skin reddened above his beard. "I thought I'd hit the jackpot. Not only could I pay off my student debt far earlier than ever expected but my employer was willing to pay for me to advance my degree to a Masters." He shook his head. "I was so naïve. I wish I'd known I'd been signing a contract with the devil."

He looked so forlorn. I wanted to wrap my arms around him to offer what comfort I could. Instead, I locked my muscles into place so I wouldn't do something I'd regret later. Because I would regret getting physically close to him when he left my cabin.

"But if I hadn't taken that deal, I wouldn't have Lydia and Henry, and I wouldn't trade them for anything."

The love in his eyes for his children shone. It was a beautiful sight to see. Against my better judgment, I reached my hand forward and rested it on his knee. "I'm going to be bluntly honest here because, frankly, I lost the ability to beat around the bush years ago. Moreover, I don't like secrets or lies. So here's the truth about what I see when I look at you:

"You're right that you're not a mountain man. Whether you have certain skills or not, those can be learned. What I see above all else when I look at you is a loving father. *That's* your calling,

Adam. You are so attentive and caring to those kids that it hurts sometimes looking at you with them, because I no longer have that type of relationship with my parents. It's also a shameful reality about mankind as a species that there are millions of children out there who are in abusive homes or are starving or are kidnapped for all sorts of disgusting and nefarious reasons. To see how you are with your kids is like a breath of fresh air.

"So maybe you're not mechanical. Maybe you need to learn a thing or two about mountain life. First and foremost being that jeans and snow don't mix." His lips twitched but he didn't crack the smile I was hoping to see. "Being a man, especially a mountain man, is more than how much you can lift or if you're willing and able to skin a deer you just shot. It's about accepting nature, respecting it. It's about the need to escape the noise of the world and fill it with the sounds of nature."

He put his hand on top of mine. Immediately I felt the difference between the two. Mine were rough and callused while his were smooth. I didn't mind the contrast. In fact, it felt nice.

Our eyes met once more and my breath caught. I'm not sure who started leaning in first, but soon I found our mouths only centimeters apart. I could taste his breath, could feel the coarse hair of his beard against the side of my face. Our hands were now clasped between our chests, though I didn't remember lifting them.

My eyes fluttered closed. Our foreheads met. Neither of us tipped forward that final step to press our lips together.

I felt like crying. It was a feeling I hadn't had in a very long time. All of this was. The attraction I felt towards him had been almost instantaneous. I'd thought him a good looking man when he'd been unconscious, but that had been nothing in comparison to when his revealing eyes opened.

But there was no future here. It would only be one night.

My chin started quaking. I wanted this, but the regret would be palpable come morning. Because I would want more.

I was about to back away when he suddenly lifted his head, pressing his lips to my forehead. As soon as his lips made contact with my skin, I felt a tear escape my eye and make its way down my cheek.

He was respecting my wishes. I should feel grateful. Yet I felt like I couldn't breathe. The tightness in my chest prevented me from catching my breath.

Adam gripped me tight, pressing his lips hard against my forehead. I wasn't sure how long we stayed there like that. It could have been five seconds or five hours. I felt my heart crack a little when he eventually pulled back.

He lifted a hand to cup my cheek, his thumb brushing against my tear trail. I was taking short gulps of air, just trying to keep myself together.

"If I was a different man, living a different life, I would kiss you without hesitation or regret. I would take you into my arms and make love to you all night long, Brooke." He let his hand drop. He pulled away completely. I felt immediately cold, despite the roaring fire behind me. "But that's not my life. I have to put my children first. I have to protect them. And you, my beautiful mountain goddess, are a distraction I can't afford. My attentions are already divided."

Adam stood up. I watched as he took a deep breath and then walked towards the bedroom. He didn't look back and I didn't call out to him. He was clearly as torn as I was, but that fact didn't make me feel any better.

Chapter Ten

Adam

The roar of a snowmobile had never been so welcome. I was sitting in the living room playing tic-tac-toe with Lydia while Henry sat on my lap sucking on a bottle. He wasn't eating much anymore, just gnawing on the nipple. I didn't mind as it was entertaining him for a time and exercising his gums. He'd started teething just before we had gone on the run.

Yesterday had been long and painful. One could have cut the tension between Brooke and me with a knife. Corbin had been unable to come down. His mom wasn't feeling well, and he hadn't wanted to leave her. I understood, and sympathized, but I'd been really counting on the company to fill the silence between Brooke and me.

We were avoiding each other, and I hated it. She had barely spoken to me since our night on the couch. When she did speak, it was a simple question like, "Did you eat enough?" or informing me that "I'm going outside."

I didn't know how to fix it, to fix *us*. And the worst part of that desire was that there was no *us*, and never could be. When Brooke walked into a room, she took up my whole attention. She was like a magnet, automatically drawing my eyes to find her, follow her, study her... If I didn't know of her equal attraction to me, I'd call myself a creep and blindfold myself to spare her my obsession. I wanted to walk up to her and kiss her. I wanted to be able to call her *mine*. I had never felt so possessive over a woman before. I'd never understood the Neanderthal desire to claim a woman until I met Brooke.

But taking her, even with her permission, would be selfish. I needed to protect my kids. I couldn't risk any distractions from that, or it could cost us our lives.

I'd gone to bed with the kids again last night, but I hadn't fallen asleep when they had. Instead, I laid awake and fought the growing urge to walk out into the living room and make love to Brooke in front of the roaring fire. At one point, it had gotten so bad that I had lifted a sleeping Henry onto my chest and held him as if he weighed enough to anchor me down.

So by this afternoon, after almost two days of near silence between us, I was about ready to explode. When I finally heard the snowmobile outside, I let out a sigh of relief. Corbin would get my mind off Brooke.

I went to the window, and my jaw nearly dropped. I hadn't seen him in eighteen years. When he'd been arrested, Corbin had been a tall, gangly teenager. He'd been malnourished and downtrodden.

The giant that climbed off the snowmobile looked nothing like the teen I remembered. Actually, with that black beard and long shaggy hair, he could have been Hagrid's younger brother. I placed him a foot taller than my five-ten.

Brooke opened her front door for him, and he had to duck to enter. I couldn't believe how large he was. His biceps were bigger than my waist! Goddamn. He was pure muscle.

My eyes flew to Brooke, recalling the *babe* comment over the radio. Was there something between them? In comparison, how was I even in the running for Brooke's affections when she had a man like Corbin so near?

"Whoa," even came from Lydia.

Corbin looked over at me, then behind me at Lydia. A huge smile appeared on his face, and, despite my irrational jealousy, I found myself smiling back. "Jesus, Adam, it's so good to see you." He dropped the duffel bag he was carrying, came over and wrapped his massive arms around me. Since I was holding Henry, he didn't grip me too hard, but I still felt the squeeze.

When he released me, he clasped me on my shoulders. This was definitely familiar, our height difference. In high school, Corbin used to rest his elbow on my head because, per him, my head was the perfect height to be used as an armrest.

"Holy sh— I mean, cra—" He winced, biting his tongue. "Wow, I've never had to curb my language before. This is going to be hard."

I laughed. "You get used to it or get creative with alternatives. My preferred are 'sugar-snaps', 'fudge-sicles', and 'H-E-double hockey sticks'."

"I'll try to remember those." He looked around me to where Lydia had pressed herself against the back of my leg. She was peeking her little blonde head around my leg. Her natural curiosity and my greeting likely kept her from being scared of the stranger.

Corbin knelt down in front of her. Even kneeling he was huge, but at least he wasn't towering now. "Hi, sweetheart. What's your name?"

She looked up at me. At my encouraging nod, she looked back at Corbin. "Lydia."

"Lydia? That's a pretty name, fit for a princess."

She shrugged but didn't say anything.

"Hm," Corbin hummed. "Are you afraid of me?"

Again, Lydia looked up at me. I didn't indicate which way

she should answer though. After some contemplating, she pursed her lips and looked at Corbin. "No. You're Daddy's brother and my uncle."

He smiled so wide, it must have hurt his cheeks. I hadn't told him I'd been referring to him as her uncle as an explanation as to who we were seeing. I could have called him a friend, but I wanted her to feel like she had family beyond me if anything happened to me. It was my hope that by calling him her uncle, she would trust him easier.

"That's right." Cautiously, he opened his arms. "Can I have a hug?"

Lydia stepped forward slowly. She kept her hands at her sides. When she got close enough, she lifted one hand to his outstretched one. Her entire spread hand fit in the palm of his. She journeyed down his arm, touching his jacket, which looked like it was made of real fur. Her exploration brought her closer to him. Corbin remained perfectly still, letting her choose how close she got.

I watched, waiting to see what would happen. Lydia wasn't very trusting with strangers. I think she attached herself so quickly to Brooke because, one, she'd saved us and, two, Brooke was a woman. Lydia had learned from a young age not to trust men other than me and her brother.

She was in between his outstretched arms but still hadn't gone in for a full hug. Lydia scrunched up her face. "Are you going to keep my daddy safe?"

Corbin's eyes flew to mine before immediately going back down to her. "I'm going to try. And not just your daddy, but you too."

Lydia thought about this for another moment before nodding. Her seven-year-old curiosity satisfied, she closed the distance between them and wrapped her arms around his neck. She had to stretch up on her tippy toes to reach.

Corbin's arms came around her, holding her tightly to his chest. He rose to his feet with her still in his arms. Lydia's legs dangled high off the ground. She lifted her head to look down, way down, at the floor. Her grip on Corbin's neck tightened but she didn't look scared. Instead, she turned to me with the biggest grin on her face.

"Look, Daddy, I'm taller than you!"

I chuckled. "I see that, Angel."

Corbin patted her back. "Stick with me, kid. I'll give you as many piggyback rides as you want so you can stay taller than your daddy."

She was so small in his arms. If he tightened his hold, he could crush her like a bug. But I knew that would never happen. I knew those arms could and would protect her.

Henry, finished with his chewing on the bottle's nipple, let out a large burp. Thankfully there was no spit up this time.

Corbin reached over and draped a large hand over his head. "Good to meet you too, little guy."

"His name is Henry," Lydia supplied. "He's six months old."

"Yeah?" Corbin jostled her playfully in his arms. "And how old are you, little miss? Twenty-one? Twenty-two?"

Lydia giggled. "No! I'm seven!"

"Oh, how silly of me. You look so much older when you're this tall!"

Movement from behind Corbin drew my attention to Brooke. I was reminded of the first morning I'd woken up here, when I'd held my kids on the kitchen floor. It was the way she stood, her hunched posture, almost like she feared she was intruding on a private moment.

I wanted so much to pull her into my arms then, to include her. It would have been so easy, so right. To hold her against my side, one arm around her waist, the other holding Henry. I could picture it perfectly, like a family portrait.

I cleared my throat, needing to get that vision out of my head. "Brooke, would you mind taking Lydia into the kitchen for a snack? Corbin and I need to talk."

While there definitely were things that I didn't want Brooke to know, I also needed space from her. It was the excuse I needed to prevent myself from doing something stupid.

I didn't miss Corbin's eyes as they volleyed between the two of us.

Brooke stepped forward. "Of course." Corbin lowered Lydia to the floor and Brooke offered her hand. "Come on, Lydia. Let's see what goodies we can dig up."

She didn't look at me as she led Lydia from the room.

Corbin, however, did. He raised his bushy eyebrows in question. I shook my head, not ready or willing to talk about that.

Chapter Eleven

Adam

I led him into Brooke's bedroom so we could close the door. I knew how voices echoed around the cabin, and I didn't want our conversation overheard easily.

Henry was still in my arms, but the kid was currently being entertained by his own foot. It was a fascinating discovery that took up his whole attention.

"What the hell, man?" Corbin asked, keeping his voice low. "What happened?"

I sat on the edge of the bed. "I don't even know where to start."

"Jack told me some of it. I didn't know this before, but when I sent you that postcard years ago, he looked you up. He's protective of those of us who live up on the mountain and he wanted to make sure you were a good person if you tried to contact me."

I wasn't sure how I felt about that, but his previous research explained a lot about our first conversation. As well as how Jack was able to jump into action so quickly to help us. Any other situation, I probably would care a lot more than I did right then.

I was just grateful Jack had been able to help my kids and me out.

"It started eight years ago, right when you sent the postcard actually. When I received it, I was in the middle of packing. I'd been offered a new job and it included live-in quarters. I'd given up the lease on my apartment." I shook my head at my own stupidity. "I should have done more research. Or I should have asked more questions. Hindsight is always twenty-twenty though. At the time, I just knew that this millionaire was moving me into his mansion to tutor his fifteen-year-old son. He would pay me to tutor him and pay for advancing my degree."

"Sebastian Gunther?"

I nodded. "He seemed like your everyday millionaire. Stuck-up, condescending, and did not accept failures. When his son—Trenton is the son's name—failed a math test, he was furious. Took a crystal vase that probably costs more than my annual salary and smashed it against the wall. The only reason I wasn't fired within my first month of being there was because Trenton copped to not being the one that took the test at all. He'd ditched class to have sex with another student and had paid yet another student to take the test for him."

Corbin snorted. "I really want to say something like 'kids today...' but we were probably just as stupid at fifteen."

I couldn't argue with him. Corbin and I had ditched class more than once too. Mind, neither of us did it to have sex. We weren't exactly popular with the girls in our school. I'd only managed one kiss before graduation. Sex hadn't happened for me until I'd gone to college. As far as I knew, Corbin hadn't had sex before he'd gone to prison—and I certainly wasn't going to ask him to verify the accuracy of that statement.

"Gunther was so proud of his son for having sex, called him a man, that he didn't even care about the test. Looking back on it, maybe I should have seen something then, but I was just so thrilled to still have my job that I pushed any concerns I had aside. Gunther instructed me to continue tutoring him, and then added like it was a funny joke that I should also add Sex Ed to my curriculum.

"Less than a month later, it became common knowledge around the mansion that Gunther's *mistress*, not his wife," I clarified, "was pregnant. She was one of the maids. There were rumors that this was not the first time he'd gotten one of the staff pregnant. However, the difference this time was that the wife had recently moved out. They were living in separate households in different states. I guess Gunther didn't care anymore if she knew about his affairs or an illegitimate child.

"He approached me about a change in my job responsibilities and title. Rather than being a tutor for his almost sixteen-year-old son, I would be the sole caretaker and nanny for the baby when he or she was born. Apparently now that the son was sexually active, he didn't need a tutor anymore." I shrugged, to this day still not understanding that logic. "I was honestly thrilled. Trenton was a horrible student. As bad as it is for me to admit this, I was happy to be leaving that position.

"I spent a lot of time with Helena, the pregnant mistress. She was excited about the baby and was completely convinced that Gunther was going to divorce his wife to marry her. What she didn't know, and that I accidentally found out, was that most of Gunther's business connections came from the wife's side of the family. He was never going to divorce his wife and risk losing that standing with her family. Helena was so sure, though. She was utterly convinced that Gunther was going to marry her. The last couple of months of her pregnancy, she even started to refer to herself as his fiancée.

"Then Lydia was born, and Gunther didn't show. When Helena was brought to the hospital, I had called and texted him, but all I got back was a single acknowledgement text of 'fine'.

Man couldn't even be bothered to come to his own daughter's birth.

"A couple of days after we brought Lydia home, I was informed by Gunther that Helena had been dismissed from her services and was no longer welcome in the mansion. It took me by surprise. How could she leave her daughter? I didn't understand it. I was instructed by Gunther to care for and raise Lydia. He was fine with her being in the house, but he was not to see or hear her. Again, I didn't understand. The man didn't want his own daughter either.

"It was Trenton who informed me what had really happened. Surprisingly, he was actually attentive to Lydia. She was his half-sister after all. I was proud of him for showing her affection. Anyway, Trenton told me that Gunther had paid Helena a lot of money to sign away her parental rights to Lydia. She signed another document saying that she would never try to contact Lydia or come near the mansion again. If she did, she would forfeit her monthly stipend."

Corbin, who had been silent for most of my story, shook his head in disgust. "What sort of mother does something like that?"

"A greedy one, I suppose."

"What happened next?"

"Not a lot for the next several years. Lydia grew into a beautiful little girl. She is so smart and absolutely loves puzzles. Around her fifth birthday, though, things started to change. Up to that point, Gunther hadn't paid any attention to Lydia. He would occasionally ask for a status update on her, but he'd never visited her. Lydia didn't know him as her father. In fact, she called me her father. I corrected her when she was younger, but eventually I stopped. I knew it was wrong of me to call her my own, because I was being paid to care for her, but, Cor, she was *my daughter*. I raised her, I loved her, I taught her, I *named* her. Gunther was nothing more to her than a sperm donor. She didn't even know who he was. She'd never even seen his face. She knew Trenton was her brother, but she knew nothing of her biological father."

Corbin gave me a sympathetic look. "I get it, man. I'm not a dad, but I know I'd do anything, have done everything, to protect my mom." I nodded, having been there for the aftermath of that protection. "What happened when she turned five?"

I cleared my throat. "Gunther suddenly started wanting her around. She was to be dressed up and presentable. She was to attend meals with him. It was a complete one-eighty to the first five years of her life. Lydia was confused. She did everything I asked of her, but she didn't understand it. She would sit at these big meals and parties Gunther was hosting and look for me in the crowd. I wasn't allowed to sit or talk with her during the parties. I was the *servant*," I spat the word, "and could only attend to her from a distance.

"I relied on Trenton a lot during those parties. He was the one allowed to be near her, and she knew him. We coached her on making sure to call Gunther 'Father' and to never call me 'Daddy' in public. Trenton told me that the change in Gunther's behavior was from some new investors that Gunther had. He was trying to impress them by presenting himself as being a family man. He always explained his wife's absence by saying she was 'shopping in Paris' or was 'on a cruise' with some girlfriends...

"Things went on like this for a couple of months. New investor, new party, and Lydia was dolled up like a piece of art to be shown off. And then..." My voice trailed off as a flash of that horrible night came to the surface.

Corbin came forward, resting his hand on my shoulder. He gave me a reassuring squeeze but didn't speak. I appreciated him keeping his silence so I could get my thoughts in order.

"We were summoned to Gunther's office. Trenton wasn't

there. It was Gunther, two bodyguards, and two other men I didn't recognize. Lydia was to be brought in for a show of sorts. We'd rehearsed it numerous times. It was a skit Gunther put on for the investors. Lydia would barge into his office, run over to Gunther, and hug him. She would say what a great time she had at the park and try to tell him all about it. Gunther would then say that he's got a friend over and she could tell him all about the park at dinner. In the last couple times we did this, Gunther would even *boop* her on the nose for effect. Lydia was to smile, wave to the investor, and then run back to me. I was always by the door. I was not allowed further into the room than the wall by the door.

"I always hated when Lydia had to do this, but we'd done it numerous times by then. I assumed this time would go just as smoothly as the others." I flinched, the echo of the gunshot still in my head. "I was so wrong. The investor didn't allow Lydia to run past him to come to me. Instead, he grabbed her by her skirt and brought her towards him. I started forward but Gunther gave me this look that told me I was to stay in my place and..." I had to fight through my shame to admit, "I froze. I stayed where I was told to stay like a good little servant while *my daughter* was dragged up onto the lap of a stranger."

Bile rose in my throat. Henry curled up closer to me, as if he sensed I needed his comforting touch.

"The investor started talking about *stock*. I didn't understand. Gunther was a businessman who dealt in trades. I wasn't really paying attention to what was being said though because all my attention was on Lydia. She was sitting stiffly, her thumb in her mouth. She was so uncomfortable. And I just *stood there*."

I hated myself for that. More than I would ever admit aloud.

"And then the investor put his hand *under* Lydia's skirt. She was *five*. I started forward again. I didn't care what Gunther said at that point. I was not going to stand by and watch Lydia be molested. But then Gunther, who was just sitting calmly behind his desk at this point, casually raised a gun and shot the investor in the head. *With Lydia still on the man's lap.*"

There were no words to describe the fear I had felt in that moment. Lydia had screamed so loudly I'd thought she'd been shot too.

Corbin took Henry from my arms. I hadn't realized until then that he'd taken off his jacket. He was wearing a long sleeve beige shirt. His pants looked like the same polyester material of the suit Brooke donned before going outside.

I appreciated him taking the baby. As much as it comforted me to have Henry in my arms, I needed space right then. I needed to move. We silently swapped seats. He sat on the bed holding Henry and I started pacing the room.

"I felt like I was running through *Jell-o*. I couldn't get to her fast enough. The man started to slump over. She would have been crushed under him if he'd fallen with her still in his lap. I caught her just in time. She was *covered* in blood. It was all over her face, her hair, her pink dress... She was screaming and crying, clutching me like I was her lifeline.

"Out of the corner of my eye, I saw Gunther put the gun down. Then he instructed me to take Lydia out of the room and he'd find me later." I shuddered. "He was so *calm*. It was... unnerving. He'd just shot a man with his own daughter on the man's lap, inches from where the bullet had passed by, and he was just sitting there cool and collected.

"I knew the man was cruel. I knew he was calculating and ruthless when it came to business. I'd been working for the man for six years at that point, I'd picked up on some things. But a *murderer*? A psychopath?" I shook my head. "I never saw that coming."

I continued my pacing. I could feel my palms sweating and

my fast heartbeat. I was grateful I'd eaten a light lunch, or it probably would have already come back up by now.

"I knew I had to call the cops, but Lydia was my priority. I had to get her cleaned up and she was so hysterical. I kept going over and over in my head what I needed to say to the police. I didn't want to forget a single detail, including which drawer in his desk Gunther had put his gun in. That would be evidence. It hit me then that I didn't even know the man's name. I hated him for having touched Lydia, but I'd also seen him be murdered. And I didn't even know his name.

"I guess I was in shock myself. My thoughts just kept whirling in my head like my brain had been thrown into a blender. I remember thinking that nothing had to change once Gunther went to jail. Trenton would inherit the mansion and would take guardianship of Lydia. He'd let me stay and continue caring for her. Nothing had to change." I shook my head, looking up at the ceiling. "I was so foolish. Of course, a man like Gunther was prepared for me to go to the police.

"I had just gotten Lydia calmed down enough to sleep when Gunther came to my rooms. I hadn't had a chance to make my phone call yet. In the all the years that I'd been there, Gunther had never come to my rooms. When he needed to talk to me, I was always summoned to his office. It was where he held the most power and authority. That was *his* domain. So, for him to show up in my rooms... I truly thought he was there to kill me. Sick as it was, I was grateful Lydia was asleep, so she didn't have to watch my murder too.

"Up to that point, despite the heinousness of the murder itself, a part of me believed or wanted to believe he'd done it to protect his daughter. After all, the man had had his hand up her skirt." I turned to Corbin. "Cor, he didn't even care about me seeing the murder. He didn't care about the man touching

Lydia. What he cared about was that I never repeated what I'd overheard about the shipment coming in."

"What shipment?"

"Exactly. I had no idea what he was talking about. I'd been so concerned about Lydia that I hadn't even paid attention to what was said between Gunther and the investor. Still, I swore that I'd never repeat what I heard. It was the truth, as I had no idea what was said anyway, but I knew he wouldn't believe me if I said that. Gunther nodded once and told me that I wasn't to bring Lydia around again until he specifically said otherwise. I was starting to get my hopes up that that was it and he would leave, then I could call the police and report the murder.

"But then, Gunther pulled a gun out of his coat pocket. I froze. Gunther waved off my concern like my reaction to the weapon was foolish. When Gunther held up the gun, I realized it was in a plastic bag. Now I'm no expert on weapons, but even I could tell that this gun was different than the one he'd used to shoot the investor. I didn't understand why he was showing it to me.

"Gunther then reminded me of how I was fingerprinted at the start of my employment. He never came out and said my fingerprints were on that gun, but the implication was there. He said something along the lines of, it would be a shame if the police were made aware of what had happened that night because the only weapon they would find would be the one he was holding, and it wasn't *his* fingerprints that were on the gun.

"Before I could even fully process the threat, he was gone."

"Fuck. And you were fingerprinted when you started?"

I nodded solemnly. "I thought it was all part of the background screening required to take the job.

"Later, after Trenton had heard what happened, he came to my room to check on Lydia. After I'd taken the job as Lydia's nanny, I'd been moved to a bigger room that was attached to her then-nursery, now-bedroom. It was late and she'd already woken up screaming from a nightmare, so I had had her in bed with me. Trenton sat on the bed on her other side. For all his faults as a teen, he truly did care about his sister. *That* was when I discovered why that man had died. He'd been skimming money from Gunther. Trenton told me he would have died whether he'd touched Lydia or not. Then Trenton made me swear that, no matter what, I never repeated that I now knew his family money came from human trafficking."

"Holy fuck," Corbin breathed out. Then he winced when he looked down at the baby in his arms. "Oops. I mean, holy fudge-sicles."

Despite the story I was telling, a humorless laugh escaped me. "Thankfully, he's too young to remember any of this."

"A good thing." Corbin looked at the closed door then back at me. "What does Lydia remember?"

"Too much, unfortunately. She still has nightmares, wets the bed, and she knows that her birth dad is a very bad man."

"I'm sorry you had to go through that."

I gave him a sorrowful look. "It gets worse."

"Well, shit."

"Gunther didn't summon Lydia again for about six months. I tried to make her life as normal as possible, tried to get her to open up about what had happened so she could process it, but she was *terrified* of Gunther. Sometimes when Trenton came in to visit, she was scared of him too before she realized he was her brother and not her father. Trenton never held it against her, but I could tell it bothered him.

"Lydia was six by then. She knew what had happened wasn't right or normal. I started studying child psychology more in depth so I could better help her. She'd been making progress, less nightmares and she hadn't wet the bed in a couple of weeks, but I didn't know what facing Gunther would do to her. I was so grateful when it was Trenton who came to get us. I knew he would protect her if I couldn't get to her in time.

"Lydia was very quiet during the meal. She hadn't acknowledged Gunther as he demanded she did when she attended these gatherings. I could tell he was not happy about how she entered the room without greeting him, but he didn't draw attention to it in front of his guests.

"Dinner came and went. Trenton was even able to get a smile out of Lydia by making funny faces at her from across the table. Then, after dinner, we were summoned to his office. Trenton, Lydia, and me." I swallowed hard. "As soon as we entered, Gunther slapped Lydia across the face."

"Fuck."

I seconded the expletive. "I jumped between them. Biological father or not, no man strikes my daughter. Trenton got her off the floor and cradled her to his chest. She was crying. And then..." I let out a shaky breath. "And then Gunther informed me of the choice I had to make. Lydia was my responsibility. Therefore, her failures and wrongdoings were my own. I either had to step aside while she was punished, or I could take her punishment for her. But if I took it, it would be twofold."

"I'm not going to like this, am I?"

I shook my head. "Trenton tried to talk his father out of it. He kept saying that she was just a little girl, and she was getting over a trauma, but Gunther didn't care. I could see it in his eyes. He *would* punish Lydia for not greeting him in front of his guests when she entered the dining room." I swallowed around the lump in my throat as I admitted, "I said that I would take her punishment for her."

"Goddamn."

"Gunther went over to his desk. I didn't know what he intended. A part of me thought he was going to get his gun. All I knew was that I was not going to allow Lydia to be punished. I told Trenton to take her back to her room and stay with her until I returned." I hadn't said the *if I returned* to Trenton back then, but we had both known it was unspoken. "But Gunther told Trenton to stay. He wanted Lydia to see what happens when she misbehaves. I begged him to let her go. Told him that he could do whatever he wanted to me as long as Lydia wasn't subjected to it." I would never forget the stricken look on Lydia's little face as she figured that I was going to be punished for something she had done wrong. Never. "Gunther still told Trenton to stay."

I fell silent, terrible memories whirling around in my head. I wasn't sure how to admit what happened next. Sometimes it still felt like a bad dream. If it wasn't for the scars on my back, I might have been able to convince myself of that too.

"What did he do to you?" Corbin's voice was low and gentle. It didn't take a genius to figure out how hard admitting and reliving all this was for me.

"He flogged me."

"He *what?*" It was probably a good thing he was holding Henry just then or I had a feeling Corbin would have thrown a fit of rage with how angry he was at my admission.

"My daughter and her brother watched as I was stripped of my shirt, told to stand up against the wall, and then I was flogged with a whip. I don't know if he would have used the same whip or a smaller one for Lydia, but I received twenty strikes, which meant she would have gotten ten. The man was going to *flog* his six-year-old daughter."

"Dear God. Did you go to the hospital? What happened?"

I turned my back to him and lifted up my sweater to my pits. I had three scars from my ordeal. One was long and went from my right shoulder blade, across my spine, and ended at my left side. That had been one of the first to bleed when I'd been struck. Most hadn't broken flesh, but the ones that had were permanently with me. The second scar was shorter than the first and almost directly below it. The third went from the left side of my spine around my side to almost my bellybutton.

"That rat bastard. I'll kill him."

Coming from a convicted murderer, I wasn't sure how seriously to take that statement. I lowered my shirt and turned back around. "If you're going to kill him, do it for what he did next to Lydia and not for what he did to me. I took that punishment to save my daughter. I'll never regret that."

"You're a better man than I am, Adam. I don't know if I could have done what you did."

"When you have kids, you'll understand. There isn't anything you wouldn't do for them."

A haunted look crossed his face. It was there and gone again in the blink of an eye. "I don't think kids are in the cards for me."

That was a conversation for another time. "To answer your question, I didn't go to the hospital. That would have raised too many red flags. Instead a physician came to the mansion to check on my wounds. Trenton called him, by the way, not Gunther."

"I'm actually starting to like this kid."

I gave a wry smile. "Me too. He took charge of Lydia while I couldn't. He'd bring her in to me so I could see her and spend time with her. Otherwise, he was with her twenty-four-seven while I was laid up. He even changed my bandages and put the medication the doctor had prescribed me on my back."

I had been stuck on my belly for over a week so the cuts could heal. The doctor had said I could get up if I felt up to it, but any movement would break the cuts open again. It was better to let them heal as quickly as possible to lessen the scarring.

"One night, it was super late, probably around two or three in the morning, I woke to find Trenton sneaking into my room.

He'd been sleeping in Lydia's, but he'd never come into my room like that before. He told me he had a plan to get Lydia out of the mansion and away from their father. After what had just happened to me, I was all for it. But we had to do it safely. We had to somehow escape and assume new identities that Gunther couldn't track or trace. Trenton said he would start to work on it, but he wanted to make sure I was willing to leave with her. I never even hesitated. I told Trenton to do what he had to do and, when everything was ready, we would leave and never look back.

"It took almost a month for Trenton to get everything together. But fate had a plot twist neither of us were expecting." I gestured to Henry, now asleep in his uncle's arms. "Trenton found out another one of Gunther's mistresses was pregnant."

"Wow, this guy needs to learn to glove up or pull out."

Surprisingly a snort escaped me. "I truly don't think the man cared."

"Obviously, you stayed."

I nodded. "We had to. I wasn't about to subject another child to that life. Trenton and I considered Lydia and I leaving before the birth and then Trenton would somehow get the baby to me, but we nixed that idea almost as soon as we had it. Once I was away with Lydia, I couldn't ever contact Trenton or risk leading Gunther back to Lydia.

"So, we stayed. Once again Gunther came to me and told me that I was to be his son's nanny too. The woman was further along than I'd expected. I was with Helena for almost six months of her pregnancy. This woman was almost eight months along when I met her.

"There were complications with the birth, though. The woman had preeclampsia and her heart gave out during delivery. Henry was a preemie too, so he was in the NICU ward for several weeks because his lungs weren't fully developed yet.

"Once again, Gunther wasn't there for any of this. Trenton took care of Lydia at home because I didn't want her in the hospital. I stayed with Henry until he was released to go home. There was actually a clerical error when they made the birth certificate, and I was named as Henry's birth father."

Not that that mattered now. I didn't have that document with us. Plus, I doubt a piece of paper would stop Gunther from claiming Henry as his son.

"By the time I brought Henry home, he was almost six weeks old. Trenton and I didn't know what to do. We now had a baby to get out of the mansion too. A baby needed more supplies and care than a seven-year-old did. Trenton said that Gunther was so ecstatic about having a son that he was actually acting nicer. We decided to wait until Henry was a year old to leave. He would be bigger by then, able to handle more. Lydia would be eight by then too, so she'd be able to help out more."

If only, if only...

"Then, three weeks ago, Gunther called us to his office again. We hadn't been summoned there since the night I'd taken Lydia's punishment. I didn't know what to expect. As soon as we entered, though, I saw the look of horror on Trenton's face... I should have run then. I had Henry in my arms, I had Lydia's hand... I should have just run then.

"But we would have been stopped. We would have been caught if I'd done that. And yet, what I wouldn't give to have spared Lydia that next hour."

"Shit, man. You don't need to tell me if you're not ready."

I shook my head. "You're taking a risk protecting us. You need to know. You have a right to know why I'm risking your life too."

Corbin hesitated but then nodded his agreement.

"There was a group of men in the office with Gunther. From the way they held themselves and the weapons I could see, I guessed them to be gangsters or maybe even the mafia. Hell, I still don't know what organization type Gunther was in. Not that that matters now.

"Lydia was instructed to walk forward for 'inspection'," my tongue soured at the word. "She looked at me and Trenton, but we couldn't tell her no. She walked over to where Gunther stood with the group of men.

"This time, I paid attention to what was said." Yet, there were times when I wished I hadn't. I had that image of Lydia's intended future permanently stuck in my head for the rest of my life. "And from the moment I understood what was happening, I was beyond horrified. Gunther was arranging Lydia's *marriage* to the other boss's son. His *late thirties* son."

"The fuck!" Corbin's exclamation was so loud it woke Henry, who started crying.

I reached for my son, rocking him to my chest to calm him. "Cor, it was disgusting. Apparently, the one boss wouldn't do business with Gunther unless there was a family connection. They needed to be bound with more than just a handshake. Since his only adult child was male, Gunther offered up his daughter—who is still a little girl!

"The deal was struck. I watched them shake hands before ordering champagne to be brought out like it was an engagement party. Lydia was to go live with her intended husband at his estate. She would leave in the morning. Gunther instructed me to pack *her* things, just hers. I was not going with her. Then he stated like he was assuring me that the actual wedding wouldn't take place until she was twelve. As if that would make me feel better about him selling off his daughter or the statutory rape that would follow."

Corbin made a gagging sound. I wasn't that far behind him.

"Trenton was outraged. I was so shocked I'm not even sure I uttered a single word during the entire meeting. He started shouting that his sister was not one of his father's *inventories* that he could sell off. He called his father a child molester and a murderer. He told the other boss that he shouldn't want to do business with his father because he would double cross them and cheat them out of their share." I shook my head in shame. Henry had finally started to quiet down. "I should have seen it coming. I'd seen that look in Gunther's eye before, that eerie calm that meant something bad was about to happen.

"Cool as a cucumber, Gunther picked up his gun and shot Trenton."

"No!"

I nodded morosely. "He didn't kill him, but he shot him in the shoulder."

I didn't know Trenton's current fate, and that haunted me. Had he died while I'd kidnapped his brother and sister? As far as the law was concerned, I *had* kidnapped them. I was not their legal guardian. To anyone other than my children, I was just the nanny. The law didn't take actions and love into consideration or the fact that I was the only father either child had ever known. If we were caught by the police, I would go to jail, and maybe for more than just kidnapping if that gun Gunther had with my fingerprints on it was also found. The children would go back to their psychopathic father. If we were caught by Gunther... Well, I doubted I would live long enough to learn what would become of my children.

I had to finish. I had to tell Corbin everything, to get it off my chest. "Lydia started screaming and that woke Henry up. He started crying. On top of the children's hysteria, the other boss had pulled a gun on Gunther. His bodyguards pulled theirs and the other bodyguards pulled theirs." I flinched, still hearing the piercing echoes. "Trenton was lying on the floor. I could see the pain in his eyes, but he looked right at me and yelled 'run!'

"I'm still not sure how Lydia got to me. She had been across the room next to Gunther. Then suddenly she was next to me. I took hold of both kids, and I ran out of the office. Seconds later, gunshots were fired.

"Other guards started running towards the office. In the chaos, I got the kids into my car. I had grabbed the diaper bag, which already housed a spare set of clothes for me and Lydia, and, at the last second, your postcard." With a heavy sigh, I ended my story. "You know the rest."

Chapter Twelve

Brooke

They'd been in my bedroom for over an hour. It annoyed me that I was excluded, but probably not for the reason it should. I didn't like that Corbin was learning something about Adam that I wasn't. To top that feeling off, I also didn't like that Adam was *confiding* in Corbin, and not me.

Not what I would call rational feelings. Just a silly response that was not like me. I was not a woman who was prone to hysteria. Never had been. I made logical, sound decisions based on facts, not emotions.

It made absolutely no sense why it would hurt that Adam felt he could trust Corbin with his secrets and not me.

Lydia sat at the table, nibbling on the cinnamon apple crisps I made her. She was humming as she ate, swinging her little legs under the chair.

It reminded me of my sister and I sitting in the swings in our childhood backyard. We were thick as thieves back then. She was my confidant and I had been hers. We'd sit for hours in those swings—even into our teen years—giggling, sharing secrets, and telling stories.

A glance out my window brought my attention to a large tree on the edge of my property. It had a low hanging branch. Come spring, I could build a wood swing for it. I hoped Lydia would enjoy it. Henry too when he got older.

I could see it so clearly. Lydia laughing on the swing while I pushed her. Adam keeping a tight hold on Henry's hands as he guided the walking toddler across the lawn. Adam's and my eyes would meet and would burn with the remembered passion from the night before.

"Brooke?"

I jumped, pulled from the fantasy. Adam and Corbin stood in the kitchen doorway. Well, Adam stood in the kitchen doorway. Corbin was hunched down, so he wasn't hitting his head on the frame.

"Hi, Daddy." Lydia offered him an apple crisp from her pile.

"Hi, Angel." He ducked his head and ate the crisp out of Lydia's hand. "What do you have there?"

"Brooke and I made chips."

I didn't correct the girl on calling them chips instead of crisps, nor did I correct her having helped. Lydia's version of helping was to stand on a chair and watch me slice, season, and bake. Lydia was so proud of her accomplishment of having made her own snack, though, that I couldn't burst her bubble.

"You did?" Adam leaned over and placed a kiss on his daughter's forehead. "Nice job, Angel."

He let her feed him one, praising her cooking skills as he ate it. His eyes, though, were on me. Our eyes held the other's like magnets, unable to break away. My heart started thundering in my chest and I found it hard to breathe. The stress that had been weighing him down seemed less somehow. I wondered if, in telling Corbin his troubles, he felt freer. I hoped so. Above all else, whether I ever learned his secrets or not, I hoped he was able to lessen his burdens by confiding in his friend.

I just wished *I* was the one who could have relieved him of his troubles. That he had come to *me*, leaned on *me*, trusted *me*—

Corbin cleared his throat, breaking the intense staring between Adam and me. At his knowing look, I felt my cheeks burn.

This was the first time Corbin had ever been inside my cabin. He'd seen it from the outside numerous times but had never been invited in before. It made me wonder if *his* cabin was little. With his mother already living with him, did he have the room for one more adult and two children? Mind, neither child took up that much space now, but they would grow up.

I wanted to offer for them to stay. I wanted Adam to *ask* to stay.

I quickly scolded myself for that notion. Adam couldn't and wouldn't stay. He'd made it perfectly clear that protecting his children was his priority and he was putting my life in danger by staying. It also wasn't like I had the spare rooms either. When I'd built my cabin, the prospect of having a partner and/or children had been ludicrous. The bigger the cabin, the more resources I would need to maintain it. An extra room meant an extra fireplace too. There'd been no point. Yet, I was regretting that decision now.

Maybe I could turn the loft into a bedroom? *Our* bedroom...

Stupid, I called myself yet again. I was acting like a lovesick teenager, trying to plot different ways to trick the boy I liked into dating me. I was far too old to play such games. And while my maturity level was currently up for question, I knew I needed to stop myself from hoping. Hope would only lead to heartbreak.

Adam would leave and he would take his kids with them. I

would once more be alone. There would be no giggling Lydia in the kitchen taking credit for my cooking, there would be no watching Henry's first steps or hearing his first words, there would be no swing in the yard, and no Adam to play twenty questions with.

For the first time in almost a decade, the idea of being alone was not a comforting one.

"The ride down here was a lot easier than I'd anticipated," Corbin was saying. I hadn't been paying attention to what he'd been saying, but that caught my attention. "As long as it doesn't snow again, I think it'll be safe to get you and the kids up to my land tomorrow."

My stomach plummeted. The expected week I'd had with Adam just turned into one more night. It took all my concentration to keep myself from crying. Tears were senseless, they solved nothing. I'd learned that the hard way a long time ago. My nose burned with my efforts to keep mine at bay.

I couldn't look at him. I couldn't bear to see the relief on his face that they would be leaving the next day. "I need to go check my stores."

Then, like the coward I was, I fled the room.

Chapter Thirteen

Adam

I watched Brooke leave. This time, I didn't stop her. What would stopping her prove? We had feelings for each other, that was obvious, but that didn't solve any problems. In fact, it complicated them. Unlike in fiction books and movies, love did not conquer all. If I stayed, it could get Brooke killed.

The further up the mountain we went, the safer my kids would be. Even when the snow cleared, making traveling easier, the terrain would still be difficult to cross. The number of hiding places on a mountain were endless.

I needed to leave with Corbin tomorrow. Then Brooke could get back to her life of solitude and peace. That was the right thing to do.

When I finally turned my attention back to Corbin, he was now leaning against the kitchen counter with his arms crossed over his massive chest. "Want to tell me about that?"

"No."

He looked like he was about to press and then changed his mind. "Fine." He went to the front door and brought back the duffel bag he'd brought down the mountain with him. "I wasn't sure how soon we'd be able to get the kids out of here, so I over-packed just in case. You can thank my mom for all of this too. I had no idea what to get when it comes to babies."

He put the bag on the table opposite of where Lydia sat finishing her snack. I came forward to see what he had.

"Jack, thankfully, had a lot of this in stock. We knew once the snow fell, getting down for more would be virtually impossible. My spare room is overflowing with baby supplies." He reached in and pulled out a Disney princess coloring book and a box of crayons. "And this is for the princess."

Lydia grabbed the book, thanking him profusely.

"I know you said she loves puzzles. Unfortunately, I didn't know that while I was getting all this, and I don't have any kids' ones at the cabin. My mom has puzzles, though. Maybe Lydia can help her with those."

My gratitude towards my best friend grew. "Thank you. I'm sure she'll love it."

"Beyond the baby food, diapers, rash cream, formula, and pacifiers, I also brought these." He pulled infant and child snow-suits out of the duffel. Henry's suit was dark blue with red stripes. Lydia's was bright pink. Lydia reached for hers with glee. Corbin handed it over with some advice, "First lesson about living in the mountains in the snow, kid: *never* wear clothing that can blend in with the snow. Wear bright, reflective clothing that make it easier to spot you at a distance."

She nodded. "Gotcha."

"Second lesson: learn how to make a snowball."

Lydia giggled. "I already know how to do that."

"Good. I'll be testing out your skills later."

"You're on, Uncle Corbin."

Corbin's cheeks reddened at the title, but I also saw pride on his face. He turned to me. "I wasn't sure what you had either, so

I brought gear for you too. We had given you winter clothing in the *Jeep*, but I wasn't sure what you were able to bring here and what you had to leave in the car."

"Unfortunately, we left too much in the car. I'm sorry about that. I don't know what survived in this cold."

"In a few days, I'll be going out to where you left it. I'll see what's salvageable and what needs to be tossed. Then I'll get with Jack about dumping it."

I didn't have the guts to ask for confirmation if it was stolen or not. I couldn't add more crimes to my conscience.

"My mom is really excited about seeing you," Corbin went on.

"I'm excited to see her too." I hadn't seen Mrs. Mullaney since that final day in the courtroom when the verdict had been read and Corbin had been led away in chains.

As if Corbin knew where my mind had gone, he reached for my arm. "I've moved on. You should too."

"You should have never been convicted. It was wrong."

He shrugged, a little too nonchalantly. "I survived. My dad put me through—" He paused, his eyes landing on Lydia who was now coloring in her new book. "Um, H-E-double hockey sticks. J-A-I-L was a cakewalk after eighteen years with that man."

I couldn't help but grin at his attempt to keep his tale kid friendly. "I'm still sorry it happened to you."

He nodded once. "I know, and I appreciate it."

"How did you end up out here?"

"Jack, actually. He was my..." Once again, his eyes flicked to Lydia. "My first roommate," he evasively said. "This is his hometown. He'd moved to New Jersey after college. I won't share his story, but, after he got out, he decided to come back here. He gave me an invitation to join him when, uh, it was my turn to leave."

I had yet to meet Jack. The respectful way Brooke and Corbin talked about him, as well as my own phone conversations with him, I was very curious about the man. He'd gone through great efforts to protect my kids and me. His criminal record did not concern me; if Corbin trusted him, so did I.

"Mom had moved to Florida after my conviction. She didn't want to go, but I told her to. She needed a life outside of that house with those memories. She would travel up each year for my birthday, even though I kept telling her it wasn't necessary. After I got out, I went south, got her, and we came here.

"Jack had already had my cabin set up for me. It was like he knew I was coming, even though we hadn't talked in years."

"Jack seems to know a lot of things."

Corbin nodded. "He's like this secret superhero. By day, he runs a general store. At night, he works with a network of people who help hunt—" His eyes went to Lydia. "Wow, how do you have any normal conversations?"

I laughed. "Very creatively."

"This is going to take some getting used to. I hope I don't mess things up around them."

I shook my head. "Mistakes are okay," I assured him. "It's expected in parenthood. It's how you handle those mistakes that they remember."

"Geez, no pressure."

"You'll do fine. You'll be their favorite fun uncle who lets them get away with things that their mean old dad won't."

Corbin grinned wide. "I can do that."

I laughed at his confidence. Movement outside the kitchen window caught my attention and I saw Brooke walking around outside. She was bundled up similarly to how I'd first seen her when she'd knocked on the *Jeep*'s window.

Corbin followed my gaze. "Takes a rare woman who can survive out in these parts."

"She's certainly one of a kind."

Lydia piped up then. "Brooke is Daddy's new friend. I asked her and she said she'd play with him."

Corbin's eyebrows rose.

My face flushed hot. "It's not how it sounds. She means that literally how a seven-year-old would think of playing."

Corbin laughed. "Pretty sure some adults are into that too."

I glared at him. "Nothing happened."

"But you want it to." Statement, not a question.

"It doesn't matter if I do or don't. Nothing can."

"Why not?"

I looked pointedly at my daughter, sitting innocently at the kitchen table coloring. "My kids have to come first."

"And they have. You got them out. They're safe here. You weren't followed. No one knows where you or they are. Getting stuck in a snowstorm definitely was not in the plan, but it also added to your protection. No one would be mad enough to climb a mountain in this weather."

"And what about when this weather passes? Will we have to move on? Will we be stuck up in your cabin for the rest of our lives?"

Corbin shook his head. "Not forever. Jack is working on new identities for you. Once that paperwork is ready, you'll be able to go anywhere you want. Do I hope you stay here? Yes, of course, but I know this lifestyle isn't for everyone. You'll still need to be careful. No social media, no public pictures. But, after some time passes and you want to leave, you'll be free to go."

"We'll never be free."

"Then stay. The mountain provides its own freedom. Between you and my mom, you can homeschool the kids. We'll figure out getting them socialized with kids their own age later on." Corbin leaned towards me. "Your kids are safe, Adam. You can relax. After everything you just told me, you deserve some happiness too."

I shook my head. "I can't drag her into my problems any more than I already have. She doesn't deserve that."

"Your problems? You act like you caused this."

"Didn't I?" I shot back at him. "If I had gone to the C-O-P-S when I wanted to, then none of this would be happening."

"And you'd likely have gone to J-A-I-L. There's no fighting a man with that much money and influence. Waiting likely saved your life as well as your kids." Corbin ran his hand down his face, pulling on his long beard. "Look, everyone has regrets. Everyone looks back on a situation and wonders what they could have done differently. You think I don't regret picking up that shard of glass? My revenge cost me ten years when he was going to D-I-E anyway. But think about Henry? If you'd acted when you say you wanted to, where would he be right now? Maybe he would have never been born or maybe he'd be in an even worse situation."

"You're not making me feel any better." I couldn't imagine a world without Henry. It was inconceivable.

"Rather than kicking yourself for the things you should have done, praise yourself for the things you *did do*. You got those kids out. You protected them when it mattered most."

I let out a long sigh. "I know you're right. Logically I know that. But it still doesn't make me feel any better."

Corbin tipped his head towards the window. "There's someone out there who might be able to help you feel *really good*."

"Really?" What were we in, high school?

"Hey, just trying to keep it PG."

I rolled my eyes. "What time do you need us ready in the morning?"

"Early," he said, allowing me to change the subject. "The

sooner we get you and the kids up the mountain, the better. I'll fill Jack in on the plan. He'll be happy to hear we're finally moving you."

Chapter Fourteen

Brooke

Sleep evaded me. Normally the crackle of the fire lulled me to sleep like a lullaby. But tonight, my remedy failed me. I stared at the flames but all I saw was Adam's smile as Corbin was leaving, saying he'd see them early tomorrow.

That smile *hurt*. I knew Adam liked me. I knew he wanted to kiss me. But he didn't seem to have any hesitation about leaving me.

Sure, he wasn't leaving *me*. He was leaving to go live with his friend, which happened to not be where I lived.

I'd never wanted kids. I'd never had that baby fever like my friends did. My mother would constantly ask when she was going to be a grandmother and I would always tell her when my brother or sister made her one. Kids had never been on my radar.

It had been six days, almost a week, since I had found Adam stranded in his car with those kids. I should be thrilled to no longer have the crying, the midnight feedings, the laughter, the scamper of little feet...

I loved silence. It was peaceful to me, cathartic. I could close my eyes out here and hear myself think. For nearly a decade, silence had been my companion. It always felt claustrophobic to me whenever I had to go into town. That was one of the reasons I loved winter as much as I did. Winter was my excuse to avoid going into town for months on end.

I was dreading the silence that would fall when Adam left in the morning. It would be deafening.

It was foolish for me to even want them to stay. I didn't have the room for them. We'd only known each other less than a week. What was I supposed to say? What logical argument could I present that would make them want to stay?

Adam wasn't a criminal, I knew that. But someone *was* chasing him. I didn't know why, but I did know that. I believed my mountain could keep those kids safe. But could *I*?

I had my hunting rifle. I was a good shot. There was a big difference, though, in hunting animals to survive and killing another human to protect another. As a police officer, I knew this better than most.

The others knew this too. Tommy certainly would shoot any trespassers on his land. Dalton would shoot to warn before he shot to kill. Corbin was the same way. There was no doubt Walter and Huck would too. Mind, someone would have to make it past Tommy's, mine, Dalton's, Walter's, and Corbin's lands to reach Huck's. That took intent.

Adam and his children would be safer the further up the mountain they were. Even if I did send out an SOS on the radio that someone was on my land, it would take Dalton and/or Corbin a while to reach me, weather permitting. The lands were vast in these parts and traveling the most direct route couldn't always be done in a vehicle.

It was entirely selfish to want them to stay. They would not be as safe with me as they would be with Corbin. Above all else, keeping those kids safe was the priority.

With a resounding sigh, I came to the conclusion that Adam

was right. He couldn't stay. It might take some time, but I'd get over my feelings and I'd move on. I'd done it before, and I could do it again.

"Can't sleep either?"

I looked up and around at his voice. I hadn't even heard him come into the living room. In the glow of the firelight, I could make out his silhouette by the couch.

"What are you doing out here?" I shakily asked.

"Trying to decide between right and wrong."

I sat up in my lounge chair. The back rose with me, but I didn't push the footrest down. I needed a barrier between us.

Adam walked forward but didn't approach me. He sat on the couch in the corner closest to me. For a long time neither of us spoke. My heart was beating fast, my breaths were a little short. My reaction to him being here didn't calm the longer we sat in silence.

Slowly, hesitantly, Adam reached across the small wood table between the chair and couch. He left his hand there, palm up. Waiting.

I swallowed, roughly. It felt like there was a boulder sitting on my chest. My hand moved to his. Our fingers laced together. We stayed like that for the remainder of the night. I didn't sleep, and I don't think he did either.

Maybe it was enough, just that touch of hands. Maybe we didn't need some quick, fleeting romance that would haunt us for the rest of our lives. Maybe all we needed was just to know the other one cared.

I was such a bad liar; I couldn't even fool myself with that bullshit.

I needed more, wanted more. But if this was all I could get, then I would take it all and hold onto it for as long as I could.

The sun began to rise over the horizon. A tear escaped down my cheek. Adam had packed what he could the night before, so the kids could sleep as long as possible in the morning. Corbin would be heading out soon now that the sun was up. We had about an hour before his arrival.

I slowly lifted myself to sit up in the chair. At some point during the night, I had slumped over onto my outstretched arm. Adam started sitting up as well. He looked as tired and weary as I felt.

We said nothing as we stood, our hands still gripped tightly together. I could feel my chin start to tremble and my vision blurred as more tears came forward. As one, we walked toward the hallway. I started towards the kitchen, and he started towards the bedroom. Our arms gradually stretched to their limits, our fingers' grip failing.

It would only take one more step and we would have to relinquish our hold. The tightness in my chest intensified. My teeth started chattering as the tremble worsened.

One of us stepped forward. I'm not sure which. Our fingers untangled, the tips just barely touching. I couldn't look back. I'd break if I did. Clenching my eyes closed, tears streaming down my cheeks, I took that final step.

Our hands fell.

I kept walking.

Chapter Fifteen

Josephine

Four Months Later

I sat outside *Jack's General Store* in Whitefish, Montana and, not for the first time, wondered if this bounty was worth all the time and money I'd spent on it.

For starters, I'd been given false information by the children's own father as to *when* they'd been kidnapped. That alone had sent me on a wild goose chase that had taken up the better part of two months. Then a hefty bribe to one of the household servants had told me the actual date of the kidnapping. Except the father claims to have been out of town that day, according to his calendar and the plane ticket stubs he had. Which is in complete contradiction to the father's claim to be the only witness to the fact that his nanny, Adam Greene, had taken his children. No other staff or security guards could or would corroborate the man's story. Per the head of Gunther's security, Greene, a former schoolteacher, had disabled the cameras, motion sensors, and gate locks to make his Great Escape.

None of which made any sense. He was no Virgil Hilts, after all.

Gunther was offering a million-dollar bounty for the return of his daughter and her kidnapper. A million dollars was still a million dollars, but any idiot would know that million had blood on it. That was the type of man Sebastian Gunther was. I didn't need to see his bank records to know that. It also struck my notice that there was no bounty out for the safe return of his infant son.

I was very protective of children, and most women. I added the 'most' before the women because I knew firsthand that being my gender did not automatically make them harmless or innocent.

Adam Greene was being labeled as a pedophile, as well as a murderer. Gunther was portraying himself as the concerned and grieving father, but he was enjoying the media attention too much for me to buy it. The children's older brother was also suspiciously absent during every press conference.

Whether Greene had nefarious intentions or Gunther was the psychopath I believed him to be, it didn't change the fact that there were two missing children. I was determined to find those children. Other bounty hunters would be out for the money, not caring about the children. While I certainly wasn't going to turn down a million dollars—girl's got to eat—my main concern was the welfare of those kids.

When I'd first taken the case, I'd reached out to a contact of mine who specifically specialized in making abused and vulnerable women and children disappear. For the past fourteen years, Art Jackson had made a name for himself as a protector. I'd never met the man, but I knew his reputation and, more importantly, I knew his phone number.

I'd come across Jackson's group, the Mountain Mutineers, several years ago when I'd been hunting a pedophile who had escaped custody. A single phone call with the man had revealed just how big a reach he had. We'd come to an understanding that, while I was in it for the profit and he was in it out of the goodness of his heart, we both had similar goals.

Problem was, when I'd reached out to Jackson initially, I'd had misinformation. Everyone, including the police, did. I'd nearly given up on this case entirely, which was not something I did lightly, when I'd decided to go to the people who saw and noticed everything within the household.

Donna Novak had been a maid in the Gunther household for nearly twenty years. I'd approached her at the bus stop on her way home from her shift. It had taken some prodding, and most of the cash I had on hand, for her to tell me the children were not taken on the date their father claimed. That was all she would say, but it was enough to get me to look into the claim further.

One month. The children had been gone twenty-nine days before their father had reported them missing. When I'd confronted Gunther, he'd told me I had been misinformed and, if I wanted to get my bounty, I should be more careful about who I bought false information from.

My first conversation with Jackson had been more informative on my part to clue him in to the situation. While I didn't want to give away my chance of getting the bounty, I also knew that, if anyone would know about the missing children, it would be Art Jackson.

My conversation with him a month ago had been far different. I'd told him about how suspicious the father was acting. While Gunther's actions were strange, it did not prove that Greene was not the pedophile he was reported to be. Jackson had thanked me for the updated information and assured me that he had not heard anything but that his contacts were still looking. Frustrated that a schoolteacher with no history of criminal activity could disappear so thoroughly, I started back at square one.

It was convenient for Gunther that, on the date of the real kidnapping, the security tapes were also suspiciously blank. I had no video evidence to prove or disprove Gunther's version of events. But Donna Novak's story seemed more believable than Gunther's, so I started looking into it further.

A contact at the NYPD traffic watch had let me pull up the license plate scanner readings for Greene's car. It had cost me front row tickets to *Hamilton*.

By the time I'd finished with this case, I wondered how much of the million I would even have left after all these bribes. Not to mention the ones I'd wasted before I'd known the correct date of the kidnapping.

That really did not sit right with me. Why would a father lie about the day his children were kidnapped? If I had been on a wild goose chase, I can't imagine what information the police were following. I'd read the profile that had been released on Adam Greene and had to wonder if someone had doctored some of the information.

It was hard to believe a powerful man like Sebastian Gunther, who could afford to hire the best and the brightest tutors in the world, would specifically choose a man who had already been arrested once on suspicion of child molestation to be his children's nanny. While Greene hadn't been charged with the crime, the arrest was on record.

Gunther claimed this was why the elementary school had let Greene go eight years ago. Gunther, giving the perfect performance as a grief-stricken father who was so worried about his children, had claimed he'd foolishly believed Greene's story about being falsely accused, which had ruined his career and reputation. Gunther had hired Greene out of the goodness of his black heart.

I wondered if the man even had a heart. If he did, it was probably old and decrepit with cobwebs around it.

The police had record of the last time Greene's car had been seen in the city before the kidnapping. Exactly twenty-nine days before. I knew then that what the police believed to be a regular ride through the city a month earlier was the actual kidnapping in progress.

What I found interesting is the gap of time between when Greene's car had been spotted crossing Park Ave and again when he'd reached the Lincoln Tunnel. There was a partial plate of a parked car that could be Greene's read on Twenty-Fifth Street, but that would have been off the direct route to the tunnel from NoHo. Since nothing so far about this case was what it seemed to be, I decided to work off the assumption that it *was* Greene's car parked at that intersection. It would explain the extra time between Park Ave and when he'd reached the Lincoln Tunnel. So what had been on Twenty-Fifth Street that had been so important he'd made a stop with two kidnapped children in the backseat of his car?

The partial plate had been read near the intersection of Twenty-Fifth and Sixth Ave. Upon arriving at that intersection, my first thought was he'd stopped at the Goodwill NYNJ store across the street. It was diagonal and in the line of sight of where the plate had been read. None of the clerks claim they remember seeing Greene in the store, and they immediately recognized his face from the wanted announcements on TV. That made me believe that they would have connected him to a customer if he'd been in the store.

From Goodwill, I went to a grocery market. If Greene was going on the run, he'd need food and supplies. Based on what was left in Greene's and the children's bedrooms in the police report, Greene had not taken much with them. A couple hundred to the wannabe cop in the security office had let me see the tapes on the day of the kidnapping. I watched specifically for a man with a little girl and a baby in or out of a carrier. Since

Greene likely would have been wearing glasses, a hat, or some form of a disguise if he was taking kidnapped children into a public place.

Except there was nothing. I had the urge to check on the day Gunther reported the kidnapping but knew it would be a waste of time. By the time Gunther had reported his children missing, Greene had already had them for twenty-nine days.

I was beginning to wonder if I was chasing ghosts. The children could have been dead and buried before Gunther had even noticed his children were missing. The man clearly was not an attentive father. I still found it interesting that the oldest brother, Trenton Gunther, was not available for questioning. The police had been unable to locate him at the resort in Maui that Gunther claimed he was at.

An interesting thought had occurred to me as I had walked the block of Sixth Ave and Twenty-Fifth Street. What if the reason Trenton Gunther couldn't be found was because he was *with* Adam Greene and his siblings? What if *Trenton* was the real kidnapper? Could Greene have been taken against his will or been a willing participant in the kidnapping of his charges?

I had to put a pin in that thought.

I hit pay dirt when I checked the surveillance footage at the CVS on Sixth Ave, less than a block from where the partial plate had been recorded. I watched as a clearly flustered Adam Greene walked into the pharmacy with a baby carrier and an upset little girl in his arms. He went immediately to the register and bought a burner phone. At the last minute, he threw a coloring book that was in a magazine rack by the register and a box of crayons on the counter too.

He paid in cash.

By the time I left the CVS, I was out nearly a thousand dollars, but I had the footage of Adam Greene, Lydia Gunther, and a baby carrier which I could only assume held Henry

Gunther, though I never saw the baby's face to make a visual confirmation, *and* I had the number of the burner phone Adam Greene had purchased.

A former military buddy who now worked in private security was able to get me the phone records for that burner. I was out a couple thousand dollars, a promise of a date when I got back into town, and a no-questions-asked favor. While I had no romantic feelings towards him, a date wasn't the worst thing in the world, and he was too honorable a man for the favor to be something morally questionable. It was worth the trade.

The burner phone had called a Chinese restaurant in Lansing, Michigan once but the call had only lasted nine seconds. Enough for him to realize he had the wrong number? Several hours later, he called another number, which led me to *Jack's General Store* in Whitefish Montana. That call had lasted eleven minutes.

While I didn't know where Greene had been when he'd called Whitefish, the fact that the call had lasted eleven minutes this time meant he had spoken to someone specifically. Two hours and forty-one minutes later, Greene called the number again. This time, the call had lasted only nine minutes.

The fact that the second call had taken place at eleven o'clock at night struck me as odd. Was the General Store open twenty-four-seven? There was no website for me to find out that information on and Google hadn't had hours of operation on their site. Still, Greene had called the store twice for a total of twenty minutes.

A lot could be said in twenty minutes.

I felt this warranted an in-person look at the store and to speak to whomever was working from eight-thirty to eleven-thirty that night. Which was how I found myself standing in snow slush in a small town in Montana at the end of April.

The town was small. It had a single main road with a single

traffic light. There was a sign on parallel light posts proclaiming a Spring Festival this coming weekend. There was a raffle to dunk the mayor in a bucket of slime.

It was obvious that outside of the winter months when the ski resort was open, there was not much going on in this town.

I spotted a diner down the road from the General Store and wondered if that was the only place to eat in this town.

The store itself was nothing special. It was on the corner of a block of buildings and probably took up four times the space as the other shops on the strip. There was a single door with a glass window that held an OPEN sign on a chain. No hours of operation sign was posted either.

A cowbell above the door rang as I walked in. A quick glance around showed no surveillance cameras or sensors on the display windows. The single lock on a wood door with a glass window was also a big indicator this was not a high-crime area. Geez, I really was in the middle of small-town America.

I'd lived all over the country since getting out of the Corps, but this was definitely the smallest 'small town' I'd ever stepped foot into.

Upon walking in, I saw shelves of canned food. There was a single stand-up display refrigerator that held dairy products to my right. I hadn't seen a Walmart or any grocery store driving into this town. Was *this* their version of a grocery store?

A display near the register proclaimed *local jerky* was for sale, which did look hand-bagged rather than factory made. Guess so.

There was a man at the counter talking to the older gentleman at the register. The man purchasing the items was *huge*. No other way to describe him. He was probably six-foot-seven or eight. He had shaggy black hair that fell past his shoulders and a long beard that was braided. A pink bow tied off the end, which I found peculiar. The man looked tough. He was clearly not a stranger to hard work. Having seen a lot of those guys in the military, I knew the man's man persona very well. None of the men I'd served with would ever be caught with a pink ribbon in his beard—in public, that is. They'd rather do a thousand burpees before running ten miles in full gear.

A chuckle from behind the counter drew my attention to the older guy. He was tall too, though nowhere near the giant's height. He was maybe six-foot. He had salt and pepper hair, a clean-shaven face, and kind green eyes. You could tell a lot about a person from their eyes. It was one of the reasons I knew Gunther was lying about caring for his children.

I unintentionally wandered closer to the men in my perusal of the store. In the back was more outdoorsy gear than grocery. Hunting supplies, including a lot of guns.

My Glock was tucked away in the holster at the small of my back. I wore a longer jacket that hid the bulge. I'd need to keep in mind that this area had a lot of gun owners.

"...so excited. She's been counting down to her birthday since the start of the New Year." That was the giant who spoke. He had a very deep voice with a slight New Jersey lilt if I had to guess. A quick glance at his items on the counter and I saw birthday gift supplies. Not surprising, given the conversation the men were having.

"Belle deserves a great birthday after the winter she's had." The cashier finished ringing up the items on a manual cash register. Did this place even have internet? The giant handed over cash.

"Yeah, Mom's making her a spaghetti birthday cake."

"A what?" The cashier paused in counting out the man's change to ask for clarification. I also had no idea what a spaghetti cake was.

"You heard me. I have no idea what my mother is doing or

how she is going to do it, but she swore to Belle she would have her cake."

The cashier seemed to ponder this for a moment. "I'm sorry I'll miss that."

"You're invited, you know that."

"I know and I appreciate the invitation, but I have a lot to do around here to get ready for spring."

I looked around the store and did notice a mixture of winter and summer supplies. It must take a lot of time to switch things over with the seasons. *Disney* boasts that they can do it in one night, but I doubt the owner of this store has that much help.

The cashier reached under the counter and brought out a wrapped gift with a pink bow. "Tell her this is from Super Jack."

Ah, Jack. As in *Jack's General Store*. Good, I found the owner.

"Will do." The giant took his purchases and the gift. "Thanks for everything, Jack."

He nodded once. "You never have to thank me."

The giant left, and I was alone in the store with Jack. I tried to look like I was examining a plaid shirt that was in front of me. I'd never be caught dead in plaid. Leather was more my style because it provided better protection.

Jack came around the counter. "You know, it's not polite to eavesdrop, Josie."

I froze. What. The. Ever. Loving. Fuck.

I turned in time to see Jack lock the door and turned the OPEN sign to CLOSED. My hand went to my Glock at the small of my back. I did not like being locked in.

"Take it easy," Jack brushed off my concern. "If I meant you any harm, I would have stopped you long before you arrived here."

Before I'd arrived... What the fuck? Who was this guy? How did he know my name or that I would be here?

He kept his hands in plain view as he approached me. The guy was probably in his sixties. I doubted he was a physical threat to me, but I knew well that there are a lot of other types of threats that most people didn't see coming.

Something tickled in my brain. This conversation was far too similar to one I'd had years ago with... Oh fuck. I'm an idiot. Jack. Jackson. Art Jackson.

"Son of a bitch," I breathed out. I dropped my hand from my gun but didn't drop my guard. "*You're* Jackson?"

I'd never met the man in person. Only had a number that I called to leave a message that I needed to talk to him and then he'd call me back. Always from a different number that never traced back to the same location.

The man's lips twitched like he was fighting a smile. "I was impressed with your investigation from the start. You cared more about the welfare of the children than you did the million dollars. I figure that's the difference between you and the others, who are still chasing their tails."

He tipped his head, indicating for me to follow him. While I wasn't keen to follow him into an unknown room behind yet another door, I did appreciate that he walked in first and didn't block my exit.

"I don't understand. *You're* Jackson? As in the man who runs a vigilante group that secretly hunts down murderers, rapists, and pedophiles?"

"I don't like the word 'vigilante'. It always makes me feel like I should be wearing tights and a cape—and believe me, you do not want to see me trying to fit this ass into a pair of tights." He shuddered for effect.

Walking into the back room, I saw what appeared to be a standard stockroom for a grocery/convenience store. Jackson, or Jack, continued to the wall opposite the door we entered, and pulled the fire alarm.

Except, no alarm went off. Instead, a series of beeps occurred and then a hidden door sprang open. Jack took the time to put a chair in front of the door to hold it open. I assumed that was for my benefit, because it made no other sense to prop a secret door open. That kind of defeated the purpose of a secret door.

My jaw dropped as I walked into this room. Holy Mother of the Internet. Tony Stark would have an orgasm walking in here.

An entire array of monitors decorated the one wall. There was a single desk in the middle of the room, facing the monitors. I saw videos of intersections with cars passing through, what looked like a baby's bedroom, the outdoor view of someone's house from a door camera, some big shot's office with the Chicago skyline, and so many more. He was monitoring all of these cameras? Why?

Jack pointed to the monitor of the baby's room. "That baby was abducted from the hospital right after her birth. She was thankfully located but her kidnapper got away. When I heard about it, I hacked into the nanny-cam in her nursery in order to catch the perp if there was a second attempt."

He pointed to what looked like a kids' soccer game. "That's the camera closest to the park with the clearest view of the playing field. There have been numerous reports of a strange man watching the toddler games. I plan to get a look at his face next time he shows so I can identify him and figure out why he's stalking the park."

Next was what I assumed to be a big shot's office in Chicago. "Warren Barrington the Third has had six secretaries in four months. The last reported that he raped her in his office. While a rape kit and police report were made, both have myste-riously disappeared, along with the hospital records. Multiple sexual harassment reports have been made against him over the years and all have been dropped. I have a suspicion Claire

Conrad was not the first woman he's assaulted. One of my men snuck into the high rise and planted the camera in his office. It's unfortunate that we have to wait for another attack, but, if one occurs, I'll catch it and my men will take care of him."

I didn't know what take care of him meant but I could guess.

"This is...insane." This wasn't like Big Brother's watching; this was like Creepy Uncle is watching and waiting for you to fuck up.

Jack sat down in his chair in front of the keyboard. Since all the monitors were on the wall, there wasn't one on the desk too. Instead, it was just the keyboard, a notepad with a pen, and a picture of a little girl. It was an older picture from the hairstyle and clothing, maybe from the 90s or early 2000s. The girl was posing with a smile. School photo?

Jack typed into the keyboard. All but one monitor went blank. I was shocked to see myself on the screen. It was last week when I'd been at the *CVS* store getting the surveillance video. "It wasn't until you led me here that I even knew he'd made a stop before exiting the city. He told me he'd gone straight to the motel. The man was clearly frazzled, and this stop likely skipped his memory of the events. I've deleted the video off the backup servers, but unfortunately you made a copy of the video. Did you show it to anyone?"

My eyes were stuck on myself. "You were following me?"

He spun around in his chair to face me. He seemed extremely calm. "I've been following all the heavy hitters who pose a threat to Mr. Greene and those children. You are the only one who figured out Gunther is lying to the police and media. Since I've planted enough false trails to keep the others busy, I know they will not become a problem. You, however, might be depending on what you did with the copy of the surveillance video."

I swallowed hard. A problem that needed to be taken care

of, like that CEO bastard who raped his secretary? My heart started thumping in my chest.

"Why bring me here? Why show me any of this? I could have asked you questions, and you remained anonymous. I never would have guessed Jack the General Store owner was Jackson my mysterious contact."

Jack swiveled around in his chair again to face the keyboard. He typed in something else, and the monitor changed.

Again, it was a picture of me. This one was an actual picture though, not a video. I was in my military uniform surrounded by my squad of Devil Dogs. Good men, men who had lost their lives needlessly.

I both loved and hated that picture. It was one of two pictures I kept in my wallet as a constant reminder of how fleeting life could be.

"Josephine Gonzales, age thirty-eight. Single, never married. Born to Hector and Isabella Gonzales in San Jose, California. Parents were illegal immigrants. Your parents were caught and deported when you were seventeen and your sister was fifteen. Your parents could have taken you with them, but they begged Immigration to allow you to stay since your sister and you were born in this country. You were only months shy of eighteen. You received your emancipation status and took guardianship of your sister, Constance Gonzales, or Connie as you called her."

The picture on the screen changed and I was faced with a picture of Connie and myself outside our school. It wasn't a posed picture. In fact, we were in the background of the intended picture. But I knew this picture so well. I'd studied it for hours on end until I knew every pixel, line, and color.

It was the last picture ever taken of my sister Connie before her disappearance.

I had walked into our high school. She had said she was

going to wait for a friend. I left to go to class. I left my sister outside our high school, alone and vulnerable.

Her friend Gabby claimed she never saw Connie outside the school and had gone inside, assuming that's where Connie was too. Then the bell had rung, and it hadn't been until lunchtime when I'd seen Gabby but not Connie at their usual table.

Connie had vanished into the ether, never to be seen or heard from again. I'd taken guardianship of my sister and I'd failed within months of accepting the responsibility.

A couple of days after her disappearance, a garbage man had called the police to report an unusual find. The police had collected Connie's purse, backpack with her schoolbooks, and her bloody shirt, pants, and—worst of all—torn panties. Her body was never found.

I'd long ago accepted that Connie was dead. She'd died a horrible and gruesome death while I'd been sitting oblivious in math class. After graduation, I joined the Marines. I refused to ever be so helpless and powerless again.

And I hadn't been...until that RPG that had taken out my squad. Three of us had survived the initial blast. One had succumbed to blood loss before the EVAC could reach us. The other had taken his own life after returning to the States. He'd been a triple-amputee. His wife had taken one look at him, turned, and never looked back. Rogers had signed the divorce papers before putting a bullet in his head.

So much pain. So much loss.

First my parents, then Connie, and then my squad.

I refused to cry at their memories though. I'd shed tears for each of them a long time ago. I was done crying.

"What does any of this have to do with my investigation to find the Gunther children?"

Jack turned back around to face me. "You and I first met

when you were hunting an escaped pedophile six years ago. I came across your name before that, but that was the first time I ever reached out to you." I remembered. I thought the call was a hoax before I'd figured out that the mystery man's information was too accurate to be a prank call. "I realized then how similar you and I are. We hunt evil, not for money, but because they're evil."

I raised an eyebrow. I was a bounty hunter; I hunted the scum for money.

"You might receive a paycheck at the end of your job, true. But your resume is filled with rapists and murderers. You pass over the thieves and other white-collar criminals."

I crossed my arms over my chest. "So? I still don't see what any of this has to do with Adam Greene, which by the way you lied to me about *both* times I called you. Clearly, you've been helping him."

He narrowed his eyes at me. "And what makes you think I would help a child abductor and pedophile?"

I paused. Jack *wouldn't* help out a child abductor or a pedophile. He'd made a reputation out of hunting those scumbags. Hell, rumor had it that he even had a serial rapist murdered his first night in jail. Other rumors said that he had a secret prison where he held the criminals he caught and made them suffer, Hammurabi style. I wasn't sure I believed either of those stories.

What I *did* believe was that he would not help someone who had abducted two children unless there was a damn good reason.

I let out a loud sigh. "Fuck. Greene's innocent, isn't he?"

"Of being a pedophile? Indubitably."

"And you're helping him hide like you help out the other victims who can't get away otherwise." Shit. There goes my million-dollar payday.

Jack's lip twitched. "I help out anyone who needs it."

"And you're showing me all this because you want me to stop hunting Adam Greene?"

Jack bobbled his head side to side. "More of, take your investigation down another path that someone might also try to follow. Preferably if that someone has a badge."

"I won't tamper with or plant evidence," I warned.

"Of course not. I'd never ask you to. I have others who can do that for me or," he indicated to the computers behind him, "I do it myself."

Jack was playing a dangerous game. I looked up at the computer monitors, the squares on the wall making me think of a chess board. I guess it wasn't quite as dangerous when you could see the whole board.

"And if my investigation led me back to Sebastian Gunther…?"

Jack smiled. "Well, then, I certainly won't stand in your way."

I nodded. If Adam Greene was innocent, the man had a huge uphill battle to clear his name.

Still, I wasn't one to take someone solely at their word. I liked evidence. And I wasn't willing to risk those two children's lives just on one man's claim of innocence. I'd take my investigation back to Gunther. If that man had hurt either child, I'd make him pay. But I would find Adam Greene eventually too. Even if it was just to verify the kids were safe, I would find them.

Chapter Sixteen

Elijah (formerly Adam)

"Annabelle Louise! Don't you dare jump down from there!"

My daughter, laughing from her perch on the tree branch, looked down at me, who was safely on the ground, with glee. "Come on, Daddy! It's not that high!"

It was high enough to break a bone if she didn't land correctly. "You climbed up, you can climb back down."

Annabelle, or Belle, as we now called her, grumbled as she started her slow descent but thankfully listened to me. I was not yet used to the number of trees, rocks, and a variety of other high items in the forest surrounding our cabin that Belle could get herself into trouble climbing. I thought winter was bad, with her constant begging to play outside in the snow. Corbin generally obliged, because my daughter had him wrapped around her little finger. He did anything she asked, just so he could make her smile or laugh.

Overall, living in a cabin in the middle of nowhere on top of a mountain wasn't as bad as I was expecting. While we were stuck where we were, we weren't stuck inside as much as I'd thought we would be. Lucas, as we now called my son, even joined us outside a lot. The snow had been like a barrier to the real world, caging us in but also setting us free.

As the months went by, we fell into a rhythm. Mornings were the times for lessons. Mrs. Mullaney, or Gertie as she insisted we call her, was a lifesaver. While I did lessons with Belle, Gertie entertained Lucas. Both kids were growing fast and had gained weight since our days of being on the run. Gertie kept us all fed, and sometimes overfed.

Corbin's cabin only had one extra room besides his and his mom's. When they'd learned that the kids and I were in danger, Gertie had immediately started rearranging their old storage room into a bedroom. Lucas slept in a crib that Corbin made himself. Apparently, my best friend was a carpenter now and made a living off of beautifully crafted homemade pieces he would bring down to Jack for him to sell in his store. Sometimes he received a commission for something specific too.

My bedroom furniture was mismatched pieces he'd had in storage that were already completed but hadn't been brought down the mountain yet. The dresser, bed frame, and nightstand were well-crafted pieces, and I felt bad that my taking them meant Corbin wouldn't get any compensation for them. He assured me it was fine, but I had to wonder.

Lucas's crib was in my room. Belle slept in Gertie's room. They both had twin beds, again ones that Corbin had made. Corbin had added a small dresser for Belle. Once we were able to get off the mountain, I wanted to get a bedside lamp for her. Corbin was already working on building her a bookshelf. That man was going to spoil my daughter rotten.

After lunch, we would generally go outside. Belle called this playtime, and it was for the most part, but it was also the time when Corbin was showing me his equipment and explaining how his cabin functioned.

Changing our names had been weird. I was grateful for the

time secluded in the cabin for us to get used to calling each other the different names. Corbin was the worst. I would hear "Adam!" shouted from across the cabin, followed by "Fudge! I mean, Elijah!" His messing up always made Belle laugh, and a part of me wondered if he did it on purpose just to get a rise out of my daughter.

Belle loved her name. She thought that Annabelle was pretty, but Belle was better because it made her a princess. My little angel was adapting to mountain life wonderfully. Lucas was too young to register the change in his name. He definitely had a slower reaction time to 'Lucas' in the beginning, but now responded immediately when someone said his name.

My nickname for Belle had not changed nor had her referring to me as 'Daddy'. Corbin *loved* that she called him 'Uncle'. Gertie had become 'Grammy'.

After the kids were asleep for the night and adult conversations took place, Gertie, Corbin, and I figured out contingency plans for if we were found. Some nights Corbin would set up his radio so we could also speak with Jack. I had yet to meet the man who had helped save us. Belle had a pile of colored pictures to give him as a thank you. She'd overheard Corbin refer to him as a superhero and now called him 'Super Jack'.

Jack was positive no one from New York knew where we were. He said that if his contacts heard anything, he would let us know immediately. I also learned that Trenton had survived the shootout. I was beyond relieved to hear that. His possible death had been weighing heavily on me. He'd sacrificed himself so I had time to get away. I owed him everything for that.

The worst bit of news was that there was a warrant out for my arrest for kidnapping and murder. Gunther had followed through on his threat to release the gun to the police with my fingerprints on it. I didn't recognize the name of my supposed victim when Jack said it, but I felt sorry for the man, whoever he was. According to Jack, Gunther hadn't reported the children missing for almost a month after we'd left. I had to wonder if that was because he'd been injured too and wanted to play the grieving father without a bullet wound, or perhaps that they had to hide the bodies from the shootout and didn't want to draw police attention to the mansion until they had staged everything to look like it had never happened.

Jack said that there were private investigators and bounty hunters looking for me. I asked him to look in on my parents and sisters. The police had talked with them, but phone records and social media posts proved that I hadn't been in contact with them since before I'd kidnapped the children. Jack told me my parents denied the charges and refused to believe I was guilty. I hoped like hell no one casually mentioned Corbin, which would point the police in our direction. As far as they knew, I hadn't spoken to or of Corbin in eighteen years. My family shouldn't be mentioning him to anyone.

My car, the one I'd driven away from the mansion in and left at the train station Jack had instructed me to go to, had been found within days of the reported kidnapping. Per Jack, they had not yet found the security footage of me walking the kids through the station to get to the locker where we found the supplies Jack had left for us. He believed it was because no one was looking that far back, due to Gunther's delayed report.

Gunther wasn't counting on the police finding us, though. That was just smoke and mirrors. He had issued a million-dollar bounty on me, dead or alive, and for the safe return of Lydia Gunther. Jack said there was no mention of a reward for Henry Gunther's return. The man couldn't even care about his own infant son. What if I was a real kidnapper who meant to do harm to his children? The man didn't even care. It was disgusting.

I didn't ask where or how Jack got us new identities. Once

the snow cleared enough where we could come down off the mountain, Jack said he had all the documents I needed to claim my new persona. Including a backlog of data that indicated my children and I had been living in Whitefish our entire lives. There was even a death certificate for my 'wife' and the children's mother.

I didn't know how I felt about leaving the safety of the cabin and Corbin's land. Corbin had said he would get the documentation from Jack if I didn't go down with him for his first trip into town since the snowfall. While I appreciated Jack's efforts to cover our tracks, there still were ways to prove we weren't who we claimed to be. DNA, for one. Also we still looked the same. My face was on hundreds of thousands of wanted posters around the country. Surely, someone would recognize me and turn me in.

I hadn't shaved my beard for that reason. It was now past my chin. Belle was looking forward to the day it was long enough to braid, like she did with Corbin's. The man usually walked around with glittery barrettes or ribbon bows in his hair and/or beard.

Gertie suggested I dye my hair. Corbin argued that my sandy brown hair would match the town's populace better and suggested I keep it. He had some extra ball caps around too and offered them to me to wear when I went out in public.

We cut Belle's hair. She cried for an hour after we made the suggestion. She loved her beautiful blonde hair—so did I—but cutting it meant less maintenance during the winter months. In exchange for allowing us to cut it, I promised she was allowed to dye her hair whatever color she wanted come springtime.

Pink hair dye was now on Corbin's shopping list for when he finally got to town. We probably should have seen that one coming.

When the snow started to melt and the air became noticeably warmer, my old fears and stress returned. The snow kept us in and barricaded from the world.

It also meant there were no more excuses as to why I couldn't bring Belle down the mountain to visit her friend Brooke.

Every time I thought of Brooke, it was like a punch to the solar plexus. Any time her name was mentioned, especially when I wasn't expecting it, I couldn't breathe for several seconds. To this day, months later, I could still feel the imprint of her fingers in mine. At night I would dream about holding her, kissing her, making love with her. The best dreams, though, were of a family, a mother for my children.

I was a wanted man. I could never be with her. She deserved better. The nights when Jack would get on the radio to give us updates about the manhunt for my children and me, it always hammered that fact home. I was living on borrowed time, and I refused to bring her down with me when the axe fell.

Because it would. Living up here in the mountains was a sanctuary. I didn't know how long it would last, but one day, maybe not one day soon, but one day we would be found out. Brooke could not be standing next to me when that day arrived.

The times when the mountain men—and one strikingly beautiful woman I was trying my damndest not to think about— would do their check-ins after a storm or a brutally cold night, it was both heartbreaking and soothing to hear her voice. When she came across the radio, I would wonder if she was thinking about me, maybe hoping that I was there listening. She never asked about me or the children, and I had yet to determine if that was good or bad.

With my permission, Jack had informed the mountain men of the additions to Corbin's cabin. While he didn't give details, he made it clear that there were to be no strangers on the mountain. He implored all of them to be on the lookout for signs of others on the mountain and to send up a signal if found. They all agreed, though one was just a series of clicks that Jack said was an agreement. I had no idea what that meant. Corbin didn't say anything about it, so I remained quiet. One, I think his name was Dalton, even offered to babysit. According to Corbin, while the men who lived on the mountain were formidable and not ones you wanted to cross, they were extremely protective of their land and each other. The fact that Corbin now had children living on the mountain with him meant extra protection.

Belle finally landed safely on the ground next to me. She automatically reached for Lucas's hand. I had his other. We slowly walked back towards the cabin at Lucas's wobbly pace. My son was getting so big. His eagerness to follow his sister everywhere had driven him to start walking sooner than I'd expected. He was even talking. Mind, his vocabulary extended to "mik" (which was milk), "Da", "Bee-Bee" (which was Belle), and, my personal favorite, a short and precise "yeah". He was very good at pointing to get what he wanted too. When Corbin was around, that was usually a silent "up" command.

Gertie was waiting for us at the cabin's door. As a child, I always compared Mrs. Mullaney to an old lady. She'd had a rundown, gaunt look about her. Her shoulders were always hunched and her hair prematurely gray. Now, the woman looked beautiful. She stood tall, had some meat on her. Her hair was still gray but now looked healthy and washed. The biggest difference to eighteen years ago, she looked *happy*.

Belle let go of Lucas's hand and ran towards her. "Is it ready?"

Gertie smiled down at my daughter and nodded. "Darling, it is a masterpiece beyond measure. Even I surprised myself."

Belle cheered before rushing into the house. I picked Lucas up so I could pick up my pace. "Did you really make her a spaghetti birthday cake?"

Gertie nodded. "The girl wanted spaghetti and chocolate. I'm not sure she's quite right in the head."

I laughed. "I think it's the altitude."

We entered the cabin. I set Lucas down in the playpen Corbin had constructed for him in the living room. While it was warmer outside where we didn't need heavy winter jackets, it still had a chill in the air when the sun set. Corbin let the fires in each room go low during the day before building them back up at night.

When putting together our new identities, Jack had asked if I wanted to keep the kids' birthdays. He said it was safer to change them, but it was my call. In the end, I chose to change them. I would always know their real birthdays and what day we celebrated on wouldn't matter in the long run.

Belle's birthday was now two months sooner, which she was ecstatic about. By her logic, this meant she would always get her presents earlier.

Lucas, who was about to turn eleven months, would be waiting an extra month before we celebrated his birthday. In fact, his birthday was now what his predicted delivery date had been if he hadn't been born a preemie.

So today we were celebrating Belle's eighth birthday. To which, my unique daughter asked for a spaghetti cake. Dinner was going to be interesting.

I heard the sound of an engine in the distance. I still wasn't used to that sound intruding on the silence of the mountain. Corbin had taken his four-wheeler out this morning. He said he was getting Belle's birthday gift. I wasn't sure what that meant and wondered if he was going all the way to town. While the snow had mostly melted, Corbin wasn't expecting to go back to town with all the furniture he'd built over the winter for another couple of weeks.

Even though I knew the chances that it wasn't Corbin

were low, I still tensed at the sound approaching. I automatically moved so I could see both my children. Gertie noticed but didn't comment on my reaction. I appreciated her discretion.

Once I saw it was Corbin approaching, I relaxed. When I saw there was another vehicle following behind him, I tensed back up.

Gertie looked out the living room window. "Ah, don't worry. That's just Dalton."

I knew the name and his voice from the radio check-ins, but I had never met the man. I wondered what he was doing here.

Belle ran to the door as soon as she heard the vehicles approach. She rushed outside just in time to see them park in front of the porch. "Uncle Corbin!"

Corbin climbed off his vehicle, taking his helmet off. He opened his arms just in time to catch my little daredevil as she flung herself off the porch at him. Geez, I was going to have a heart attack one of these days if she didn't stop jumping off of things.

I remained in the doorway so I could watch outside while also keeping an eye on Hen—damn it. *Lucas.* At least that slip up wasn't out loud.

The second four-wheeler pulled up next to Corbin's. The driver was dressed all in black and had his helmet on. My divided attention between my children was my only excuse as to why I didn't notice the passenger on the back of the vehicle with him until she got off.

Blonde hair came piling out of the helmet as she raised it off of her head. She shook her hair free, and I realized I was seeing it loose for the first time. Before, she'd always had it braided.

Our eyes met, and my mind went blank. Had her eyes always been so blue? I couldn't think, I couldn't speak. She was gorgeous. I wasn't even sure I was breathing. My chest hurt, but that could either be lack of oxygen or the punch I had felt at seeing her again.

"Brooke!" was screamed so loudly it broke me out of my stupor.

Belle climbed down from Corbin's arms and ran over to Brooke. Thankfully, she didn't jump this time. Instead, she wrapped her arms around Brooke's waist and squeezed as tightly as she could.

"Hi, sweetie," Brooke smiled down at her. She put her hand on Belle's shorter hair, pulling on the ends. "I love the new hairdo."

Since Belle was looking up at Brooke, her chin resting on Brooke's flat belly, I could see her scrunching her nose. "I look like a boy."

Brooke shook her head. "No, baby. I think you look very pretty. I also hear you'll be dying it pink soon."

That got Belle excited again. "Yes! Will you do it for me?"

"Well, I've never dyed mine or anyone else's hair before, but, if your dad allows it, I'll try." She didn't look up, even though she'd mentioned me.

"Great!" Belle let go of her waist. She turned towards the cabin and then spun around so quick she nearly toppled over her own feet. Thankfully, Brooke caught her because neither Corbin nor I were close enough to have. "Oh, and my name is Annabelle now, but everyone calls me 'Belle.'"

I winced at her wording. Brooke was the only other one on this mountain who knew Belle's birth name. Hopefully she would just introduce herself regularly in the future and not add in the 'now'. I still would have a talk with her later about making sure she never admitted or hinted that she once had a different name.

Brooke smiled indulgently at her. "I know, sweetie. I think the name 'Belle' suits you perfectly."

Movement behind Brooke brought my attention to Dalton as he approached. He'd taken off his helmet. I was surprised to see he was African American. I hadn't guessed that by his voice. He was tall, maybe six-two, and bald. When he walked up behind Brooke, he placed his hand on the small of her back. He leaned in close to whisper something in her ear.

Red clouded my vision as she leaned into him. Well, that hadn't taken long. Here I was pining over her, still struggling whether I'd made the right decision to leave, and she'd already moved on. Guess her feelings weren't as deep as I'd imagined they were.

Before they reached the stairs, I turned my back and walked into the cabin.

Chapter Seventeen

Brooke

All evening Adam had been glaring at me and I didn't know why. Shit, I mean *Elijah*. That was going to take some getting used to. Belle and Lucas were easy enough to remember and their names flowed naturally when I needed to use them. Elijah's, though... I cringed. He was still *Adam* to me. I'd spent months dreaming of *Adam*, not Elijah. 'Elijah' felt like a stranger while Adam felt familiar.

I needed to break that train of thought, though. I knew better than most how important it was that there wasn't even a suspicion that someone named 'Adam' lived up on this mountain.

Elijah continued to glare. He was all smiles around the kids and sang 'Happy Birthday' just as loudly as the rest of us but would turn cold when I approached.

I don't know what sort of reception I was expecting. When Corbin had showed up at my cabin this morning to ask if I wanted to come to Belle's birthday party, Dalton had already been there. He was helping me fix a leak in one of my sheds. The heavy snow had caused the roof to crack. As usual, Dalton was the first to volunteer his services. I could have done it on my own, but four hands were easier than two to get the job accomplished.

So Dalton had come to the party too. Since the little girl didn't have anyone her own age to invite, Corbin wanted to make sure there were enough people there to still make her feel special. Apparently, Dalton also had not known that Corbin's mother, Gertie, was also living on the mountain.

Dalton offered to drive me on his four-wheeler and to take me home at the end of the evening. He truly was a sweetheart. I understood that he needed space from society due to his PTSD, but it was a shame he was all alone. Years ago, he'd described himself to me as a perpetual bachelor.

Then again, who on this mountain wasn't?

I'd been dreaming and fantasizing about Adam since the moment he'd left, so I had been nervous about seeing him again. Best case, Adam—damn it, *Elijah*—would run to greet me, kiss me, and declare his love for me. Worst case, he'd offer me his hand and tell me it was nice to see me.

I never expected to be ignored and glared at throughout the entire party.

In fact, I was angry about it. I wanted to shout at him and demand to know what his problem was. If I was here for any other reason except it being Belle's birthday party, I would have, but I was not going to ruin the girl's birthday with my petty love issues.

And here I thought I'd left all this drama behind me when I'd moved to Montana. I really did not need this sort of anxiety and stress in my life. That was the whole point of me living outside of society. I wanted a drama-free life. I deserved that after everything I'd been through.

I saw my opportunity to corner Elijah when he went into the kitchen to refill his coffee cup while Belle was opening her gifts. I hadn't gone shopping for her and didn't have much in my supply shed that was appropriate for an eight-year-old. However, I'd recently finished crocheting a blanket and decided that was a good gift. And then I realized I didn't have wrapping paper or a gift bag. Corbin gave me one to use, clearly having come from town.

It surprised me, since Corbin usually wasn't the first to come down off the mountain after winter. Generally, it was Dalton or me. I guess he made a modification to his schedule this year for his new niece.

Since Belle had already opened my gift, I followed her father into the kitchen. In a hurried whisper, I demanded, "What the hell is your problem?"

He turned around, having not heard me enter. "I don't know what you mean."

I snorted. "So, we're going to be childish about this. Fine. You've been glaring at me all day and you haven't even acknowledged me. A 'hello' would have been nice, maybe even a hug."

"Really?" He turned to the counter to put his mug down and then faced me again. "And how would your boyfriend out there feel about me hugging you?"

My jaw about fell to the floor. "Dalton? He's not my boyfriend. He offered me a ride."

Elijah's eyes narrowed. "You two looked pretty cozy together."

"He's a friend! I've known him since I moved up here. There's nothing between us and there never will—*oh!*" Before I had finished my sentence, Elijah had moved. He rushed forward, took my face between his hands, and kissed me. I was so shocked by the action that it took me a moment before I gripped his sweater, pulled him closer to me, and kissed him back.

And, damn, the man could kiss.

It had been nearly a decade since a man had kissed me, but I still remembered the mechanics. Yet, I didn't remember it being like this. The rush, the elation... The way his beard tickled my jaw or the way his hands tangled themselves in my hair. I don't recall any kiss being so fulfilling before.

"Daddy! Come look what Uncle Corbin got me!"

We broke apart at Belle's summons. Both of us were breathing heavy, and neither relinquished their hold on the other. Without looking away from me, Elijah called back to his daughter, "Be right there, Angel." Gently, he lowered his lips to mine again. It was just a simple peck on my lips, but it still sent a shudder all the way through my body. Then, without a word to me, he left me in the kitchen to rejoin his family.

When I finally got myself together, I turned to reenter the living room. Corbin stood in my way. From the look he gave me, it was obvious he either knew about or had seen the kiss. I wasn't sure what I was expecting him to say or do. Elijah was his best friend after all. But he let me pass by without saying a word.

I wasn't sure how to process any of it. Elijah's now obvious jealousy, the kiss, Corbin's reaction... Was there even an appropriate response to any of it? If there was, I certainly had no idea what it was.

I'd told Elijah once that I didn't do casual hookups and I didn't do relationships. He'd said that there wasn't much in between those two. And he was right. But what if I made an exception to my rules? Clearly, Elijah hadn't gotten over me any more than I had him. Where did that leave us?

Was this just a kiss or did it mean more?

Christ, I sounded like a fucking teenager. Does he love me, does he love me not, does he love me...? I was starting to get a headache. I'd spent four months pining over the man and yet I had no answers when he finally kissed me.

Maybe I should walk away. Kiss or not, that was the

soundest choice. Less drama, less risk of heartbreak. Walking away would be safe.

Elijah's deep brown eyes met mine from across the room. Fuck it, I didn't want safe. I wanted *Elijah.*

The party seemed to drag on. Per the birthday girl's request, we had spaghetti cake for dessert. That was a new one for me. Mind, I also hadn't been to a child's birthday party in a very long time so maybe this was a new fad.

My brain was having a real Ross-and-Rachel dilemma going on. Fact of it was, though, that no decisions could be made until Elijah and I talked. This *will we, won't we* spiral that was going on in my head right now was pointless.

Eventually, we journeyed outside to sit around the fire pit. Since Corbin only had two lawn chairs, we brought out some of the kitchen chairs too. A little bit later, the party goers started to drop off. Lucas went down first. Gertie took him in, claiming she was done for the night too. Belle tried to hold out, but the excitement of the party and the day finally got to her. She crashed on Corbin's lap, the princess tiara he'd gotten her falling to the side of her head.

Corbin stood with her securely in his arms. He elbowed Dalton's shoulder since his hands were full. "Mind following me in? I've got a project I want to run by you once the ground thaws."

And then there were two.

Elijah let out a low chuckle as soon as the door closed behind them. "He's not exactly subtle."

"Most of us out here aren't. We gave up drama a long time ago."

Elijah caught on to my double meaning. "Look, Brooke, I'm not going to say I shouldn't have kissed you. That would dampen the moment for both of us. Truthfully, I'm glad I did it."

"But," I prompted when he stopped talking.

"It's not a *but*. More of a concern that I need to talk through with you. You need to understand what you're getting into if you choose to be with me. I've tried to fight this, I really have. I was almost grateful for the snow because it kept me from going out and stupidly trying to find your cabin again. I want to start something with you."

"I appreciate your honesty." We were sitting opposite the fire from each other. It made it easier to see his face, which I was glad for. "So let me be honest in return.

"I like you too, Ad— I mean, Elijah. That's not even a question at this point. We liked each other when we were stuck together in my cabin, and we like each other now. Our separation over the winter has proven that the attraction between us is real, not fleeting. But if we're going to start something, I need you to be *completely* honest with me. About everything, even if you think it's too dangerous for me to know. I *need* that honesty between us. I can't be constantly wondering if today is the day you go on the run again and leave me behind without answers or at least knowing why."

"I don't want to run again. My kids are safe here. But there's always a risk. That's never going to go away."

"I know. I knew that before." Once I'd figured out he wasn't a lost tourist, that is. "I'm not expecting you to tell me everything right this minute, but it will need to be soon. Certainly before sex is even considered an option for us."

Elijah gave me a cocky smirk. "Oh, it's more than an option. It's inevitable."

I stuck my tongue out at him. He chuckled.

"I also feel I need to be honest with you. You once asked why I was living on this mountain. It's a long story, but I'd like for you to know."

Elijah stood and came to sit in the other lawn chair next to me. He took my hand, lacing our fingers together. I tightened my grip, remembering the pain from the last time we did this. His look was sympathetic, telling me he remembered too.

"Tell me as much or as little as you want to."

I nodded, taking a deep breath. "I haven't talked about this in almost a decade. Not exactly easy, remembering your faults and mistakes.

"First of all, I need to tell you that I was married." Elijah looked shocked but didn't interrupt. "Tyler was the love of my life. I'm not saying that to hurt you or even to compare the two of you, but you need to understand my devotion to him. Tyler and I met our freshman year of college. We were inseparable. We did everything together. Our friends called us 'sickeningly in love'. We were each other's firsts too. I loved how he would always reach for me, like he couldn't stand not to touch me. When we had separate classes, he would risk being late to his own so he could walk me to mine. The dorms were split by gender, but he would sneak in after visiting hours were over to stay the night with me.

"He asked me to marry him at the start of our senior year. I, of course, said yes. We decided to wait until after graduation to get married. My parents and my siblings were thrilled for me. My best friend since she was born was my younger sister, Kate. Even though we'd gone to different colleges, we were still close. 'Thick as thieves,' our mother called us.

"Tyler and I got married. We bought a house, we started our jobs, and we were still sickeningly in love. He supported me when I went for my detective's shield and I supported him when he changed marketing companies. Tyler would text me heart emojis throughout the day to let me know he was thinking of me. I wrote love notes to him and put them in his lunch bag. We talked about kids, but I honestly wasn't interested in becoming a mother. I was being selfish. I wanted

Tyler all to myself and he said he was fine with not having kids.

"So, ten years ago, four years into our marriage, I was completely shocked and taken by surprise when I picked up his phone to find an unread text message from 'Unknown' on the front screen reading 'Tomorrow at lunch. I won't wear panties this time.'"

"Oh fuck." Elijah's jaw dropped. "I was not expecting that. I thought you were going to tell me he died."

I snorted. "If only I had been so lucky. As awful as it is for me to say, I think it would have been easier to get over.

"Tyler was still in the shower after getting home from work. That was why I had picked up his phone. When I saw that message, I opened his phone and clicked on the text. There was an entire thread of messages going back a while, including nude pictures and even a sex video. I couldn't believe it. I *didn't* believe it. I was so sure it was a prank of some sort. Tyler would *not* cheat on me. It was impossible.

"But then I saw a picture of the girl's face, and it was like a final nail being driven into the coffin. It wasn't some random girl that I didn't know. It was my *sister*."

"Are you fucking kidding me?"

I nodded, confirming, "My sister, my *best friend*, was having an affair with my husband."

"My God, Brooke. I'm so sorry. What did you do?"

"That day? Nothing. I took pictures of the text thread, returned the phone to where it was on the counter, and went back to cooking dinner. I was in shock. A part of me wanted to demand answers, but another part knew that it didn't matter. Nothing Kate or Tyler did or said would ever make it right. My relationship with both was over. Tyler and I would never reconcile, and Kate and I would never be friends or sisters again."

"I can't even fathom how you felt. Weren't there signs? Like he was home late from work or had a business trip out of town?"

I shook my head. "That was what made it so hard for me to accept. I was a fucking *detective* and I had no idea my husband was *cheating* on me? But, to this day, I swear there were *no signs*, nothing. I had no odd occurrences or wife's intuition about any of it. He was attentive and loving as he'd always been, and we still had an active sex life. I couldn't remember seeing Kate and him acting differently around each other either. I had caught no lingering looks or touches between them. And we got together regularly, the three of us. So it wasn't like they never saw each other outside of holiday family gatherings. She was always over to our house and we were always over at hers.

"The next day, Tyler went off to work and I called in sick to work. The first thing I did was call a divorce lawyer. I had no idea who to choose, so I honestly just went with the first one that came up in Google. My lawyer gave me steps on what to do next. It would take some time to process the paperwork and serve him. First thing, I needed to separate our accounts. We didn't have any separate accounts other than the trust that was left to me by my grandmother. He knew about it, but we'd never touched it, thinking we could use it to remodel the kitchen or build an entertainment patio out back. I had to go to the bank and take my name off the joint accounts. I split everything down the middle, fifty-fifty.

"Then I went to see the attorney in person. I gave her the pictures I took of the text thread, including the blown-up picture of my naked sister on his phone *in my bed*."

"Jesus..."

"Then I went home and packed. I took all my clothes, jewelry, and toiletries. By the time Tyler came home that day, I was on my way to my parents' house. Kate had tried calling me earlier in the day, but I ignored it. My lawyer warned me not to block Kate or Tyler until the divorce was finalized because any admissions or accusations they sent to me could be used against Tyler in the proceedings.

"It was around dinner time when I arrived at my parents' house. They welcomed me in and that was when I collapsed. I told them everything, including that it was Kate whom he was having the affair with. My dad was outraged, but not for the reason you would think. Kate was the youngest, the baby, and a real daddy's girl. She could, and did, get away with anything in my father's eyes.

"My dad actually accused *me* of staging the text thread to get Kate into trouble. Like we were five and I was trying to get her grounded."

"That's fucked up." Elijah stood up, clearly outraged on my behalf. "You're his daughter too! And the facts were right there in front of the man. You had the evidence!"

I nodded. "He didn't care. He told me that if I chose to divorce Tyler over 'this little incident' that was my choice, but he did not support it. Then my mom put the icing right on the proverbial disaster that was now my life. She actually told me that if I had just given Tyler the babies he'd asked me for, he wouldn't have strayed."

Elijah lowered his head. "Goddamn."

"I went to my parents for support, and I got spit on. So I left. I'd just checked into a hotel when Kate started blowing up my phone. When I didn't pick up, she started texting. Calling me a bitch and a liar. Telling me that it was my fault all this happened anyway. That I wasn't woman enough to hold onto a man like Tyler.

"Per my lawyer's instructions, I didn't respond to any messages and took screenshots of each one as they came in. Then Tyler's messages started to come in. Clearly, someone had told him I knew about the affair or he'd come home to find all my things gone from the house. He demanded to know where I was, apologized, and begged for forgiveness. He claimed it had only happened once, but I knew that wasn't true because of how far back the text messages went. Also, Kate had already thrown it in my face that they'd been fucking behind my back for months and I never knew. My personal favorite of his excuses as to why he had the affair was because he was a man, and all men cheat."

"Well, that's a load of shit. My parents have been happily married for forty-four years and my dad's never even looked at another woman."

I agreed. Cheating was a choice, not a biologically driven action. "At that point, I'd had enough. Not wanting to deal with it anymore, I put my phone on silent and went to bed. I had to figure out what I was going to tell my boss in the morning, what I was going to do with the house, our belongings, our entire *lives* were mixed together. Tyler had been the first and only man I'd loved, and he'd taken my heart and ripped it right out of my chest. Then he gave it to my sister to stomp on with one of her ridiculously high heeled shoes."

Elijah sat back down next to me. He wasn't any calmer. Frankly, neither was I. Rehashing all of this was dredging up all those old feelings of heartache and betrayal.

"I hope you understand now why honesty is so important to me, Elijah. You have one shot," I held up a finger for emphasis, "one chance. One lie—well intended or not—and we're done. I'm not going through what Kate and Tyler put me through again. I came out here to be *alone*. The affair divided my family. It killed my marriage. Friends chose sides and it was like a war line was being drawn. Tyler refused to sign the divorce papers for months. He dragged the proceedings on and on, claiming I too was having an affair. Once that was disproven, the judge granted me the divorce against Tyler's very loud wishes.

"The straw that broke the camel's back though was at Thanksgiving that year. I had told my mother that I wasn't going to come to the family meal unless Kate wasn't going to be there. My mother swore Kate was not. I went. Then Kate walked through the door with Tyler on her arm."

"Fuck," Elijah breathed out. "Now I know how Corbin felt when I told him my story. This is like an emotional rollercoaster when you're sitting on the other side of it. What an asshole, both of them."

I let out a wry laugh. "Wasn't exactly an easy ride living through it either. My mother didn't understand why I was so angry or why I insisted on leaving as soon as I'd seen the happy couple. I was on my way out the door when I heard Kate announce, proudly and happily, that she was pregnant. Suddenly, it didn't matter anymore if I was present or not, I realized I'd become chopped liver to my entire family. My brother and his wife didn't try to stop me from leaving. My father was over the moon and my mother immediately stopped her argument against my departure. Kate was once more the center of attention, standing there so proudly with my ex-husband. And my family saw nothing wrong with any of it.

"I left and immediately started researching how to get away. I needed to escape, even if some might consider it cowardly. I saw a post about mountain life, and I was hooked. I took the money from the settlement, plus my trust fund from my grandmother, and built my cabin. I've been here ever since."

"And your family's never tried to find you?"

"I have an email account that I communicate with my mother on. If I didn't have at least that, she would file a missing persons report on me. Jack sometimes emails her for me when I can't get off the mountain or when I just don't feel like dealing with her. I don't think she's sorry for the way she acted. I truly believe that she thinks I overreacted and abandoned *them*."

"I can't believe how they turned their backs on you. Kate was clearly in the wrong."

"And yet..."

"And yet," he mimicked. We were both silent for a moment. Elijah reached for my hand. I gave it. "Brooke, I can't promise to be upfront about everything. Believe me when I tell you it's an even longer and more gruesome story than yours. That was not a comparison," he added quickly. "Just a statement. I'll tell you what I can and I swear I'll never lie to you—unless it's to save you or my children's lives.

"My kids come first and, the more people who know my story, the more chances that the wrong person will eventually hear about it too. I'm not saying that I think you'll tell anyone, but my silence is to protect you too."

"Protect me from what?" I asked. "You keep talking about protecting me, but I don't understand from whom. How would the person chasing you even know about me?"

Elijah sat back in his chair. He ran a hand down his face. I could tell he was working the nerve up to say something, so I remained quiet.

"There are warrants out for my arrest."

My heart nearly stopped. I ripped my hand out of his. "*What?*" I recalled asking Elijah if he was a criminal, and he had assured me that he wasn't—but something had felt off about that response. I'd brushed it off at the time. I wasn't going to now. "For what?"

Elijah swallowed hard. "Murder and kidnapping."

Well. Fuck. Suddenly I recalled Elijah telling me that Lucas's mother had died in childbirth. What if...? Oh God. What if Elijah had *killed* her?

Then I paused in my hysterical rantings.

Elijah wasn't a murderer. He didn't have an evil bone in his body. I *knew* Elijah. We might not have talked as much as I would have liked while he was staying in my cabin, but I *knew* him. I'd watched him. A lot. He was so warm and loving to his children. He was sweet and kind.

That couldn't have all been an act. Could it?

My insecurities, a parting gift from Tyler, crept forward. I clearly wasn't a good judge of character like I'd always thought I was. I'd trusted Tyler and look where it got me. I'd quit my job as a detective because I didn't trust my instincts anymore. Tyler's betrayal had left me questioning *everything* I thought I knew about myself.

"I need you to explain that statement. Right now."

"I didn't kill anyone, I swear. Brooke, I've never even held a gun before in my life. I heard something I shouldn't have, and my employer was blackmailing me to stay silent with a gun he put my fingerprints on. When I ran, he turned the gun over to the police. The police believe I killed the man who died by that gun, but I swear I didn't. I'm innocent."

Tyler had claimed to be innocent too—before he realized how much evidence I really had against him.

Was Elijah being framed? Didn't every murderer claim he was being framed?

"Who are you accused of murdering?"

Elijah shook his head. "Jack told me the name, but I didn't recognize it. I'm assuming it's a business associate of my employer's, but I don't know who he is." He looked me straight in the eyes. "Brooke, I am not a murderer."

Even in the low lighting of the fire, I could see him clearly. He looked sincere. I wanted to believe him. I really did.

"Jack can verify all this?"

Elijah nodded. "He can. He's been helping the kids and I since the beginning."

I recalled that from his stay in my cabin. Jack was the 'friend of a friend' who'd been helping them out. I trusted Jack, and from the little of what I knew about Jack's history, I knew he would not blindly trust Elijah. Should that mean I could trust Elijah too? I wanted to.

"Do you understand now why I stayed away? I don't want you tangled up in this. If I'm caught, I don't want you in trouble for harboring a fugitive or obstructing justice."

It did make sense now. The longing in his eyes, yet always pulling himself away. I got it, but if he was innocent... There had to be a way we could clear his name.

Then I remembered the second charge he'd said he was wanted for. "You kidnapped your own children?"

Elijah shook his head. "They are mine in all ways, except biological."

"Holy shit, Elijah!" My voice echoed through the trees. I stood up in shock. He might not be a murderer, but he *was* a kidnapper. "You mean, they're... They're not... Fuck!"

Elijah stood too. He frantically launched into his explanation. "I need you to understand. I *had* to get them out. They have an older brother in his twenties. He helped us to escape. That place, that man..." In the firelight, I saw Elijah's complexion take on a greenish hue. "Brooke, their birth father tried to *sell* Belle to a man in his thirties to seal a business deal."

My stomach rolled at the implication. He had to have been mistaken. My time on the force had proven there were some sick fucks out there, but still... "That's disgusting. Why would you ever think that?"

"Because I was there. I saw and heard the whole thing. Lyd —*Belle*, her father was marrying her off. She was seven fucking years old, and he was selling her like she was a brood mare."

I felt sick. "Oh God." I didn't want to believe him because believing him would mean that Belle's biological father had tried to sell her. That was beyond heinous.

What if he was lying? What if Elijah had taken two children that were not his from a loving household? What if that was why he was on the run?

That conclusion didn't feel right. Even though believing him was a worse reality for Belle, I couldn't make myself believe that Elijah was so cruel and selfish a person to take two innocent babies from their home. It didn't fit with the man I had come to know.

Then again, I'd only known him for six days and he was unconscious for one of those days. So maybe I didn't know him well enough to trust my intuition about him. But it was those five plus days and nights that I had seen Elijah with his children that didn't let me believe he was capable of such cruelty.

When Elijah had collapsed in my kitchen, Belle hadn't been happy he'd fallen unconscious. She hadn't said anything that indicated Elijah had been anything but loving to her brother and her. I recalled how protective Belle was of her baby brother those first couple of nights while Elijah slept. No matter how much I coaxed or tried, she would not rest. She was guarding her brother against...something.

And that something hadn't been Elijah.

If Belle and Lucas were strangers to Elijah, or even if they were familiar with him and had been taken from a loving family, wouldn't Belle have given some indication of that? She was old enough, even at seven, to know right from wrong. Yet, instead of telling me that Elijah was a stranger who had kidnapped her and her brother or ask even once where her parents were, she'd been attentive to Elijah. She'd tuck him in tighter when the blanket would start to fall and had put moisturizer on his lips when they'd been cracking and bleeding from being out in the cold. She'd called him 'Daddy'. She'd never once slipped and called him 'Adam' or another name.

Didn't they say that kids and pets could always tell the true character of a person? If Belle had been cautious in any way towards Elijah, it would have sent up red flags to me the day I'd rescued them. But she hadn't. She'd shown clear devotion and love towards Elijah.

Elijah continued talking while I tried to wrap my head around what he was confessing to. "Her older brother and I were already planning on escaping with her when we learned about Lucas. His mother was still pregnant with him then. We knew we couldn't subject another child to that life, even if it meant stealing the children away from their biological father. We knew the implications, and I didn't care. Brooke, the man is a psychopath—and I knew that long before he tried to sell his own daughter. Their brother and I decided to wait so we could get the baby out too. We had it all planned out, but everything went wrong. Neither of us were expecting..." He cringed. "There was a shootout between their father's organization and the one he was trying to marry Belle into. Their older brother was shot protecting us. I didn't think. I just took both kids, and I ran."

For a moment, I thought I was going to throw up. Belle's laugh, the joy on her face tonight... And some bastard who didn't even deserve to be called her father had tried to take that away from her.

Neither of us spoke for a while. I was trying to process all he had told me. Clearly, he'd left out some details. A lot of details. But God! How could the law be on the side of a murderer and pedophile? Because, whether he touched his daughter himself or not, he was *allowing* another man to. Worse, he was getting money or some exchange for it. I was fairly certain that fell under human trafficking too.

If what he was saying was true, I couldn't blame Elijah for running. But he could have run to the police! I get that he thought of those kids as his own, which was another thing I had to address, but surely the police could have helped him.

But it also sounded like his employer was a powerful, manipulative man. I recalled Elijah referring to his contract as signing a deal with the devil. What had seemed like an exaggeration then was now an understatement. Plus, his employer had been blackmailing Elijah. He'd known about the gun with his fingerprints on it, and he'd still taken those kids and run.

"Belle calls you 'Daddy'. Does she know?"

Elijah looked more ashamed answering that question than he did when he'd admitted to kidnapping two children. "Belle knows far too much. No child should know or have seen the things she has." The disgust was plain on his face as it was in his voice. "I'm working with her, though, helping her process. Since she could speak, she's called me her dad. We had to be very careful about who heard her call me that. Biology never mattered to me. From the moment I held her in my arms in that delivery room, she was *mine*."

In any other situation, I would call that statement crazy. The man was claiming another man's child as his own. But given the facts I had, not even knowing the facts he hadn't yet told, I could understand why Elijah felt justified to take the children out of that situation.

But there had to be other options than going on the run with them like he had. Witness protection or protective custody?

"Jack and Corbin can verify everything that I've told you. I know you'll trust their word over mine. I get if this changes how you feel and think about me. You were right that it wasn't fair to you to start something without you knowing the truth, or at least part of it. But I beg of you, Brooke, don't tell anyone about us. If not for me, for those children. They are finally *happy* and, above all, they're safe. If their birth father finds us, I'll be killed. And those kids? Belle will likely be sold or married off to benefit his business. In his mind, that's all women are good for anyway.

Lucas will likely grow up to be ruthless, heartless, and to follow in his father's footsteps. I couldn't bear that."

I couldn't either. It was clear Elijah believed what he was telling me. The disgust and the passion rang true in his voice. I also believed that if a man could sell his own daughter into slavery, then he would not hesitate to kill the man who'd tried to keep him from those profits.

But just because Elijah believed something, didn't mean it was true. Humans had once believed the Earth was the center of the universe and that the world was flat. Others believe that the moon landing was a hoax and aliens walk among us. And don't even get me started on the countless religions in the world that have sparked brutal and unnecessary wars.

I'd always been taught to uphold the law. Right versus wrong. It was why I'd longed to become a cop since I was a little girl. When I'd discovered what Tyler and Kate had done, I hadn't hesitated to take action. There'd been no forgiveness, no listening to stories or reasons. I'd cut both of them out of my life completely and immediately. And when my family had chosen to support them, the wrongdoers, instead of me, the victim, I'd done the same with them (with the exception of my mother's monthly email to prove I was still alive).

So why was I hesitating now?

Elijah was in the wrong. He'd taken two children that were not his, claimed them as his own, and gone on the run with them.

But blood wasn't everything. Corbin and Elijah were as close as brothers and look at the extremes Corbin had gone to protect Elijah. Yet my own sister, who had also been my best friend, had been screwing my husband, the love of my life, behind my back for four months and now had a child with him. I'd never inquired about the child, and I'd never asked my mother if Kate and Tyler were still together. My own blood had completely blown up my entire reality.

And if I believed Elijah, which I was ninety-nine percent sure I did, then Belle's biological father, her *blood*, had tried to sell her off to a man who would claim to marry her—because that sure as hell would never be a legal union—before raping her. A child.

Hadn't Elijah proved he was more of a father to the children than their biological one was? But did that give Elijah the right to take the children away from their father and their home?

Right versus wrong.

I looked towards Corbin's cabin. I'd never been invited inside before today. It was weird, because he'd never been inside of mine before he'd made it down the mountain to reunite with Elijah. We had a birthday party for the first time on this mountain tonight. Elijah had done that by bringing those kids to our mountain. I saw Belle's face when Gertie had put her birthday spaghetti cake in front of her. That was a look of pure joy and innocence that only a happy and healthy child could portray.

I wanted to believe Elijah. I really did. It wasn't that I needed more facts or to verify his version of events with Jack or Corbin. My hesitation came from my own morals. Was Elijah right or wrong to take those children?

I stepped forward and put my hand on his arm. My hand traveled down until I was able to lace our fingers together. I stepped into him. "I need time to think about all this. I think you were very brave to remove Belle and Lucas from such a grotesque situation. I can't even begin to imagine the horrors Belle would have gone through if you hadn't. I understand now the risk you were talking about as well as your desire to protect me." I pressed my lips to his shoulder. "But I still need time. Your secret is safe with me. I'd never do anything to endanger those children. I just... You gave me a lot to process."

Elijah pulled me into his chest. I felt his lips in my hair. I pressed my face into his sweater. He was so warm. "I know. Thank you for believing me. I know the story sounds farfetched, but it is the truth. I swear it to you. All I ask is that you take care when asking Jack or Corbin about this. Make sure there's no chance of you being overheard." He clenched me tighter before adding, "Please don't ask Belle about any of this. I've been working with her on processing the things she saw and heard. She's finally to a point where she's ready to move on."

I squeezed him tighter too. From one perspective, one could argue that Elijah was taking away my option of asking the only witness who had actually been there. From another, it was obvious Elijah was only trying to protect his daughter.

I remained silent, knowing I'd never do anything to endanger those children. We stayed like that until Corbin and Dalton came back outside.

Chapter Eighteen

Brooke

I was torn. Once again, I suffered through a sleepless night due to Elijah, but this time it had nothing to do with sexual fantasies.

Elijah had kidnapped two children that were not biologically or legally his in any way. He had been their nanny. I thought he'd said he was a teacher, but that was something to be clarified with him at a later date. Regardless of job title, Belle and Lucas were *not* his children.

I believed him when he said Belle's life and welfare was in jeopardy. He'd said something about a shootout too and her older brother getting shot. I would need to get more information about that too next time I saw him.

Maybe I should start making a list...

No, anything I wrote down could potentially be used against Elijah if it got into the wrong hands. So, I'd just have to rely on my memory. I could probably ask Belle for some ribbon to tie around my fingers. I looked down at my hands and realized I probably would need more fingers once I was through processing all he'd told me.

I also had to process the fact that I'd told someone, for the first time in nearly a decade, about my failed marriage. I hadn't talked about Tyler since the incident that awful Thanksgiving at my mother's house. I'd told Elijah though. It had felt *right*. Not because I was keeping anything in, but because I needed to be open with him if I wanted to start a romantic relationship with him. He needed to understand my past and my trust issues.

Opening up to him might have also made him feel more comfortable about opening up to me. Mind, he wasn't kidding when he'd said his past was far more complicated and gruesome than mine.

But now I knew.

Everything from that week he'd spent in my cabin now made perfect sense. He'd taken the kids and somehow gotten in touch with Corbin, who put him in touch with Jack. Since Corbin didn't have reception or internet at his cabin, I didn't know how Elijah had reached out to him. My eyes landed on the postcard I'd pulled out of Elijah's jeans pocket when I'd undressed him that first night. I'd saved it for him, but it had remained here when Elijah had left with Corbin. It had resided on my nightstand for the past four months. All that was written on it was a phone number to an area code that was not local. I recognized the picture on the other side, though. In fact, I'd asked Jack once why he sold postcards with pictures of the ocean on them in a town with no ocean access. He'd just smiled and said, "What's life without a little whimsy."

The postcard had no doubt come from Jack's store and was likely sent by Corbin. I didn't recognize the phone number, but it explained how Elijah had been able to get ahold of his friend after eighteen years apart.

It still frightens me, the thought of what would have happened to Elijah and those kids if I hadn't been passing by exactly when I had. If I'd gone to Tommy's earlier, I would have been home before they'd even driven up the mountain. If I'd taken a different route home, I never would have seen them. If I'd looked away before the glow from the taillight had caught my eye, I might have driven right past them without even knowing they were there.

All I knew was that I was beyond grateful that I'd been in the right place at the right time to help them.

As I stared up at my ceiling, I knew that while what Elijah had done was in a morally gray area, he'd done it with good intentions. His goal had always been, and always would be, to protect his children.

I wasn't sure how I felt right then calling them his children. Technically, they were the children he'd stolen. *But* Elijah did say that Belle had been calling him her dad since she learned to speak. That had to mean that her real father hadn't been around or attentive enough to his own daughter for her to form any relationship or bond with him.

There was no doubt Elijah loved those children. It must have been so terrible for Belle if she was suffering from, what I assumed, was a form of PTSD. It was possible Elijah was too, with how protective he was towards those children.

Bottom line was, I *did* want to start a romantic relationship with Elijah. I understood that there might be some heartache down the line if he and the children had to relocate, but I felt it was worth the risk. I didn't know if I would fall in love with Elijah. I liked him, certainly. Love was a different story. I wasn't sure I was capable of that anymore.

I didn't still love Tyler, but I still remember the feeling and elation of loving him. I had been so devoted and utterly blind that I'd missed my own husband having a four-month affair with my own sister. Tyler no longer held a piece of my heart, but I wasn't entirely sure my heart was whole enough to be given out again.

Time would tell, I supposed. It wasn't like I had to fall in love with Elijah by a certain date and time or my carriage would turn back into a pumpkin. We had time. That was the great thing about this mountain. *Time.* Time had no meaning up here, beyond the change of the seasons. We could go as fast or as slow as we wanted, and there was no external pressure from family, culture, or society.

Elijah and I hadn't made plans to meet up again when I'd left Belle's party. I think he was leaving the ball in my court since I had said I'd needed time to process. I had a bunch of questions, there was no doubt about that, and maybe it was foolish of me to even contemplate a relationship with a man who was a self-admitted kidnapper—good intentions aside. When Dalton and Corbin had come back outside, Elijah and I had stepped away from our embrace. He'd kissed me on the cheek and gone inside for the night. Dalton had driven me home.

He hadn't said anything about what he'd seen at the party between Elijah and I. Mind, he'd also been introduced to Adam as 'Elijah'.

Dalton just gave me a knowing smirk before driving off to head to his cabin.

I'd planned on going hunting in the morning. The big game was starting to come out of their winter hidey-holes. It was prime hunting time before mating season turned many of them aggressive, especially the males. I also needed to start setting up my regular traps for the small animals. I had specific places around my property that I liked to catch rabbits, squirrels, and (once) a wolverine. I checked them every day or so throughout the warmer months and usually caught something in two out of five traps.

Geese would also be prime in a few months as they headed north to lay their eggs. There was a stream on my land that attracted ducks sometimes too. Pheasant were also popular come summertime.

There was always plenty to do. I was never short on work.

Yet, I knew that tomorrow (after I'd gotten some much needed sleep) I would be heading up to Corbin's cabin to see Elijah.

Chapter Nineteen

Elijah

I had a rough night. I kept waking from vivid dreams of police kicking down the door and taking my children away from me. At one point, I'd even gone into Gertie and Belle's room to verify that Belle was in the cabin, safe and sound asleep after her big day. Her tiara had still been on her head. Corbin probably didn't have the heart to take it off her. I did so it didn't get tangled in her hair as she slept.

My precious angel.

Lucas was also sleeping soundly. He didn't wake much through the night anymore. Generally, once he was down, he was down. I was usually grateful for that, as it allowed me to sleep uninterrupted too. Tonight, though, a part of me wished he'd wake up so I could have an excuse not to go back to sleep.

I knew Brooke wasn't going to go to the police. I wouldn't have told her a single thing if I'd had any doubt about that. I'd taken a chance in telling her what I did, but it needed to be said if she was going to take a risk on me.

If Brooke and I did start dating, and that was still a big *if*, I needed to have a conversation with Belle. I knew she considered Brooke a friend and I didn't want Belle to think I was taking away from that friendship at all. I would also need to pay close attention to Belle's relationship with Brooke to make sure she wasn't becoming overly attached to Brooke. As a female figure, and a potential mother figure, Belle might become attached as a way to disassociate from her past. In her previous life as Lydia, she didn't have a mother. She might try to make it so *Belle* did have a mother, essentially forming a completely new life around that relationship.

I was getting ahead of myself, though. Christ, we'd only kissed once before we both revealed some painful experiences from our pasts.

I couldn't believe Brooke's husband and sister. How could they do that to her? Regardless of blood or vows, they had started an affair *knowing* Brooke would find out. They might not have known when, but they had to have known she would eventually. Or maybe they were the type of cheaters who believed their actions were justified by something Brooke had said or done. Regardless, they had not started an affair knowing that Brooke would not be hurt as a result.

Yet both claimed to have loved her.

Fools.

If I was lucky enough to one day win Brooke's love, I'd hold on tight to it and never let it go. She was an amazing person, strong and independent. She was made of steel after surviving her ordeal with no familial support. I was glad there had been no children caught up in the mix.

I remembered Brooke confessing that she didn't want to have children. When she'd said it, she'd made the comment that she was selfish and hadn't wanted to share her husband. I could understand that. Children were certainly attention-seeking monsters with big appetites and curious minds. I just hoped she understood I was a package deal. I was never going to leave my children or abandon them. Despite what I had done to claim them, they were *mine.*

I must have fallen asleep again because no sooner did I have the attention-seeking monster thought than forty-eight pounds of spaghetti-filled child land on me. *"Hmph!"* came out of me as I quickly put a hand over my family jewels to protect them from bony knees.

My little angel devilishly grinned down at me. "Hi, Daddy."

"Hi, Angel." I couldn't help but grin back at her. I looked over at the crib to see Lucas standing up, holding onto the rails. "Did you sleep well?"

She nodded like a bobblehead. "Can we have pancakes?"

If Belle was up, that meant Gertie was also up. Likely, Corbin's mother was already in the kitchen getting breakfast together for us. Corbin would be outside working. I really needed to start figuring out a way to help him with that. The one time I'd tried to help him chop wood, I'd fallen on my ass.

Belle still brought it up on occasion, to my utter humiliation.

I picked my daughter up as I got out of bed. I wore sweatpants and a white undershirt. I always made sure my back was covered when around Belle, not wanting her to regress and have flashbacks about watching my flogging. It was bad enough that I still had nightmares about the experience.

She giggled as I flipped her upside down and held her by her ankles. Her nightgown fell down around her face. Belle frantically tried to squirm out of my hold, but I kept ahold of her until I lowered her into the crib next to Lucas. "Stay with your brother while I go to the bathroom."

Her giggles were soon joined by his as she tickled him. It was the best sound in the world. Sometimes I wished I still had my phone so I could record times like this or take pictures for them to look back on when they were older. I hoped they understood as they grew why anything like that would be too dangerous for us to keep around just for sentimental reasons.

But I still wished.

I wanted my children safe. I knew that was the priority. But at what expense? What would happen when Belle got old enough to want to go into town on her own or to go on a date with a boy? I cringed at the last one. Lucas might want to play sports or go to a summer camp.

At what point would I think enough time had passed for me to let the reins loose?

I wanted to say never, but I knew how unrealistic that was. And hypocritical, given what I'd told Brooke last night.

When I was done in the bathroom, I got the kids together and joined Gertie in the kitchen. I gave her a peck on the cheek as I passed.

"Angel, what do you say to Grammy for creating your cake last night?"

Belle was sitting on her knees. She drew herself up on the table. "Thank you, Grammy! It was awesome!"

Gertie came over to the table with a plate of bacon and eggs for Belle and a bowl of oatmeal for Lucas. I took the oatmeal out of grabbing range while I got up to get a spoon.

"You're welcome, sweetie. It's nice to know, even after all this time, I can still be surprised by some things." She gave me a knowing look.

I met it with a grin of my own. My daughter certainly was unique.

Belle was mostly through her breakfast, and I had more oatmeal on me than in Lucas's belly, when Corbin came stomping into the cabin. He was so tall that any doorway was a hazard for his head.

Belle's breakfast was abandoned. Maybe I shouldn't be so concerned about her attaching herself unhealthily to Brooke, given how attached she already was to Corbin. The two had a special bond. I couldn't find fault in that. Especially when the relationship was so beneficial for both parties. Gertie had told me in confidence that she'd never seen Corbin so happy as he was around Belle.

When it came down to it, I knew Corbin was big enough and strong enough to protect Belle from anything. I viewed him as her bodyguard. I didn't have to worry so much about her when she was with him.

Maybe I was actually transferring my concerns about getting overly attached to Brooke myself onto Belle. That woman was like a drug, and I was just pining for my next fix. How could I protect my children if I was constantly wanting to be with her?

Shit. I stopped that thought. I was doing it again, creating excuses as to why not instead of concentrating on why I should. I needed to remember that she had choices too. She was a grown woman who was intelligent enough to make her own sound decisions. If she chose to be with me, understanding the risks involved, I needed to respect that.

I also needed to respect her decision if she chose *not* to be with me.

Lucas slapped his hand down in the oatmeal bowl, knocking it out of my hand. "Dragons!" I let out in place of a curse.

I looked up at the ceiling, asking the Lord for patience as oatmeal dripped down my shirt to my leg and onto the floor.

Gertie quickly came over with a towel. Lucas burst into laughter. Corbin walked in carrying Belle over his shoulder like she was a sack of potatoes. It was chaos, but it was familiar. Corbin met my eyes, and we both started laughing too. We were making such a ruckus that we didn't hear the motor outside until it was nearly here.

Everyone quieted down except for Lucas. Gertie quickly

took control of the baby. Corbin put Belle down, grabbing his shotgun from above the refrigerator where small hands couldn't reach it. I didn't like that there were guns in the house, but Corbin went through where each one was with me and I approved of their locations. We also had a talk with Belle about gun safety.

Corbin cocked the gun before heading for his front door. I ushered Belle behind me with Gertie and Lucas. My heart was pounding so hard, it likely resembled a drum line. I needed to calm down to keep my wits about me, but I could feel the start of a panic attack coming on. How could we have been found? What had we done wrong? Who had found us? What would happen next? If it was the police, I had a chance to plead my case, but I'd likely never see my children again. If it was Gunther... Well, I still would never see my children again.

I planted myself in front of my family, knowing I would do everything possible to keep them safe. Including Gertie.

Corbin took a glance out the window and immediately his shoulders sagged. He lowered the muzzle of the gun before turning to me. "It's for you, lover boy."

At those words, my panic ceased. No one had found us. My children were still safe.

I came forward just as Corbin opened the door for Brooke. She came in, a smile coming across her face when she saw me.

My heart started pounding hard again, but for an entirely different reason this time.

And then I realized she wasn't smiling at me because she was happy to see me. No, her smile was full of humor. She tried to cover her mouth with her hand, but it was too late. I'd seen it.

That's when I recalled the oatmeal. I looked down at myself and cringed. Oatmeal covered my shirt from my left nipple down to my stomach and onto my pant leg. I was barefoot, despite the cold flooring. It wouldn't surprise me if I had some on my face or in my hair too.

I looked back up and squared my shoulders. "Well, I'd like to see you try to feed a ten-month-old who's teething."

She held up her hands and took a step back. "That's okay. I'll leave it to the professionals."

Belle came running out of the kitchen. "Brooke! You're back!"

Brooke nodded. "Yeah, I came to talk to your dad." When she saw Belle's face start to fall, she quickly added, "And maybe play some games with you later?"

Belle immediately agreed and then ran off to her room to get dressed for the day. Brooke was wearing a heavy turtleneck sweater and leggings. I assumed the leggings were lined given the briskness of the morning. On her feet were work boots. They didn't go with her outfit per se, but the boots totally went with her personality.

Corbin nudged her shoulder. "Why don't you and I head outside to get some work done while lover boy gets himself presentable?"

My cheeks flushed and I scratched my nose with my middle finger. Corbin just smiled. Brooke followed him out the door after a lingering look back at me.

I turned. Gertie was behind me with Lucas still in her arms. He was rifling through her hair as if searching for buried treasure. "I'm happy for you."

"You don't think it's risky and foolish, given my situation?"

Gertie didn't know all of it, just enough to make her aware of the danger hunting us. She shook her head. "I think the two of you would be a good fit, as long as your head doesn't get in the way of your heart." She turned back towards the kitchen before throwing over her shoulder, "Both of them."

It took me a moment to catch on. When I did, I slapped my forehead with the palm of my hand. I did not need sex advice from Corbin's mother.

Chapter Twenty

Brooke

Thwack! I brought down the axe hard on the stump on Corbin's chopping block. After a long winter like we had, and especially because he had extra people in his house, Corbin had gone through a lot of wood over the past four months. He was down to bare bones. In addition, all his tanks and stores had taken extra usage. There was also some damage to his workshop where he constructed his furniture. A tree branch had fallen on the roof. Thankfully it hadn't punctured through, but the roofing needed to be patched again. Especially before the spring and summer rains.

Corbin was doing a thorough inspection of all his buildings, including the cabin, while I started rebuilding his wood pile. For some reason, he'd been extra encouraging to have me be the one chopping the wood instead of checking for damage.

Regardless, I'd offered to help, so I took the man's axe and started chopping away. After a few rounds, I felt the pull of familiar muscles that I hadn't used all winter. Soon after that, I started warming up despite the chill in the air and rolled up my sleeves. I'd worn the turtleneck to look nice for Elijah, not anticipating being put to work. I really should have known better.

"If I make a comment about how sexy you look right now, will that axe come down on me next?"

I smiled at his voice and took one more swing to split the stump completely in two. Corbin and the other mountain men probably could have done it in one but some of the larger stumps took me a couple extra swings.

I put the axe down, handle up against the chopping block. Elijah was standing a couple of yards behind me, which was a smart decision considering the weapon I'd been wielding. He was freshly showered and his clothing oatmeal-free.

I tipped my chin towards his pants. "Thought I warned you about wearing jeans out in these parts?"

He at least looked a little sheepish when he admitted, "I don't really have a lot of options when it comes to clothing. Not like I'll fit into anything of Corbin's. I could probably fit one of me into each of his pant legs."

I knew he meant it as a joke, but I heard the underlying tone of self-condemnation too. Like he was less because he wasn't a raging hulk of a man. I crossed my arms over my chest. "Elijah, you know there's nothing wrong with not being as big or as strong as some of the others. Mountain men are big because they've earned it through the hard work it takes to survive up here. It's okay that you're not as bulky as them." I added just to boost his ego a little, "Plus, I like you just as you are."

"Now when you say it's okay if I'm not as big, you are referring to their *muscles*, right?"

I snorted, allowing the joke. "Yes! I mean their muscles. Trust me, you spend enough time up in these parts and you'll start getting them too."

Elijah took a step forward. "I plan on remaining here. I still have to find ways to be useful, but I do plan to stay." He stepped forward again. "I'll learn the ways of the mountain and I'll figure out how I can fit in up here. I also plan on figuring out where I am so I can come and go as I please." He stepped forward again. "If I happen to wander down towards your cabin, would I be welcome?"

I grinned. "Depends on if you bring me any treats."

"Just treats?" He reached his arm forward and snagged me around my waist. I went willingly. "Or maybe something else too?"

I tipped my chin up towards him. "Maybe a bit of both."

He grinned before touching his lips to mine.

I wrapped both arms around his neck. We were closer in height when I was in my winter boots, which made the kiss all the more perfect. I felt a rush of rapture run through me. My blood was on fire for this man. I wanted him so badly, but I knew that sex was too fast, too soon. There was so much we still had to learn about each other, beyond our chemistry. But that certainly didn't stop the pure *wanting* rushing through me. His tongue prodded and I happily opened for him.

Elijah gripped my waist, pulling me even closer to him. I immediately felt the evidence of his arousal against my groin, and inwardly grinned. Yeah, he had nothing to worry about in that department.

His tongue scraped across the top of my mouth. A shiver ran through me. My core was soaked with arousal. I needed relief or I'd—

"Um, Daddy?"

Shit. We broke apart. Belle stood behind us, looking sheepish. Elijah twisted us around, so we were facing Belle, but I was in front of him. I thought that movement strange until I felt his erection brush against my butt.

Yeah, probably not something he wanted his daughter to see. Bad enough she'd seen me practically humping her father like a horny bunny. I was happy to act as a shield. Thankfully my thick sweater and sports bra—I only wore sports bras since moving up to the mountain—covered up my erect nipples. Nothing I could do about my shortness of breath though.

"Yes, Angel?" Elijah prompted when Belle didn't continue.

She was looking at us funny but didn't comment on the kiss she'd seen. "Have you seen Uncle Corbin?"

I pointed, since I had more of an idea of where he was than Elijah would. "He's down by his workshop, sweetie. There was damage to his roof over the winter."

"Thanks," Belle mumbled.

She was a few feet away from us when Elijah yelled, "If he is on the roof, do *not* climb up there. Do you hear me, young lady?"

Huh. Apparently Elijah's Dad voice was a complete and total turn on. Who knew.

I must have stepped back further into him because he tightened his grip on my hips to stop me.

Belle rolled her eyes at her father. I'd never seen her do that before. Maybe it was a new skill kids learned when they turned eight. "I know, Daddy. You tell me *every time*."

"Well, if you would stop climbing and jumping off things *every time*, I wouldn't have to."

"Fine." Belle turned and ran towards Corbin's work shed.

We watched her until we saw Corbin climb down off the roof to meet her. Then Elijah rested his forehead on my shoulder. He let out a low groan. I put my hand up to run it through his shaggy hair. I liked his unruly hair, liked his full beard even better. I was suddenly regretting the turtleneck that blocked his access to my throat.

"Belle's never seen me with a woman before."

I found that interesting. She was eight and he'd indicated he'd been there when she had been born. Had he not dated in eight years? Or just not brought his women around her?

"What do you want to tell her?"

"Well, we need to tell her something because we've kissed twice, and she's interrupted both of them!"

I laughed. I hadn't caught on to that. "Yeah, probably."

He pressed himself closer to my back. Lifting his head, he took a nip at my ear. "And I need to tell her something if we start sleeping over at your cabin again."

A shiver ran through me as his teeth scraped against my lobe. "Her daddy is just having an adult slumber party in the bedroom?" I suggested.

He snorted. "You clearly haven't been around kids much. She'll hear 'party' and invite herself."

I cringed. "Who said *you* were invited to the sleepover party?"

He hummed against my skin behind my ear. "If this is a party for one, I demand videos or pictures."

My cheeks reddened. "Too bad for you, I don't have a camera."

I felt his lips twitch into a smile. "Guess I'll just need to be there in person then."

I turned in his arms to face him. His eyes were so dark with arousal, I could barely make out his pupils. I needed to put the brakes on this before I lost myself in him again. "We need to have certain conversations before any sleepovers take place, child-friendly or otherwise."

Elijah leaned forward and dropped a kiss onto my nose before stepping back. I could see he was still aroused, but at least there were no children present where he still needed a shield. "I know you said you needed time. When you came today, you looked so beautiful that you took my breath away. I had hoped you were here to see me. I'd meant to keep my hands to myself until you indicated otherwise, but watching you swing that axe was like watching a porno. I couldn't resist touching you."

Apparently, I wasn't the only one finding new turn-ons. "Your touch was welcome. I did come here to see you." I took his hand and led him over to the porch chairs. Corbin and Belle were still by the work shed and hopefully Gertie was too busy watching Lucas to overhear us. I kept his hand in mine on my lap.

"I thought a lot about what you told me. Any doubt you may have seen last night was due to my initial reaction to hearing something so horrible had happened, or almost happened, to Belle. I didn't want to believe she could have been victimized so by her birth father. I came across some malicious and disgusting people while on the force, and it always made me doubt the goodness of humanity every time. The fact that something so heinous almost happened to Belle is beyond terrible." I didn't realize I wasn't looking at him until I saw his hand twitch between mine on my lap. "The law says you did wrong when you took the children from their father—and I use that term very loosely. I've never hated a man I've never met before so much in my life. There's a special place in Hell for those who prey on the weak, regardless of age or gender.

"But life is not as black and white as the laws that govern us. I wasn't there so I can't pass judgment on whether you were right or wrong, but I saw the fear in your eyes last night when you told me about Belle. I know any action you took was with the intent of keeping those children safe." I looked up at him, only to realize he wasn't looking at me. He was staring out into the wilderness that surrounded us. "Elijah, you were so strong to do what you did. I hope you know that and acknowledge it. Your strength may not lie in muscle." I touched his chest. "It lies in your heart."

Elijah finally looked at me. I could see the echo of the pain he'd suffered in his eyes. Along with something else I couldn't identify. "You believe me?"

I squeezed his hand between mine. "I do. What you did was wrong in the eyes of the law but not in mine. There's no doubt of the love you have for those kids and, more importantly, the love they have for *you*. We would be having a far different conversation if I didn't see the love and respect Belle has for you."

"Can I ask you a question?" I nodded for him to continue. "You came to your conclusion without verifying my story with Jack or Corbin. Don't get me wrong, you don't know what your faith in me means to me, but I have to wonder why you didn't speak with them."

"Oh, I still plan on speaking to them." Elijah's eyebrows drew down in confusion. I squeezed his hand. "But not for the reason you think. I don't need to verify your story with them because I do believe you. I believe that those children were in mortal danger, and you rescued them. Don't forget, I was there that first night. I saw your fear for their lives, saw Belle's concern for yours. You drove yourself beyond exhaustion trying to protect your kids to the point where your body literally collapsed and required thirty plus hours of sleep to recuperate. Your first question to me when you woke up wasn't for water or to ask where you were. Your first demand was to know where your kids were.

"And as horrible as it is to admit, I saw Belle's fear those first couple of days too. That wasn't some made up fantasy that made a seven-year-old guard her brother so fiercely. She jumped at every sound, refused to sleep herself because she wasn't sure she could trust me to keep her brother safe. That type of fear isn't something a child gets from a story someone told her to *be* afraid. I didn't realize the signs at first. Maybe it was because I haven't been around people in a long time or maybe it was because I didn't want to believe it. Regardless, as soon as you told me what happened last night, it all clicked, and I understood her behavior for the first time."

I reached forward and put my hand over his beard-covered cheek. "*Your* behavior made sense for the first time. I don't know if you even realize how jumpy you were that first day. Your attention was solely on those kids. It's a wonder you even noticed me in the room."

He turned his face and kissed my palm. "I noticed you far too much. I had to force myself to concentrate on my kids."

I felt my cheeks heat. "So, to answer your original question, I do plan on speaking with Jack and Corbin. Not to verify your story but find out how I can help protect you and those kids."

Of all the reactions I'd been expecting from my statement, anger was not one of them. He stood up, breaking contact with me. His shoulders were hunched, and I could see his fists clench and unclench.

"What's wrong?" I asked.

Elijah leaned forward on the rail. "You shouldn't be the one protecting me. What kind of man would I be if I let you stand between me and any danger *I* brought to your doorstep? It should be *me* protecting you."

I understood, I think. Men, good men like Elijah, were raised to protect women and children. He already had a job that others would see as feminine. I saw nothing wrong with raising and homeschooling children, even if the title was 'nanny'. I wasn't sure he did either. In fact, I think he was proud of the job, and it showed in Belle. She was smart and inquisitive, not a spoiled rich brat.

I was surrounded by alpha men on this mountain. The typical muscled men one would see shirtless on the cover of a romance novel. They might be damaged or in need of solace, like me, but they were, at heart, good men. I'd only met Walter once and I'd never met Huck, but I knew Tommy, Dalton, and Corbin well. Or as well as any of us knew each other. They didn't know my secrets and I didn't know theirs. What I did know was these men had good, though troubled, souls.

Elijah didn't see himself clearly. He may believe he had done the right thing when he'd taken the kids away, but it was evident a big amount of guilt weighed on him too. Likely not for the kidnapping itself, maybe for not taking the kids away sooner. I also believed that Elijah had been traumatized by what had happened that horrible day, and maybe even from experiences before that. After all, he'd said that Belle's older brother and he had been plotting to escape before they'd learned of Lucas's arrival. Something had to have happened to make life so miserable that Elijah had been contemplating kidnapping one child, even with her older brother's permission, let alone waiting to take the second one once born too.

Maybe Elijah wasn't physically as strong as some men. Maybe he looked at my lifestyle and thought me capable of such strength too. What he didn't understand is I didn't come to this mountain that strong. I'd had to earn that strength and skills over the near decade that I'd been living here. If he'd seen me my first couple of years here, he certainly wouldn't be calling me strong or viewing me as competent.

I walked up to him and put my arms around his waist. He'd filled out from the gaunt man I'd met all those months ago. I put my cheek on his shoulder, pushing myself flush against him.

"I get why you would think that, given societal norms of how the man protects the woman. But up here on this mountain, gender doesn't matter and cultural decrees don't matter. So how about you don't worry so much about needing to protect me because I'm a woman. How about we start this relationship off on equal footing and we work together to protect each other?"

He put his hands on mine around my waist. "Doesn't sound like too horrible a plan."

I smiled and squeezed his middle. "Most of mine don't."

214

Chapter Twenty-One

Elijah

We were nearing the end of our first summer up on the mountain. The kids were flourishing more than I could have hoped in our secluded hideaway. Lucas was showing his joyous personality a little more each day while Belle was growing bolder and stronger. I worried constantly over her safety. I knew that scrapes and bruises were a rite of passage for children, but I still cringed each time my baby girl got hurt. If I wasn't, I knew her Uncle Corbin would be there to pick her up and make it better. I was so proud of how much she'd grown past her trauma. It was very rare for her to wake with a nightmare nowadays, and her bed wetting had stopped too.

I knew that there had been some instances where she'd wet the bed in the middle of the night due to a terror dream and she had Gertie help her clean up and change. She would then beg Gertie not to tell me. Not because she was afraid of getting in trouble, but because she didn't want to add to my worries. Of course, Gertie would inform me in the morning so I could keep track. I wanted to identify any triggers that might be occurring prior to her having a nightmare and if they differed from the instances that resulted in her wetting the bed. We simply didn't tell Belle that I was aware of her secret. When we'd first arrived at Corbin's cabin, those occurrences were once to twice a week. Gradually, it became once to twice a month. Now, it had been almost two months since her last nightmare. I was so proud of her ability to move on.

Corbin had taken Belle into town multiple times over the summer. I was terrified when he'd suggested letting her come with him to drop off his furniture to Jack's store. Belle really wanted to see the town, as well as meet Super Jack. Corbin knew of my fears and assured me that, with her short pink hair, no one would recognize her. Beyond that, he swore that he would not let *anyone* take her away from him. I knew I could trust Corbin to protect her, but that didn't stop my mind from panicking as soon as they drove away on his four-wheeler trailering his furniture.

I swear I couldn't breathe the entire time they were gone. I hoped I had hidden my fear from Belle. I'm still not sure if she saw how relieved I was when they'd *finally* gotten back. Thankfully Gertie had taken care of Lucas for me, so he wasn't affected by my panic either. Corbin definitely saw it though.

Later that night, after the kids were asleep, Corbin told me that he wouldn't take Belle into town again. I was so relieved by his declaration—only to remember how excited Belle had been to go into town with Uncle Corbin. She'd met Super Jack and had ice cream and played on the playground and ate a giant hot dog and helped Uncle Corbin move his furniture and met the lady who ran the bakery... She'd be crushed if I told her she couldn't go back.

Corbin yet again questioned if I wanted to go with them on their next trip, but I quickly shook my head. I knew my anxiety would be worse if I went to town too. My face was on national television. We'd been able to alter Belle's appearance enough that I was sure no one would recognize her as Lydia Gunther. But me? A beard couldn't change my body type, height, or eyes. Plus, who would believe spoiled, rich Lydia Gunther was the happy child rolling around in the mud all day?

I couldn't do it or risk it.

So Lucas, Gertie, and I remained at the cabin all summer long. It wasn't as isolating as I figured it would be. Like winter, summer had its advantages and disadvantages. The heat was definitely something to get used to. Some days it felt like I was baking after taking only a few steps outside.

I was learning a lot from Corbin about mountain life. I could now successfully chop wood—to Belle's enthusiastic applause. I was also learning how to manage the water and food stores. I wasn't up for hunting or gutting, but I had helped Corbin cure the meat. Belle was utterly disappointed that I would not allow her to go hunting with Uncle Corbin. She stomped around the house all day, refusing to play or do her studies. Even Lucas couldn't bring a smile to her face. I was not one for rewarding bad behavior. However, I did tell her that, *perhaps*, we could revisit the *possibility* of her going hunting with Uncle Corbin next summer. While that did not immediately cheer her up, she did tell me that she would take hunting lessons from Uncle Corbin until I felt satisfied she would be safe enough to go with him.

My little angel. I knew what she was doing and, though I was aware of the manipulation, I allowed it. She had, after all, agreed to take lessons before doing the activity. I could make Corbin drag out those lessons for a very long time.

Over all, the summer was amazing and I was shocked with how quickly it had gone by. I was beginning to grow muscle too. Nothing like Corbin's, but my body was slowly becoming more defined. I certainly wasn't complaining—and neither was Brooke.

Brooke was, aside from my children, the light of my life. We didn't visit each other every day. That journey was just too far, but we remained in constant contact. She purchased two-way radios from Jack's store. They were crap during storms or high winds, but most of the time they worked wonderfully. We were able to chat into the wee hours of the night, staying up like teenagers past our bedtimes.

Corbin taught me how to drive the four-wheeler and, after many journeys to Brooke's cabin with Corbin, I eventually felt confident enough to travel there on my own during clear weather. Like Corbin, Brooke was also using the summer to prep for winter. I helped her where I could too. I usually brought Belle with me, and sometimes Lucas. While they weren't much help, it was a change of scenery for them.

The times when I went alone were pure heaven. We hadn't had sex yet, but that anticipation almost made the relationship sweeter. The *almost* was for when I thought my blue balls were going to kill me.

Brooke was so sexy and funny and brilliant. She was constantly surprising me with how adept she was at mountain life. I loved watching her work. She even built a tire swing for Belle in her backyard. I was falling head over heels for her.

When we could grab adult-only moments, we couldn't keep our hands off each other. While we hadn't had intercourse, we'd done most everything else. Just last week, I'd pinned Brooke up against a tree and made her come with my fingers. Due to the kids being close by, I'd also had to cover her mouth with my other hand. I'd never been one for adventurous, outdoors escapades, but damn I don't think I'd ever not want to have Brooke. Anywhere.

The kids and I had slept over her cabin a couple of times. The first time, Brooke had taken the couch again. But the next time, Belle had invited her into bed with us. Since then, any time we stayed over, it was in her bed with the kids between us. Some nights, we barely slept, just stared at each other with our hands clasped over the children.

It was near perfect. A glimpse of an optimistic future.

As summer started to die down, I started growing restless. Upon waking that morning, it felt like I had imaginary ants crawling all over my body. I couldn't scrub myself hard enough in the shower. I was twitching and itching all through breakfast, to the point where I caught the glances shared by all over one year old. I hadn't figured out why until I realized the day's date.

Two years ago, Belle had watched as her birth father had flogged me, scarring me mentally and physically. I hadn't even realized what my body had been trying to tell me with my increased anxiety, my dark mood, and my inability to sit still. The date explained the increase in my nightmares as well.

I knew that Corbin and Gertie could tell something was bothering me. Corbin knew about my scars and what had caused them, but I'm not sure he'd put the timeline together from the story I'd told him.

Hell, if it hadn't been for Corbin's scheduled trip to town tomorrow, I'm not sure I would have put it together either. As Brooke had once said, you stop paying attention to dates and days of the week up here. Time was different on the mountain.

But my body had still known. Subconsciously I'd still known.

I decided to take a walk after breakfast. I didn't want the kids to grow worried by my foul mood, nor did I want to say something to them I'd later regret. I figured the best choice was to remove myself from our little mountain haven for the day.

There was an overlook a few miles away from the cabin. We'd brought the kids here multiple times over the spring and summer for picnics. I hadn't even realized that was my destination until I'd arrived.

I couldn't change the past. I knew that. And I'd never for one moment, even in the worst of the pain, regretted taking the punishment Gunther had deemed his daughter worthy of. I would never have forgiven myself if I'd stood by and watched as *my daughter* was punished, regardless of whether that punishment would have been the same as mine.

Sometimes I wondered if Gunther had chosen a stricter punishment for me because he saw how attached his daughter was to me. Maybe he thought he could break that bond by making me bleed.

Regardless, I would have taken that punishment ten times over to save my daughter from that monster.

I *knew* that to the marrow of my bones. Yet...every time I saw my scars in the mirror or felt one twinge or pull when I moved in a certain way... I wondered why I had stayed all those years.

I knew why I stayed. I'd never abandon my daughter. Lydia or Belle, she was *mine*. From the moment I'd held her in that delivery room, she was mine.

It wasn't until Gunther had started bringing Belle around his business associates that things had become bad. If we'd remained invisible, I'm not sure I would have run with the kids. I might have stuck it out until Lucas was eighteen and then they would be legal to make their own decisions and choose who their father was.

I shook my head at that ridiculousness. Gunther would have never allowed us to remain invisible. I was pretty sure the only reason he hadn't bothered us for the first five years of Belle's life was because she wasn't yet useful to him at such a young age.

Arms encircled my middle. I was sitting on a large rock facing the expansive horizon of the Montana forest. Despite not seeing who was behind me, I'd know her touch anywhere.

My hands immediately went to hers at my waist. I closed

my eyes and leaned back against her. I didn't know how she'd found me, but I was so grateful she had. Brooke quieted the noise. She made all the bad disappear with just a touch.

"Do you want to talk about it?"

I shook my head.

We'd talked a lot about what Belle and I had gone through at the hands of her birth father, but I wasn't ready to talk about this. Perhaps I didn't want her to see me as damaged. In all our fondling and make-out sessions, I'd never allowed her to remove my shirt or put her hands on my bare back. I wasn't sure if she'd picked up on that but, even if she did, she didn't know why.

She moved herself closer, pressing her chest to my back. We remained like that until the sun started its descent. It couldn't disappear fast enough, ending the anniversary of that horrible day.

I'm not sure which one of us moved first, but Brooke ended up in front of me straddling my lap. Her blue eyes seemed so bright this evening. I loved her eyes. They seemed to sparkle whenever she was being humorous or mischievous. Even in my delirium from being exhausted, I never forgot how her eyes were the first thing I'd noticed about her. They were so beautiful, so emotional.

I knew she was worried about me, but I wasn't sure how to explain the turmoil going through my mind. I wasn't even sure *I* understood it.

I leaned my head forward, resting my cheek against her chest. God, I loved her tits. They were perfectly sized handfuls of goodness. The few times I'd tasted them, all I'd wanted was more. Where she thought they were too saggy, I only saw perfection. Like me, she couldn't see herself clearly.

"How did you know I needed you?"

She wrapped her arms around my head, holding me closer. My grip on her hips tightened. With our current positions, there was no way she couldn't feel my arousal pressing between her legs. What I wouldn't give to remove our clothing in that moment.

"You were supposed to meet me at my cabin this morning. When you didn't show and weren't answering your radio, I reached out to Corbin." I felt her lips brush against the top of my head.

Shit. I'd forgotten about our plans. At least she hadn't assumed I'd purposefully stood her up. Unintentional or not, I still felt bad. She'd driven all the way up here and I wasn't even in the mood to talk.

Her touch felt like a soothing balm, like aloe on sunburn. It was the calm I needed to clear my head.

"Sorry," I mumbled into her chest.

Running her fingers through my hair, her nails massaged the tension out of my scalp. "It's okay. I'm glad I found you, though. Corbin wasn't sure where you were headed exactly, but you left an easy trail for me to track."

I liked that she'd made the effort to even try, rather than just wait at the cabin for me. I felt bad about pawning off Lucas and Belle on Corbin and Gertie. I really did rely on them too much. Brooke, too.

"I know you said you didn't want to talk about it, but it's not like you to brood. I'm worried about you."

For some reason, I didn't like that description. "I wasn't brooding."

Her chest vibrated with her giggle. "Yes, you were."

"Sulking, maybe," I allowed. She smelled good. She must have been in her garden earlier; she smelled of dirt and greens.

"All right. Fine. It's not like you to *sulk*."

I knew she was right. This wasn't like me. Maybe I was due a bad day after all we'd been through. It had been eight months since we'd run.

I looked past her right ear, out at the vast horizon. There was nothing but trees and rocks for miles. I knew the land well enough by now to know which direction the mountain river was in, but it blended into the foliage too much to be seen at this distance. There was nothing like nature to make a man realign his priorities.

Up here on this mountain, we were safe and protected from everything. The influence of society, the dangers of man, the expectations of modern life... There was nothing around us and yet I didn't feel alone.

My eyes slid back to hers. I reached up, placing a lock of her hair between two fingers and threaded it down around her face. Brooke was, without a doubt, the most important person in my life—aside from my children.

She knew most of my secrets and had accepted me. It was time she knew the rest.

"Take off my shirt."

Chapter Twenty-Two

Brooke

The gruffness in Elijah's voice sent a shiver down my spine. For all our sexy times, the secret encounters away from the kids, Elijah had never taken off his shirt. The couple of times I'd started to take off his shirt, he always stopped me. When I asked him over the summer if he was embarrassed by his physique—which I felt was a logical assumption based on some of the comments he'd made about his lack of muscle and body type—but he claimed it wasn't.

The conviction in his voice now puzzled me. He had nothing to be ashamed of, but I got the feeling he thought this was a reveal of some sort.

I wondered if he'd pieced together that I'd already seen him naked during my care for him the first night he'd stayed at my cabin. While I hadn't looked at him in a sexual way, I had seen him. And I liked what I had seen.

I brought my hands down and bunched the hem of his shirt into my fists. He raised his arms as I lifted the material up and over his head. I dropped it onto the rock beside us. When I saw the apprehension in his eyes, I realized just how nervous he was. I still didn't understand but wanted to make him feel more comfortable. I quickly unbuttoned my shirt and placed it on top of his.

My sports bra was not sexy or fancy. Like everything I wore, it was practical. Elijah knew I did not own lingerie. He also was aware that I didn't shave that often. When it had just been me in the mountain, what was the point? Who was I shaving for, the bears? Since he'd come back into my life, I had started to take more care with my feminine hygiene. I might not own a skimpy, slutty outfit, but I could still do my part to make myself look nice for him. I still drew the line with makeup, nail polish, and high heels.

I was sitting on his lap, which was a relatively intimate position in and of itself. It surprised me when Elijah moved me to kneel beside him. He got up onto his knees. Again, it seemed like he was bracing himself for something.

My eyes gazed down over his chest and abdomen. He'd gained both weight and muscle over the winter and through the summer. While I had not minded his softness, I was also not complaining about his new definition.

And then he turned.

I'm embarrassed to say how long it took me to realize what it was I was looking at. At first, I didn't understand and couldn't place the crisscrossed lines marring his back. They weren't birth marks or stretch marks.

The white raised lines were jagged and non-symmetrical. He did not have a tan. Unlike the other men on the mountain, Elijah did not remove his shirt outside during the summer. The paleness of his skin only seemed to accentuate the angry lines.

With a careful hand, I stretched forward. He flinched when my fingertips made contact with his skin, though I knew it wasn't from pain. These lines were not new.

"What happened?" I knew what my brain was telling me had happened, but I didn't want to believe it.

During my first year as a detective, I came across a case involving a couple heavy in the BDSM scene. The woman had been so submissive that she would not speak to me without her partner, her Dom, present. I saw scars and even a brand on her. What I'd had trouble wrapping my head around at the time was that everything done to her had been willing. She'd consented to it all without coercion. The man, her Dom, loved her with a fierceness I'd never seen before—even in my own marriage. He was protective and possessive, but he was not cruel.

It had been another man, who was not a Dom in their scene, who had believed the woman's submissive nature meant she was submissive to *all* men. The woman's Dom had killed her attempted rapist, but not before he'd beaten and flogged her within an inch of her life.

I did not want to press charges against the Dom, but the law stated he was in the wrong by killing his partner's attacker. As I put handcuffs on that man and read him his rights, it had been the first time I'd questioned my chosen profession.

The last time had been when I'd discovered evidence of Tyler and Kate's affair without having suspected a thing prior.

I thought about that woman from time to time. I knew that the charges against the Dom had finally been ruled a justifiable homicide, but he'd still been arrested, jailed, and separated from the woman he loved during her most vulnerable time. When I checked in on her during his absence, I saw the scars that now littered her body. Though her clothes covered most, I knew that her breasts and buttocks were heavily marred. The scars that were visible, though, looked a lot like the ones I saw now on Elijah.

Someone had *flogged* him. From the shame and his need to hide the scars, I knew he had not been a willing participant. Aside from her attack, the woman submissive had gotten pleasure from the pain. It had been a power exchange between herself and her partner—a man she *trusted* and loved.

Elijah and I had talked a lot about our past experiences. He knew more about Tyler, especially the good times. I even talked about Kate and the mischief we'd caused as kids and teens, best friends.

I knew that Elijah hadn't had a steady girlfriend since entering the employment of Belle and Lucas's birth father. He hadn't even taken a single day off since Belle had started to become subjected to some of her birth father's attentions. The only person he'd felt he could trust for years had been the kids' half-brother, Trenton. There had been no woman in his life in years.

And he'd never been in love.

We hadn't said those words. I knew I was the hold up. The last time those words had crossed my lips, it had ended in catastrophe. I did not want that to happen again, which did make me cowardly.

So, while I knew what I felt and I also knew what he felt, we had not said those words.

That wasn't a bad thing. We had nothing but time up on this mountain. Even with the pending winter, there was no rush. It took time for both of us to rebuild the trust that had been broken in our pasts.

Trust that I knew Elijah had never placed in a woman before.

"He was going to punish Belle." Elijah's voice was cold, emotionless. Like he was trying to not *feel* the memory. "He gave me a choice: take her punishment or watch her punishment."

I closed my eyes, utterly broken for this man before me. He did not see his own strength. Thought himself weak or lacking because he did not have the traditional bulk generally associated with an 'alpha male'. I wondered if he would feel differently if he knew the term 'alpha male' was first coined in reference to chickens, which is also where we got the phrase 'pecking order'.

Elijah was blind to the strength of his heart. He never spoke his boss's name, but I did not need more detail to know who 'he' was that had threatened Belle and harmed Elijah. *Flogged* him.

The monster had tried to sell his own daughter, wanted to make her a child bride to seal a business deal. Should it really be that big of a shock that he would want to punish his daughter so harshly? I had to wonder too if he'd known Elijah would step in. Was the man diabolical enough to have never intended to harm Belle, knowing that Elijah would step in? Had his goal been to harm Elijah either way—emotionally by watching Belle be punished or physically by taking this punishment himself?

Because, *of course*, Elijah would take Belle's punishment. *That* was where his strength lay, in his willingness to do anything and everything to protect his children.

I crawled forward on my knees, ignoring the bite of the hard rock beneath. I pressed my bra-clad chest to his back, wrapping my arms around his shoulders. I pressed my lips into the side of his neck.

I struggled with what words to say. Were there any that could make this right? He'd been tortured at the hands of his former employer to spare the daughter of his heart a terrible fate. Telling him 'good job' would be a mockery of his sacrifice and an insult. Telling him 'I'm sorry' seemed obvious and cliché.

Before I could choose my words, Elijah spun around. He grabbed me up in his arms, kissing me fiercely. I needed no time, reacting with equal vigor. Heat flooded my veins and pooled low in my belly.

I wanted this man. I needed him like I needed air to breathe.

It took some finagling to get my tight bra off. My large breasts were confined in the material and appeared smaller than they were when I was dressed. My nipples were already hard and begging to be touched.

Elijah did not disappoint. As he raised me up onto his bent legs, he ducked his head down and claimed one of my nipples. I let out a gasp, my belly quaking. My hands gripped his brown locks as I fought to bring him closer to myself. I pressed my own mouth to his temple. Wetness pooled between my legs and I felt the hard ridge of his erection.

Words spoken or not, I knew I loved this man with every fiber of my being. I'd rescued him from a frozen death and he'd saved me from a loneliness I had not realized was slowly suffocating me. I loved my mountain life, but I loved it even more knowing I would one day share my home with this man and his adorable children.

Our pants and shoes were quickly shed. Neither of us came prepared but we were not willing to let this heat extinguish between us. We were in the middle of the woods on a cliff face with nothing surrounding us but nature and woodland creatures.

Elijah placed our clothing out to cushion the roughness of the boulder beneath us. Then he rolled onto his back. I don't know why I was surprised by this chivalrous position. He was taking the brunt of the hardness of the ground so I didn't have to.

I straddled him. Alongside heavy kissing and petting came laughter and joy. I hadn't had a man inside me in nearly ten years. Elijah, though, did not rush me or judge.

Instead, he brought my core up to his face and brought me to orgasm with his mouth. When he tried to continue, I stopped him to switch positions. Not willing to let him go on unreciprocated, I draped myself over his torso and took his erection between my lips as he made love to my pussy with his mouth.

It would have been safer for us to have brought the other to completion via our mouths and to not have vaginal sex. We had no protection and neither of us was prepared emotionally for a pregnancy. It was like the need to finally join together overrode any consideration or common sense. We moved together, completely in sync, as I moved around to straddle his hips.

I sank down on his cock, completely oblivious to the sounds of birds and critters, to the cool breeze that signaled the end of day. Our fingers laced together between us. I ground my hips down, trying to take him as deep inside of me as I could.

We never looked away from each other. Like our eyes were magnetized. We were utterly and completely alone...together. The forest could have caught fire around us and we would have never known.

There was him and me...and ecstasy. It was slow and passionate and filled with all the unspoken love we felt for each other.

At least we had the wherewithal to have him pull out as he ejaculated. As we lay there, curled around each other and catching our breath, all that mattered was each other.

We had maybe a month before the weather turned and winter would be upon us. That seemed like a lifetime away. For those few precious hours on the edge of the mountain, the rest of the world was nonexistent.

Chapter Twenty-Three

Josephine

There was nothing like the satisfaction of watching a sick sonofabitch get what was coming to him. In the eight months since Adam Greene had disappeared with Lydia and Henry Gunther and in the four months since I'd learned of Greene's innocence, I'd put all of my effort into taking down Sebastian Gunther.

It had been a long and arduous task, but I was finally seeing my reward. As I stood outside across the street from his NoHo mansion, I watched with rapt glee as Gunther was led away by the Feds in handcuffs.

News stations and various media platforms were parked outside of the police barricade to try to capture the perfect image of Gunther's downfall.

I didn't need to look that closely. I knew *exactly* what his face would look like since I'd already seen his crestfallen expression when I explained in his office just how much information I had on him. He'd tried to offer me money, power, land... It all fell on deaf ears. When he'd threatened my life, I'd taken down his bodyguards.

I'd already secretly emptied the bullets out of the gun he

kept in his desk, so I stared confidently down the barrel when he'd pointed it at me.

I would never forget the expression of utter hate and despair as he realized the Feds were already outside his office door and had listened to every single word we'd spoken.

They had his confession to the murder to Boris Rimsky on tape from his own words. Best part, they didn't need a warrant because I walked in wearing a wire after Gunther invited me over. New York was a one-party state after all.

While it didn't get Adam Greene off the hook for the kidnapping charges, it would clear him of the murder charge. Additionally, the gun Gunther had threatened me with was the same weapon he'd killed Rimsky with. He was literally holding the smoking gun when the Feds had arrested him.

Though a lot of my efforts over the past four months were grueling, I had not been working alone. I'd been in contact with Jack nearly every day and he'd even offered me a position with the Mountain Mutineers after Gunther was out of the picture. He called Gunther my 'interview'.

Jack was not my only assistance. I didn't know who was helping me here in New York, but someone was constantly feeding me information. It had to be someone close to Gunther. Since I couldn't get any information on Trenton Gunther's whereabouts, I doubted it was him. Be it greed or hatred, Trenton did have the most to gain by his father's imprisonment. However, no one had seen Trenton in months. If it wasn't for Jack swearing to me that Trenton was not with Greene, I would have been sure Trenton had escaped with Greene and his young siblings.

His absence made me fear that Trenton had met a gruesome end at the hand of his father.

Whoever the mole was reporting to me had accurate enough information that I knew *exactly* where Gunther was going to be, when, and how many bodyguards he was going to have with him. That information cut a lot of time out of my surveillance and I was able to concentrate enough on gathering evidence to take to the Feds.

At first, I wasn't sure the Feds believed me. It wasn't until I'd gotten a meeting with their district agent that anyone actually took me seriously. I still had to wonder how Jack was able to pull that one off.

I took my phone out of my back pocket. No doubt Jack was watching Gunther's downfall live on national television like the rest of the country, but I wanted to add my personal touch to the situation.

"You should be proud of yourself," was what I got in lieu of a greeting.

"Quite," I agreed. "I wasn't able to get Greene fully exonerated, but at least they have the evidence to get rid of the murder charges."

I heard clicking over the other end and pictured Jack at his desk with his hundreds of computer screens. "I'm working on getting the kidnapping charges dismissed too. I haven't been able to locate Lydia's birth mother, Helena. Gunther had her sign over her rights. If we can get her to come forward and claim coercion, we might be able to get the kidnapping charges dropped legally."

"And if we can't?" I didn't know why but I liked being included in Jack's 'we'. I hadn't been part of a team since my Marine days. There was a sense of camaraderie between Jack and I that I hadn't realized I'd been missing.

It felt really good to have someone watching my six again.

"For Henry, it's a nonissue. I looked through those files you sent me and discovered a small fact that Mr. Greene neglected to inform me of: he was named as Henry's father on the birth certificate. Legally, Mr. Greene is Henry's father."

I blinked, not anticipating that news. "Wow. How did that happen?"

"That's another story," Jack said evasively.

I wanted to argue but also took note of who might be around and listening. I was on a public street after all. "It would explain why the reward was only for Lydia. I wonder if Gunther knew."

"I have a feeling he found out when he pressed charges against Mr. Greene. The police conveniently forgot to check legal paternity."

I fought the need to scoff. "Of course they did. They're in his pocket."

"Undoubtedly. With the racketeering, arms dealing, human trafficking, prostitution, and smuggling charges on top of the murder charge, hopefully the Feds will see reason to drop the remaining kidnapping charge."

That was a long rap sheet—but Gunther no doubt had very good lawyers at his disposal.

"What about his organization?" I asked Jack. "They weren't able to make a RICO case and connect him to others, but he'll still have influence from jail unless we can somehow take that down too."

"That's why I got you some help. He should be pulling up next to you any second."

I paused, looking up and down the street. I saw mostly police cars and news vans. "I don't see anyone—" Just then a black sedan pulled up next to me. "Oh."

I expected the back door to open, given the fancy car, but instead the passenger door's window lowered. I ducked down and my jaw dropped.

Trenton Gunther took off his sunglasses and smiled widely at me. "Good to finally meet you in person, Ms. Gonzalez. We've got a lot of work to do."

Chapter Twenty-Four

Brooke

Six Months Later

Longest. Fucking winter. Of my life.

This was my tenth winter on my beloved mountain. My tasks were the same as always with the need to survive the harsh temperatures and weather. Nothing had changed—except for me. Time, which had never meant anything to me before, now seemed to drag on at a snail's pace. Additionally, I'd never felt so cold as I had over the past several months.

After my time with Elijah on the cliff, we'd worked to have more 'adult only' time through the fall. I also went down into town to purchase condoms. I felt like a teenager trying to buy their first pack as Jack rang up my purchases—because I couldn't have *just* bought condoms. He would have never let me live that down.

Thankfully nothing had come of our unprotected tryst. Elijah had apologized repeatedly for that misstep and would not accept the fact that I was equally just as responsible.

In the middle of August, we got the news that Sebastian

Gunther had been arrested—and my jaw about hit the floor. As a former NYPD police officer, I knew *exactly* who Sebastian Gunther was and it blew my mind that he had been the man Elijah had been running from. Beyond that, I could not understand how a man so corrupt could have fathered two of the most beautiful and amazing kids I'd ever met. Mind, I was a bit biased.

After that revelation, Elijah and I realized our families were nearly from the same area. He'd grown up in New Jersey and I'd grown up in White Plains. We'd both moved into the city as adults, but it hadn't been until we'd both landed on a mountain in the middle of Nowhere, Montana that we'd met and fallen in love.

With Gunther behind bars awaiting trial, Jack had gotten word to Elijah that Trenton, the kids' older brother, was working to dismantle the corrupt organization. It wasn't until I overheard on the radio Jack tell Elijah that the murder charges had been dropped that I realized my elation was premature. What if Elijah decided not to stay on the mountain? He was almost a free man. His requirement to stay was no longer valid...

But Elijah had quenched those fears almost immediately. The next time we'd met for our scheduled rendezvous, he'd skipped over common greetings and small talk to assure me that he had no intention of leaving the mountain.

"I like who I am on this mountain, Brooke. I like who my kids are. Moreover, I like who I am with you. We're staying, regardless of the charges."

Following that conversation, I asked if he wanted to return to being 'Adam'. It would have been confusing for a bit—especially after I'd worked so hard to remember to call and think of him as 'Elijah'—but he had told me that he wanted no part of Gunther to touch his or his kids' lives. They were keeping their new identities.

Jack and Corbin agreed with this decision because there were some who might want to take Gunther's downfall out on Adam Greene and the Gunther children.

As we had approached the end of September, Elijah and I knew our frequent time together was coming to an end. We had already had the conversation that he and the kids would remain at Corbin's cabin over the long winter months. My cabin, though spacious for just me, did not have the room to comfortably keep two adults, an upcoming toddler, and rambunctious little girl. I didn't know who dreaded the first snowfall more: Elijah or me. We knew what it signified.

As we watched the kids joyously play in the first snowflakes of the coming winter, Elijah and I sat under the covered front porch of Corbin's cabin. Neither one of us able to take in the beauty of the first snowfall and clinging to each other for the time we had left.

Unlike our last goodbye, though, it did not signify a lack of visits. Corbin helped Elijah bring the kids down to my cabin or I would go up to Corbin's when the weather permitted. Elijah and I remained in contact via the HAM radio, though we had to keep our conversations mostly platonic due to the potential eavesdroppers.

It wasn't the same though. Sometimes weeks would go by before we could see each other because it wasn't safe to take the snowmobiles up or down the mountain. Getting to Dalton's or Tommy's cabin was not as far a distance as Corbin's or as steep up the mountain. As much as we *could* have seen each other, it wasn't worth the risk just to do so.

Plus, winter required more maintenance. I couldn't leave my cabin for more than a day at a time without risking my stores.

February was still just as harsh, but we were experiencing an odd lull in additional snow. The snow that had fallen created a nice fluff on the ground and surrounding foliage. I was trying to figure out if I could get away for the day. If the weather turned suddenly, which was completely within the realm of possibilities, I could be stuck up at Corbin's for more than the overnight. That would place the responsibility of keeping my stores safe on Dalton—and I didn't want to ask that of him when he had his own property to look after.

The roar of a motor broke through my thoughts. Without putting on boots, I ran out to my porch in my wool socks. I knew the echo of that engine. It had been seared into my brain to announce Elijah's arrival.

I hadn't seen him or the kids since Christmas, when Dalton and I had journeyed up the mountain to celebrate with the kids. That was over five weeks ago.

I watched with bated breath as Elijah parked the snowmobile. As he hopped off the vehicle, a part of me took note that Elijah had come alone, while the other part took in his features. By the time he reached my porch, he'd stripped off his hat, goggles, face mask, and gloves. Elijah's beard was now full and past his chin, his face had filled out like the rest of him, and I swore he had more muscle, but that might have just been the bulky jacket.

In one swift motion, Elijah dropped his winter equipment, picked me up, and carried me into my warm cabin. Our mouths collided in a heated frenzy. My legs lifted up to link around his hips.

He kicked the door closed with a loud *bang*. It broke neither of our focus.

I'd never been so turned on in my life. I was thirty-six years old and divorced, yet I could not recall ever having desired a man more than I did in this moment. Elijah was a drug and aphrodisiac all rolled into one hell of a man.

I don't recall being spun around, but suddenly the door was at my back.

His lips traveled to the underside of my jaw. "Worst winter ever."

I gasped for breath, turning my head to give him better access to my throat. "You nearly died last winter."

Elijah picked up his head and stared directly into my eyes. "I stand by my statement."

I thought my heart would swell out of my ribcage at his proclamation. Tears then sprang to my eyes at the realization that this winter wasn't even over yet.

His hand, rough with new calluses, cupped my left cheek. "Corbin and I already started working on a plan and Jack has ordered the necessary lumber. The kids will take your room and you and I can turn your loft into our bedroom. It's not a great fix, since eventually the kids will need separate rooms, but it'll at least get us a few years to figure out our next step."

My eyes went over his head to the railing of my loft. I loved my loft. It was probably my favorite room in my house with the wide window. I'd fallen asleep on the small couch I had up there countless times, watching the snowfall, the sun glistening off the horizon, listening to the rain...

I absolutely *loved* the idea of turning my loft into our bedroom. I imagined a large bed taking up most of the room and lots of lazy mornings curled up in the warmth of a loving partner's arms...

A tear escaped for an entirely different reason. "You would do that? You would move in?"

He kissed me gently. "In a heartbeat. I am eternally grateful for Corbin and Gertie opening their home up to us, but it's not where I want to be."

"And the kids?" We'd talked last summer about what role I would take in the kids' lives. Neither of them had a mother-figure. Gertie had taken on the role of grandma, but that wasn't the same as having a mother.

"Not a pressing question," Elijah told me. "You'll be their friend and an authority figure. If you choose to be their mom one day, that's a discussion we can have then. There's no pressure. Belle loves you and even taught Lucas to say your name over the winter."

I smiled at that. "Yeah?"

He nodded. "I'll admit the idea of being a family with you is intoxicating, but I don't want you to feel like you *have* to become their mother." He leaned down and pressed his lips to my cheek before dragging his lips across my skin to my ear. His teeth nipped the lobe, sending a shiver down my spine. "What do you say, love? Can we move in?"

I let out the most pitiful moan as my eyes nearly rolled back into my skull. All I could manage was a groaned, "Mm-hm."

His chuckle was deep and masculine. "Good. I'll call the moving company in the morning."

I knew that was a joke. We *were* the moving company. It took a long minute for my brain to pick up on his timeline though. "Morning?" I asked.

Elijah nipped and licked his way down to my turtleneck, which I was suddenly cursing my decision to wear. "You just agreed to let me move in, Brooke. I have no intention of sleeping anywhere but your bed from now on."

Then he gripped me under my butt and carried me off to said bedroom.

Chapter Twenty-Five

Josephine

Acquitted. By a fucking technicality.

I was beyond furious.

For all the crimes he'd committed, for all the cruelty he'd displayed, Sebastian Gunther had been released and all charges dismissed. I hated the look on the smug bastard's face when he walked out of the courthouse like he was a motherfucking god. All because the recording of Gunther's admission had been 'corrupted' and the gun had been 'misplaced'.

What. The. Fuck.

If I ever learned who the agent or agents were who had tampered with the evidence I'd slaved for months to obtain, I was going to crucify them.

Trenton, despite being Gunther's son, was nothing like his father. In the six months since Gunther's arrest, I'd worked tirelessly alongside him to help dismantle his family legacy. His own mother had disowned him when she learned what he was trying to do. I'd stood as a silent witness when she'd come raging into the office that had once been her husband's to scold her twenty-two year old son like he was a child and demand he restore his family's 'honor'.

Trenton had more balls than I'd originally given him credit for. The kid stood up, leaned over his father's desk, and told his mother to fuck off.

I'd taken him out for ice cream later to celebrate. I might call him 'kid', but he handled himself better than most men twice his age. It was admirable to witness.

After the first attempt on his life following his father's arrest, I'd taken on a bodyguard role as well as advisor. I knew jackshit about finances or running a criminal empire, but I knew people and I knew the underbelly of the world. Jack had put Trenton in touch with an accountant he knew and trusted after Trenton had fired his father's financial advisors, who had been skimming money for years.

For all our success, those accomplishments meant little in comparison to his father's release. Everything that *had* been Trenton's to control as next of kin was once more his father's, including the house we were currently standing in as we watched in horror as the newscaster announced the verdict.

I was speechless.

Trenton, though, stood. "We have to go."

I turned. We were alone in the giant NoHo mansion. Trenton had dismissed all of the servants with glowing recommendation letters and a very generous severance pay. All of the bodyguards and thugs who had been in his father's employ had just been fired. More than one had since tried to kill Trenton.

Trenton was at his father's desk, packing up files and envelopes into a black leather briefcase. "With traffic, he'll be here in half an hour. We need to be gone long before then."

I knew he was right and I forced my body to move. I knew this world wasn't fair—I'd seen it firsthand too many times to count—but I could not believe the injustice served today. 'Unintentional evidence tampering,' my sweet Latina ass. This had been *very* intentional.

"I'll get your bag and mine," I told him. "Meet me at my car. We can't take yours."

Trenton nodded once.

I ran out of the office, down the hall, and up the giant, completely unnecessary grand staircase. I was used to living out of my car and motel rooms. Having been crashing in this monstrosity for the past six months had definitely spoiled me. The fact that the kitchen took up the entire basement floor, other than the underground garage, still baffled me.

It was part of my training to always have a go-bag. My rucksack from my Marine days was mine. I never went anywhere without it and I never removed my valuable items from it. Clothes, toiletries, electronics...could be replaced. The only picture I had of my parents with me and Connie could not be.

I'd instructed Trenton to do the same. Anything he could not live without needed to go into a bag and be easily accessible.

I hitched my rucksack over my shoulder and headed into Trenton's bedroom. This place had over twenty bedrooms, but I took the room next to his in case of an emergency.

I took what used to be the servant's staircase down the back. It was faster to get to the outdoor garage. I threw our bags into the trunk. When I did not see or hear Trenton come out immediately after me, I knew I couldn't sit back and wait. We needed to move.

If he was destroying evidence, I was going to murder the kid myself. He knew the rule was to take anything incriminating with us to be sorted through or destroyed later. We couldn't exactly dismantle a multi-national, multi-million dollar conglomerate legally. There were a lot of ins and outs that would have gotten Trenton into trouble if it had come to light, as his father had been using his information for years to hide certain assets.

I rushed in the side door I'd just exited. I barely made it

through to the hallway leading to the office before I was struck over the back of the head.

I didn't pass out. Not fully anyway. I was vaguely aware of the pain of hitting the floor and then the feel of someone reaching into my jacket to empty my holster. The ringing in my head and ears prevented me from hearing voices right away. I fought to rise, but my stomach rolled violently and I just barely was able to force the bile back down.

Rough hands grabbed me by the ankles and dragged me down the hallway. I tried to grab for a perch to catch myself, but my hands slid uselessly off of every surface I touched.

My senses started to come back to me when I felt my boots being ripped off my feet. I kicked out blindly. I heard a grunt but did not stop to look who made it. I scrambled to my feet, my one boot already removed and the other slipping loosely.

Two sets of hands gripped me from behind and spun me around. The room continued to spin even after I physically stopped. I fought to get my eyes to focus. I saw the silhouettes of three or four people in front of me, but not clear enough to identify who they were.

One of them moved forward and I caught the repulsive stench of cigarettes and body odor. A voice from across the room spoke but my mind took precious seconds to process the words: "Remove her clothes."

Fear gripped me in a way it had not in years. I knew that voice, distorted though it was. Somehow Gunther had arrived far sooner than we could have expected.

My vision cleared enough for me to place myself in the office, but I didn't see Trenton. I had no idea if the kid was dead or alive. Unfortunately for both of us, I was not in a position to save him. I wasn't even in a position to save myself. I wasn't so out of it that I did not know what was coming.

A face appeared before my face, hazy, but close enough for

me to make out Gunther's features. He gripped my chin painfully, forcing me to look directly at him. "I promised my men who remained loyal to me a turn with you. They're going to keep you entertained while I go teach my traitorous son a lesson."

The iron grips of the men holding my arms tightened at Gunther's words and someone let out a low chuckle. I was not balanced enough to fight or kick. I wasn't even sure I was standing on my own merit or if the thugs were holding me upright.

I gathered what spit in my mouth that I could and hocked it into Gunther's eye. A sense of twisted satisfaction filled me when he reared back in pain. It was nothing compared to what I was about to face, but it was something. Despite my current condition, I was not going down easy.

I was flung down to the floor and, despite my best efforts, blacked out when my head collided with the marble flooring.

Chapter Twenty-Six

Elijah

I woke up to the smell of cooking eggs and the sizzling sound of bacon. Before I'd come to live on a mountain in Montana, I'd never realized just how big a variety of bacon there was. I knew the two basics from the city, turkey and pig. Now, I'd had such a variety that I would probably never return to standard, store-bought bacon. Processed foods were so different. Like Brooke, Corbin too had a garden. It was mainly Gertie who took care of it, but the food grown was free of pesticides and preservatives.

Stretching under the covers, my back cracked and groaned. As much as I loved my kids, there was something to be said for alone-*alone* adult time. When there was no chance of being disturbed or interrupted, when you didn't have to sensor your volume or words due to eavesdropping ears or echoes.

Additionally, we didn't have to get dressed right away following sex.

After we finished the construction on Brooke's cabin and officially moved in, I was going to need to have a talk with Uncle Corbin about setting up some weekend trips for the kids to visit.

When Brooke had told me the story of her cheating, dirtbag

ex and how she had not wanted to have kids with him because she'd wanted him all to herself, I'll admit I was taken aback by that statement. My life was defined by my children. My world revolves around them. Every decision, every choice, I did with them in mind.

Until Brooke had knocked my world out of orbit.

My kids were still the most important part of my life. Nothing and no one could change that, but Brooke was also added to that list. I hated to think of it as a list, because it implied a hierarchy. I thought of it more as a bubble, housing safely the three people I loved most in this world.

But still, there was no arguing that the presence of my children curbed what Brooke and I could or could not do while under the same roof as them.

Like walking naked out of the bedroom in search of my lady love.

I found her in the kitchen. She wore nothing but a long shirt and a pair of wool socks.

The fire in the living room was sparking high, so she must have added wood to it when she got up. The one in our bedroom had not needed wood either from when I'd placed a large stump into it during the night. Outside the windows showed a new layer of white, indicating it had snowed during the night.

I smiled, because it gave us the excuse to not go get the kids today. I would get on the radio and tell Corbin the path just wasn't passable with my amateur snowmobile skills. He would see right through the excuse, but I was also okay with that.

Brooke turned off the stove, extinguishing the flames in the burner. She was humming to herself, swaying her hips to the music in her head. Fuck, I loved her hips. Loved everything about her, from her signature Elsa-braid, all the way down her long, toned legs to her sock covered toes. She was breathtaking.

As horrible as that night had been over a year ago when I

thought my children and I were going to die in that snowstorm, I couldn't help but feel grateful. If the storm hadn't come and Corbin had met us as planned, or if I had checked-in with Jack to learn of the pending storm and never went up the mountain that night... Well, Brooke and I might not have met. We could have been living up at Corbin's cabin, completely oblivious to the fact that the love of my life was living her own solitary life south of me.

It was hard to be grateful for something that had put my kids' lives in danger, but in a twisted, can't-change-the-past way, I was.

Brooke made no indication that she heard me or knew I was behind her. Still naked, I walked right up to her back and placed my arms around her. She let out a small yelp of surprise before pressing back against me in greeting.

I chuckled, placing my lips to her neck and nipping slightly. My hands went down to the hem of her shirt before working their way under and up to her breasts. A quick peek over her shoulder confirmed my suspicions that she was *not* wearing underwear.

My dick, already semi-hard from watching her sway her hips, filled to the brim and I felt my balls tighten. She made me feel like an uncontrollable teenager again. The only times I seemed to be soft in her presence was if she'd just made me come. And, even then, I had a faster come back than any thirty-seven year old man had a right to.

I squeezed her breasts, running my thumbs over her hardening nipples. Brooke squirmed under my touch, her ass rubbing up against my cock. Fuck. I'd never had anal sex before, and had never wanted to before, but there was something so primal about it. I *wanted* to claim her ass, like it would somehow give me possession over her.

I had never been a *man's man*. I was not a bulky gym-rat or a fighter of any kind. I certainly had never considered myself to be a possessive guy or an asshole. I was the nice guy, the reliable guy. The kind that girls felt *safe* around because I didn't have the stones to cheat or lie to them. I was, more times than not, placed in the 'friend zone' because of these traits.

But with Brooke? It was like all of the raw savagery drilled into my gender over millennia of evolution was brought out to claim, dominate, and possess her.

Her breath caught. When I pinched her nipples simultaneously, I felt her entire body shudder. My low chuckle sounded more like a rumble.

I brought my right hand from her breast down lower to find her center. Fuck, she was *soaked*. A moan escaped me as I started to gently rub her clit. Her head fell back on my shoulder as if her neck had lost control. I placed a kiss on her exposed skin.

I rolled my hips against her ass, pressing my hardness against her.

I continued to stroke her clit for a few more moments before sliding further down along her slit.

"Elijah, please..." Brooke gasped out. I loved the little whine in her voice, the plea not to stop. I can see her hands gripping the counter top before her in an effort to keep herself balanced. Then she breathed out the single word that could break my concentration: "Condom."

"Fuck," I groaned into her ear. We needed a better form of birth control. Condoms were so inconvenient. Hating having to leave her, I rushed out, "Be right back," before running from the room.

I nearly ripped the drawer off its hinges in my haste to find a foil packet. We really needed to have a talk about getting her an IUD. Or maybe the injection? I knew she would never go for the daily Pill. Hell, if we decided we were done having kids, I'd figure out how to discreetly get a vasectomy so she didn't have to worry about doctors and prescriptions. I knew how she felt about chemical treatments.

But damn, there was a part of me that hoped one day soon she'd be willing to have no form of birth control and just let nature take its course.

I could learn what we needed to and become her midwife. I paused at that wording. What was the male form of 'midwife'? The word 'accoucheur' came to mind, but I wasn't sure if that was the correct definition. 'Midhusband', maybe?

I smiled goofily at myself, rushing back into the kitchen. Where my smile utterly failed and died.

Brooke was now as naked as I was. She had moved the plate of eggs and bacon to the table, effectively placing it out of our way, and was now bent over the counter with her lower half sticking out in invitation.

I about swallowed my tongue at the sight.

Even from where I stood in the doorway, I could see her juices glistening in the morning sun through the windows.

My balls tightened and I had to shake my head to clear my thoughts enough to concentrate.

She was effectively serving herself up to me on a platter. I planned to dine my fill.

I fell to my knees behind her, trying to push my pent up arousal aside. I was *not* ready to come yet.

I ran my tongue along her slit. She whimpered. Her legs straightened, forcing my face to bury deeper against her. Chuckling, I pulled my neck back and bit the rounded globe of her left ass cheek. Not enough to break the skin, but enough to leave an impression of my teeth on her.

"Hey!" she protested, taking a step forward and away from me.

My hands shot up and locked around her hips. I dragged her

backwards and bit her right cheek to make it mirror the other. She bucked her hips.

"Stop fucking around and fuck me already!" she snapped.

Taking my pointer finger, I circled her soaked hole, running it forward towards her clit, and then back. I did this twice more before she let out a whimpering growl. Finally, I took pity on her and dipped my finger into her core. Brooke moaned and sagged further against the counter top.

I pulled my finger out, added my middle finger, and pressed both inside her. I felt her inner muscles quake around me. I leaned forward and pressed a kiss against her back hole. I checked her reaction, wanting to test how she would take me paying attention to her ass, but her only response was to moan louder and widen her stance.

Accepting the invitation, I took a long lick of her musky rear. I'd never rimmed anyone before, and fuck, I was not anticipating it being so hot. I pressed my face between her cheeks and ate her ass like it was my last meal as I pumped my two forefingers in and out of her wet heat.

Brooke practically *mewled*, writhing against the countertop. I tightened my hold on her hip to steady her.

"Please," she begged.

I laughed against her puckered hole. There was a sense of power and intoxication in making my woman feel out of control. I wanted to make her scream, to *burn*, for me. Only me, just as I burned for her. I had no idea what had come over me, as this was completely different from our previous sexual encounters, but I knew I liked it.

And, better yet, I knew that *she* was loving it.

Brooke came with a cry.

I gave her no time to recover. I stood up, broke the condom wrapper open with my teeth, and slid it down my cock. Without losing a beat, I positioned the tip of my sheathed cock at her hot, wet entrance and *slammed* myself home.

Brooke's top half arched up, throwing her head back with a wail. I took the opportunity to grab hold of her braid that I loved so much and wrapped it around my hand like a horse's reins.

I held her tight, though equally conscious for signs of pain over pleasure. I felt wild, taking her so roughly, but I had no desire to harm her. The love I felt for this woman was more powerful than any primal need to dominate.

Chapter Twenty-Seven

Brooke

The moan that escaped me was equal parts passion and surprise. He took me hard and fast, in a way that made it known that—despite what dirty words we had used in the past—that this was the first time he was fucking me, not making love. And I was *fucking loving it*.

I had only been with two men in my life. After Tyler, I never thought I *would* be with a man again. That trust had been broken. But then this single father with a terrible past came barreling into my life.

I had never felt the desire to be down and dirty *fucked* before. Like I needed to be owned, possessed, to have my body claimed and his mark on me. To know that I would still *feel* that claim even hours or days later.

My second orgasm took me by surprise. With Elijah holding my head up by my hair, I caught sight of our reflection in the kitchen window. It was duller than a mirror would have been, but still clear enough to make out our features. I saw the fierceness of his expression, but also the tenderness of his love.

He followed me over the edge, shouting out his release like a battle cry.

My body sagged, useless and limp. Elijah released his hold on my hair, breathing as heavily as I was. He gently pulled me back against his chest. He laid tender kisses to the back of my neck, shoulder, and then tipped my head to the side to reach my lips. Though I returned his kiss with equal affection, I was completely spent.

Elijah must have realized this. He gently picked up my boneless body and sat us down on the kitchen floor. He placed his back to the cabinets, somehow still keeping us connected. My legs straddled wide as I sagged against his chest. My head laid back on his shoulder, my forehead pressed against his ear and beard. Together, we were a sweaty mess.

The oddest memory came to me as my eyes landed on my kitchen entryway. Over a year ago, I had stood back as I watched this man embrace his children after having passed out for nearly an entire day trying to keep them safe. A longing had filled me that day, one I hadn't realized I still possessed, as the futile dream of joining that loving family embrace.

That dream did not seem so far away now.

I was not his kids' mother. I wasn't sure if I wanted to *be* their mother. But I knew I could be their friend. Maybe in time, the idea of being a mom wouldn't scare me so much. Loving them as a mother had no bearing on how much I loved their father.

"That was," Elijah gasped out behind me, "different."

"Very." I squeezed his hand. "Good different," I assured him.

He lifted the back of my hand to his lips. "Wanna do it again?"

I couldn't help the laugh that escaped me. "Can I at least catch my breath first?"

My body vibrated from the rumble in his chest. "I'll give

you as much time as it takes me to recover." I felt his head move around. "And possibly refuel. What kind of bacon is that?"

"Venison," I told him. "Bagged a good size buck a few weeks ago. I have the antlers ready in my shed to take up to Corbin." It was rare during the winter that I was able to catch a deer this far north on the mountain, but I was grateful for the fresh meat. While I did try to plan my hunting around mating seasons and populations, it was also a matter of survival on the mountain. We could not always follow the hunting laws, but we did try.

"Belle will love that."

"No longer upset about eating Bambi's mom?" I knew that Belle had been taking hunting lessons from Corbin. Elijah was not looking forward to when she shot more than still targets.

"She's got a stomach of iron. Girl digs right into the blood and guts to help Corbin dress the meat. She laughs when I gag at the different smells."

I pressed my own lips together to keep from laughing. First, I had to give him credit for trying. I was very grateful I had no witnesses to the first few times I had skinned and cured my catch. Also, because it felt wrong to laugh at him when he was still inside me. It was only because of the angle of our seated position that he hadn't slipped out yet.

I did not want him to leave my body. I liked holding him inside me, even though I knew that his semen was likely dripping out of the upright condom onto his balls and the floor below. Still had no desire to move.

"You can laugh," he grumbled. "I know you want to."

I shook my head, keeping my reaction under control. "You're still learning, Elijah. There's no shame in that." I pressed back against him. "I certainly am taking full advantage of your new skills and muscles."

He turned his head enough to press a kiss to my temples.

"You're sure you're okay with what we just did. I got a bit rough there..."

I laced our fingers together over my belly. "*Yes*," I squeezed. "I loved it."

"We're going to need to have a talk soon about how to lose the condoms."

I nodded, thinking the same thing. Aside from our first time together, we'd had multiple close calls where we hadn't had a condom handy. With winter approaching, it hadn't seemed necessary to have that talk back in the fall. Now that he and the kids were going to be moving in, it was definitely a conversation we were going to have to have sooner than later.

"I love the idea of turning the loft into our bedroom," I told him dreamily.

"I love hearing you say 'our bedroom'." He rubbed the coarse hair of his beard along my shoulder and neck. He was going to leave beard burns there if he pressed any harder.

Though it wouldn't be the only place on my person with beard burns. I wiggled my butt at the memory. Unfortunately, the motion made his softening cock slip from inside me. We both groaned.

"Breakfast and then shower sex?" Elijah suggested.

I smiled. We seemed to both be in unison at taking full advantage of having a kid-free house. Other than having to go outside to check my utility stores, I might not even bother to put clothing on today.

Chapter Twenty-Eight

Josephine

The swift kick to my belly woke me with a moan. My body automatically curled into the fetal position to protect myself. Cloudy memories came back at me as I braced against the sharp pain of another boot—this time to my back.

I fought to open my eyes, but my left eye wouldn't budge. From the wetness I felt as I lifted my face off of the marble floor, I was bleeding from somewhere on my head. I vaguely remembered being thrown backwards after spitting into Gunther's face. Most likely the kick to my gut had not been the first blow dealt to me while unconscious. It had just been the one to wake me up.

I was able to see out of my right eye, though all that was in my line of sight was a collection of men's boots. Since I did not know how much time had passed while I had been incapacitated, I had to check. All I could feel from my lower half was pulsing pain, but I was unable to determine where that pain was coming from. I knew I was still wearing my shirt and jacket, but that did not mean much.

When I tried to move my hand down to check if I was still

wearing my pants, I received another kick from behind me. Which would mean, I was in the room with at least four men. Three in front of me and one behind me. I jolted forward on the marble, my right hand flying out in front to catch myself. As soon as my hand landed outstretched, one of those boots came slamming down on top of it.

I cried out, feeling the bones shatter. I nearly lost consciousness from the pain again but fought to stay awake. The battle resulted in me projectile vomiting towards the boot still pressed down on my broken hand.

Someone grabbed my leg and I was rolled violently onto my back, away from my puke. The action made me lose my breath and the ceiling above me spun in circles. The only good thing that came from the rough treatment was being able to feel the seam of my pant leg pressed against my skin.

I was still clothed.

Mind, that was not going to help me in the long run. My pants were not a metal chastity device that required a key to open. Four against one, with me severely debilitated, was not going to end well for me, regardless of the fact that I was still wearing my pants. I could only take comfort in the fact that I had not been raped. Yet.

The sound of a zipper being lowered reached my ears as if amplified by surround sound. I had no idea why or how my brain could pick up on that noise when I was unable to concentrate on the words of their conversation. Like listening through a bubble, all I got was clouded garble and the knowledge that they were talking over me.

Just as I heard the *zip* of a second fly, something wet and rancid hit my face. I sputtered and coughed, gasping to catch my breath while trying not to open my mouth. As soon as the second and third streams hit me, covering my face, my torso, and my navel, I knew what they were doing. The thugs were *urinating* on me, laughing while they did so.

Ammonia filled my nostrils as I fought not to throw up again. With my broken hand cradled to my chest, I tried to raise my other hand to protect my face. A rough grip around my wrist twisted my arm out of the way as he continued to use me as a human toilet. All I could do was hold my breath—despite my protesting lungs and ribs—squeeze my eyes closed, and pray the brutes had not drunk a lot of coffee yet that morning.

I knew the action was to humiliate me and disgust me. There was no doubting that they had accomplished that goal. I was mortified by what I was being subjected to. However, the shock of it, as well as the—gag—wetness on my face also helped break me from my hazy state.

When the final drops hit my skin, I spluttered and gasped out for air. My hair and clothes were soaked. I had to blink several times, turned my head to try and dry off my eyes. My left still would not open, making me wonder if it was swollen closed.

All four men had their dicks out. One had started to rub himself obscenely in an obvious attempt to get himself hard. I did not understand the purpose or the kink of men urinating on women. I supposed there were women who also got off on the dominant act, but it was mostly a male thing from what I understood. Probably had something to do with the animalistic nature to mark one's territory.

I was very good at reading people. As my one good eye flitted about the room, I took note of several things that I had not been aware of since waking up. Sebastian Gunther was no longer in the room. I recalled his words about teaching his traitorous son a lesson and dreaded what treatment Trenton was being subjected to. I was supposed to be *protecting* him.

I realized that there were five men in the room. One was standing back, away from the others by the door. I couldn't tell from my poor vision what he was doing, but he seemed younger than the four men directly over me, around Trenton's age.

I also took note of the fact that the man who was currently rubbing his dick while standing over my urine soaked body was the leader of these thugs. Most likely he had been the first to pull his dick out and start urinating and the others followed whether they got anything out of it or not. Based on the scrunched noses from the smell now emanating from me, I guessed 'not'.

The fifth man came further into the room. Like the others, he was dressed in all black, which only made his sandy brown hair seem darker. I thought at first that he had a gun in his hand, but then he snapped it open to reveal it was an extendable baton. Was it his turn to beat me now that I had been humiliated before they gang raped me?

The man I had pegged as the leader looked up at the fifth man. He nodded in acknowledgement, clearly indicating that they knew each other. "What are you doing here? I thought Gunther had told you to stay at the—"

Before the leader could finish his question, the fifth man swung the baton. It connected with the leader's face, spraying blood, teeth, and spit down upon me as the man was thrown back off of his feet. Dick still hanging out of his fly, the leader collapsed to the floor and did not get back up.

The other three stood frozen in shock. I had to admit to being slow to process the situation as well.

The fifth man swung his baton again. The others started to fight back. I gritted my teeth through the pain as I tried to move out of the way. The urine and my blood made the marble floor extremely slippery. I ended up on my belly, using my good arm to Army crawl my way away from the fight.

A thug being thrown across the room nearly landed on me. I barely avoided being pancaked as he crashed onto a cushioned chair, shattering the expensive piece of furniture beneath his weight. I waited a heartbeat for him to get back up, but he did not. I continued crawling away.

When the grunting and groaning stopped, I heard a clatter that had me jumping and rolling onto my back. My good eye landed on the dismantled gun on the floor and then flew up to see the man taking apart another one. He pocketed the magazine clips.

Without looking at me, the man collapsed his baton and pulled out a pistol. My poor vision couldn't tell the make and model, but I knew it was a semi-automatic. I thought at first he was attaching the baton to the end of the pistol—except that made no sense. It took my sluggish brain a moment to catch up to the fact that he'd traded the baton for a silencer. I just hadn't realized it with their similar shapes and my distorted vision.

He leveled the elongated gun and, without hesitation, pulled the trigger. Four shots, four men. All now sporting bloodied holes in the middle of their foreheads. It was so fast, quiet, and thorough, I wasn't even sure it had been real.

After doing another check to ensure all four thugs were dead, he unscrewed the silencer, put both the gun and the silencer away, and then came over to me. His boots did not slide on the slick flooring.

"Shit, Josie." I had a feeling the disgust on his young face had nothing to do with my looks and everything to do with my treatment. He did not hesitate to reach out and help wipe the mess off of my skin, regardless of what it was he was touching.

"Who are you?" I managed to gasp out.

He was clearly not with Gunther, even though he was dressed like one of his thugs. He also used my nickname, not my name or my surname. It hinted at familiarity, though I was sure I had never met him before in my life.

"Jack sent me. I'm so sorry, I came as soon as I could."

My brain was not comprehending what the man was saying. How could Jack have known we were in trouble? I hadn't called him. I should have, but I figured I would do that once we were safely on the road.

"He noticed the news feed of Gunther's release wasn't live. Something about the sun placement being wrong. Anyway, when he couldn't get ahold of you, he sent me."

"You're a Mountain Mutineer," I surmised.

The man nodded. I noticed for the first time that, though young, he had a weathered look about him. Like he'd suffered more than he should have given his youth. I placed him around twenty-two or twenty-three years old. "My name's Owen. Can you stand? We need to get out of here. Do you know where Trenton is?"

I shook my head to the last question. I was walking out of here no matter what. Owen moved around to help me stand. I appreciated that. I was still wearing only one boot and had no idea where the other one was.

Noticing this, Owen surveyed our surroundings. When he spotted it, he helped me hobble over and then even knelt before me to place it on my foot.

"Come on, Cinderella," he said with a sense of humor I was surprised he could feel in our current situation. "Let's go find your charge and get the fuck out of here."

Chapter Twenty-Nine

Brooke

Elijah and I had moved my lounge chair back and then piled all the blankets and pillows I owned in front of the fireplace in my living room. We got up only to use the bathroom or grab something to eat or drink. We were completely lost in a bubble of us. I had every intention of sleeping out here in the firelight with him as my pillow, blanket, and bed.

The *beep* from upstairs broke through our reverie. I did not want to answer it, knowing it meant that someone was trying to hail me on the radio, but knew that we could not ignore it. Not with his kids elsewhere.

I tapped on the top of his head. I was lying on my back with him laid out over me, his cheek pressed into my belly. We were resting, just taking in the serenity and loveliness of the day. We talked on occasion, but mostly just stayed in the moment with each other. I had a feeling this spot before the fireplace was going to become 'our spot' when the kids weren't about.

He lifted his head, his eyes drooped with sleep.

"We're being hailed," I informed him with a frown.

He made a face that reflected how I felt. Placing a kiss

between my breasts, he rose. I instantly felt cold, despite the roaring fire beside us. Elijah wrapped one of my homemade quilts around his shoulders before he journeyed towards the stairs to the loft. I followed behind him, my blanket wrapped like a toga.

Elijah expertly turned on the radio, as mine was just like Corbin's. Seeing that I had followed him up, he caught my hand and pulled me over to sit on his lap. "You could have stayed down where it's warm."

"It's warmer here with you," I declared, folding myself against him.

He gave me a cocky grin before calling my callsign over the radio. When Jack answered, he glanced over at me in surprise. Like me, he probably assumed it had been Corbin calling regarding the kids.

"Jack, what's going on?"

"*I'm sorry to tell you this, but Gunther's free. He was acquitted this morning. Over.*"

I felt my stomach drop at the news. I remembered Gunther's reputation from my days as an NYPD detective. The Vice Department could never pin anything on him. They had nicknamed him 'the Magician' because it always seemed like he was having us look one way while pulling a rabbit out of his hat behind our backs. Even months later, I was still struggling with the realization that *Sebastian Gunther* was the man Elijah and the kids had been running from.

Elijah looked pale, and for a moment, I thought he might faint. Then he leaned forward and clicked the microphone. "What happened? Over."

His grip around my waist got tighter.

"*Officially? Misappropriation of evidence. Unofficially? He paid someone off to fuck up the evidence. Even if I find out who did it—and I will—it won't change the fact that they had to let him go. They would need to find new evidence of new crimes or new evidence of the previous crimes to arrest him again. Over."*

Both Elijah and I let out low curses. It was so messed up that the justice system could be so easily foiled. As a former cop, I knew all too well how easy it was to mishandle evidence. The first time one of my cases had been dismissed because a crime scene tech had used the bathroom at the crime scene and had unknowingly flushed a dime of cocaine. The defense had argued that the tech could have planted the trace evidence we had been able to find and the charges had been dismissed.

"Where is Gunther now?" Elijah asked into the microphone. "What about Trenton and Josie? Over."

We did not know much about the bounty hunter who had been able to track Elijah to Whitefish. *None* of us had been pleased when Jack had shared that news. However, he had quickly eased our fears when he informed us of Josie's good intentions and that he had sent her back to New York City to help bring Gunther down. It hadn't been until Gunther's arrest that I think any of us truly believed that Josie was on our side. Then Jack had kept us informed over the winter about Trenton and Josie's efforts to shut down Gunther's organization. It was unfortunate, but there were some things Trenton simply couldn't do either because the government had frozen the assets or because his father was still alive, even if he was incarcerated.

"That's where the worst news comes in. Gunther paid off several news stations to air footage of his release later and call it 'live'. Basically, made it look like he was being released when he was actually already released. Trenton and Josie were caught unaware..." Jack's voice trailed off.

Though he hadn't said 'over', I reached forward to key the mic when there was an extremely long pause. "What happened?" I demanded.

I could feel Elijah start to shake under me. His worst fears were unfolding right before his eyes—or, rather, ears.

"I wasn't able to get ahold of them. One of my newer recruits was in the area, thank God. I sent him to find them. He was able to get them out, but Gunther escaped with at least two of his men. Gunther was injured and has effectively disappeared. He used an old prohibition tunnel to escape and could have popped up anywhere in the city. Many of those link to subway and maintenance tunnels.

"As for Josie and Trenton... Well, it's not good. My guy was able to get them out but they're both hurt. Josie was beaten and..." He paused again. *"Trenton is missing several fingers and teeth. His hands had been secured to a table using a nail gun. It could have been far worse for both of them. Owen's getting them to a doctor I know."*

Elijah and I sat there in stunned silence for several long minutes. We both knew how cruel Gunther could be. Elijah's scars were evidence of that even without my years on the force and the rumors surrounding Gunther.

But to... His own son...?

Granted, this was the same man who had tried to sell his seven-year-old daughter as a child bride to make a business deal. But still... Seeing and believing were two very different things. Trenton was just a kid himself. Would his hands heal? Would he lose use of them? What about his missing fingers and teeth? If handled correctly, they might be able to be reattached.

Jack's telling of what Josie had been through had been vague enough that I had to wonder. I keyed the microphone. "Was she raped? Over."

"No," Jack assured us. *"But it was a close call. Over."*

I didn't know who Owen was, but I was grateful to him. He wasn't one of the few people who lived off of the mountain but worked for Jack that I had met. Corbin and Dalton were the two on the mountain besides me who helped secure and hide Jack's special visitors. Jack talked about Huck and Walter like they helped, but I didn't know how. Tommy was just an old man who lived a secluded life and had no part of Jack's side business.

I knew Dante, Luca, and Avery, having met them either in town or when they were handing off a visitor to be taken up the mountain. None of them had ever been on the mountain and worked with Jack around the country to help in whatever capacity Jack asked of them. I knew there were others. Jack had an extensive network of people at his disposal, but they were the three I had met.

I leaned forward. I wasn't religious but I felt the statement was valid for the situation. "Thank God. Where are they now? Over."

"There were...a lot of bodies. Owen had to get them away and wasn't able to call for medical help. Josie and Trenton both insisted they get as far away from the city as possible before seeing a doctor. I contacted a doctor I know in New Hampshire and gave her a heads up that they were headed her way. Hopefully, Dr. Souleiman will be able to help Trenton. They found all but one of his fingers." Jack cleared his throat. *"I'll keep you guys posted. I know none of you have any plans to come down the mountain for a few months still, but we might want to consider keeping Belle up there if Gunther isn't found by spring. Over."*

I knew Elijah well enough to know he was already contemplating never allowing her off the mountain again, even if Gunther was found or put back in jail.

Elijah keyed the microphone. "Thanks for letting us know, Jack. Please pass on my regrets to Trenton and Josie. I never meant for any of this to happen to them."—I was not surprised in the least that Elijah was taking the blame for what had happened, regardless of none of it being his fault. I would need to nip that line of thinking in the bud as soon as we got off the radio call with Jack.—"I appreciate your efforts as always. Over and out."

Elijah powered off the connection before Jack could reply.

I turned on his lap and wrapped my arms around his neck. Elijah buried his face into my chest.

"It's never going to end." His voice was muffled by the blanket I was wearing in place of clothing. "He's going to keep coming for us."

I pressed my lips to his hair. "This mountain is the safest place for you and your kids," I reminded him. "We can't get down and they can't get up."

"And what happens when the snow melts and the road becomes passable?"

I had no answer for him, but we had approximately two more months to figure that out.

Chapter Thirty

Elijah

The news about Trenton had been hard to hear. I'd known him since he was fifteen years old. For all of his faults when I'd first met him, he was a good kid and had grown into an even better man. He had risked his life to save his sister's *and* had worked tirelessly to right his father's wrongs. Some men twice his age weren't half as strong as he was.

It sickened me that Trenton had been born into that life. More so than Belle or Lucas, because they were still young enough to grow and forget. To let memories heal and fade away. It had been a long time since Belle had mentioned 'the bad man' haunting her dreams. Lucas, thankfully, would never know about any of it. He would grow up in a life that Trenton had never been offered.

What sort of person would Trenton be if he hadn't grown up his father's son? To be raised to *become* a criminal? There couldn't be many fates worse than that. Trenton had known from a very young age what his path in life was—and yet he had fought it at every turn. From failing in school to stepping up to be a part of his half-sister's life. Trenton had shown more gumption than I had given him enough credit for.

Like his little sister, he had a heart of gold and nerves of steel.

Several days after Jack's initial call, I returned to Corbin's cabin. I hated leaving Brooke alone and had convinced her to come up with me. Dalton had generously agreed to check on her cabin and stores during her absence. Logically, I knew that Gunther still had no idea where we were, nor could he get to us even if he did, but that old fear had taken root in my system and it was difficult to shake.

We were safer at Corbin's further up the mountain. I knew how capable Brooke was, but I still needed her with me.

When Corbin had moved the kids and me into his cabin last year, he had shown me an elevation map of the mountain. It had taken me by surprise how close to town we were. As the crow flies, it was only about two miles. However, with the terrain, the elevation, and the weather, the paths to each of our homes become a lot longer and more treacherous. After reaching Tommy's land, there was no way to get a full sized vehicle up the mountain. It was frightening to learn just how close the kids and I had come to death the night I drove up the mountain due to a miscommunication and my ignorance.

I knew better now. We had been up on this mountain for fourteen months. *I knew* how to navigate and use the mountain to my advantage. Even if Gunther located us, he did not know this mountain. As Corbin and Brooke continually tried to tell me, we had the home advantage.

It was about a week after Trenton and Josie's attack when we got word from Jack they were well enough to travel. His man, Owen, was bringing them to Montana. This was a risk, with Gunther's location still unknown, but one I was willing to take on. Trenton deserved to see his brother and sister again after all this time and after all he had suffered to protect them. Additionally, Trenton had nowhere else to go with Gunther out of jail.

I recalled all the precautions I had taken to get the kids and myself to Whitefish and had no doubt that Jack's man, Owen, would take equal measures to ensure they were not followed.

We needed to figure out living arrangements. There were only so many bedrooms available. As soon as the weather cleared enough, Brooke, Corbin, and I were going to start moving the kids' things down to Brooke's cabin. Until then, however, Corbin did not have a spare bedroom.

Brooke suggested putting Josie up with her—and I had to fight to find a reason not to do that since it did make the most logical sense. However, *I* wanted to be the one bunking with Brooke. It was selfish, given our limited housing space, but I had just spent months without her.

We still had several days before Josie and Trenton would arrive in Whitefish to figure it out. Dalton had said he would help where he could but could not offer up his cabin for anyone to sleep. The two cabins they used to house special visitors were already occupied. I didn't know by who and no one would say. Even Brooke was being close-lipped about it. I got it—I wasn't part of their group—but I did not like not being in the know.

It made the most sense to house Trenton with me and the kids. He had a right to his brother and sister. Legally, he had more of a right to Belle than I did. I knew that Trenton had no designs to take her from me, but the fact that he *could* was never far from my mind.

Then we all received a shock over the radio. Walter, who was even further up the mountain than Corbin was, had volunteered to house Josie. I had never met Walter, but I knew his voice. He had a deep bass vocal range that reminded me of Paul Robeson and the classic songs my mom listened to.

Both Brooke and Corbin looked as shocked as I felt by this announcement. According to them, Walter only aided with protection on the mountain and had never actively been involved with the people Jack took in. From what I understood, people didn't *stay* on the mountain. The kids and I were an exception because of Corbin. The two cabins they used to house people were temporary until other arrangements could be made. I didn't know where those cabins were in proximity to Brooke's or Corbin's cabins, but I had pieced together enough to know they were not high up. If I had to make a guess, they were between Tommy's and Brooke's land in elevation.

Belle knew that Trenton was coming. After Gunther's arrest, we had even arranged for Belle to talk to Trenton on the phone during her last trip to town before the snowfall. She loved her brother and missed him. Lucas was too young to remember Trenton or to have the family dynamics explained to him now.

"I'm going to tell him all about my new uncle and my new grammy and my new cabin and my new hair and my new name and my new friend, Brooke, and my new shoes..." Belle had babbled on for days after learning Trenton was going to be joining us on the mountain.

With Walter taking Josie up to the cabin, which he assured me was not an issue even with the weather, we just had to find a place for Trenton. The snow the past two nights did not help. I finally had to concede that Trenton would need to stay with Brooke while the kids and I remained a little longer at Corbin's.

Brooke and I took the time we had together before our guests arrived. We started to work on plans for her cabin's reno-vation, which we would start as soon as the weather allowed us to get the supplies Jack had ordered for us. Corbin was even working on a bunkbed for Belle and Lucas's room. I knew eventually we would have to figure out something else with their room, but it would work for now.

After some measurements and a couple failed suggestions, Brooke and I finally figured out what our furniture set up would be in the loft. I planned on using the remainder of the winter to help Corbin build us a king bed frame with storage underneath. We were only able to place a bigger bed in the room if we gave up furniture like dressers and nightstands. Therefore, our new bed would have shelving over it instead of a headboard. The couch that was currently up there was going into the kids' new room and we were going to place a shoe chest in the corner. This left the large scenery windows unblocked too.

It would take time, but we would get there.

Once Trenton was healed and adjusted, we would need to figure out what he wanted to do. He didn't have to stay on the mountain, but it would no doubt be the safest option for him. After telling his mom off, he couldn't even go to Vivian for help against his father.

Jack was having a hard time finding Gunther because most of his associates had distanced themselves from him during his trial. Even with what remained of his assets returned to him, Gunther had other resources. Per Jack, Gunther had a number of aliases through his various shell corporations. Part of why it had taken Trenton and Josie so long to dismantle his father's enterprise was because they had to track down what names belonged to actual people and which were Gunther under an assumed name.

There was no guarantee they had found all of Gunther's names and accounts.

Jack was, however, able to track down Helena Blake, Belle's

birth mother. She had taken the money Gunther paid her and had moved to London, England. In the eight years since giving up her parental rights, Helena had been through three husbands, all of whom were now dead or dying. Upon learning this, Jack had made the decision not to reach out to her regarding Belle's parental rights, which I wholly seconded. I wanted that woman nowhere near my daughter.

Until Owen arrived with Josie and Trenton, there was little to do but wait. We continued on like nothing was different or amiss for the sake of the children. Belle knew Trenton was coming, but I had not figured out yet how to tell her his condition.

Brooke knew I was worrying, even without me having to say anything. Her love and support held steady, even with our pending separation. I could only hope that the winter would come to an early end and we could get started on the construction soon. I was more than ready to move into her cabin and become a family.

I also started taking shooting lessons. Despite once having been accused of killing a man, I had never actually held a gun before a few days ago. Corbin had different hunting rifles and Gertie had an old pistol that had been her husband's. Brooke had several handguns and hunting rifles. When Dalton learned of my lessons, he also joined in to help instruct me. It was decided to start off with a handgun and then work my way up to the rifle.

Though I wasn't happy about it, Belle was also part of the lessons. Corbin had been teaching her gun safety as part of her hunting lessons. He'd started her off with a compound bow and arrows. Belle was an amazing shot and took her lessons very seriously. Unfortunately for me, Corbin was to the point where he couldn't 'add' anything else to her lessons and I would soon have to make a decision if Belle was allowed to go hunting with

Corbin this summer. After watching my lessons, Belle was also asking to learn how to shoot a gun.

I could appreciate Belle learning gun safety. I had heard a lot of stories growing up in New Jersey about kids 'playing' with their parents' guns and accidentally shooting themselves or each other. I never wanted that to happen to Belle or Lucas. Guns were a part of mountain life and they needed to learn gun safety. However, I was still apprehensive about Belle actually shooting a gun at another living thing.

Maybe that was just my own fears coming to the surface. Animal or human, I had no idea if I actually had the strength to pull the trigger to end a life. Still targets were one thing.

I had yet to hit any of my targets. My bad aim was making me the laughing stock of the group—including my own daughter and the woman who held my heart.

Watching Brooke handle a gun should not have been sexy. But damn, I enjoyed watching her in action. As a former police officer and a veteran, Brooke and Dalton were nearly matched in skill and often had shooting contests during my training. Once Dalton had joined in, Corbin had stepped back to help keep Belle entertained so she didn't keep asking when it was her turn.

"You're going to need to let her at some point," Brooke told me as we were packing up one day. The sun was setting fast and what little warmth we had been allotted that day was dying down.

"She's eight years old!" I argued back. Again.

"She's eight, almost nine, and she lives on a mountain." She leaned over to press a kiss to my bearded cheek. "There are enough of us around to help keep her safe. I know you don't like guns, but they're a way of life up here. She's a great shot with her bow. She's never goofed off or mistreated the weapon. I know a gun seems scarier, but it's no more dangerous than a bow in the wrong hands."

I still didn't like it, but I conceded. The next day, Corbin started Belle's training with an eighteen-inch Ruger compact rifle he'd purchased for her.

I stood back and watched in trepidation as my little angel hit the bullseye after only three shots.

Chapter Thirty-One

Brooke

Elijah clung to my back as I guided the snowmobile down the steep, snow covered slope. This was his first time off the mountain since he'd arrived almost fifteen months ago. It was hard to believe how much had changed, how much *I* had changed, in fifteen months.

Jack had called us this morning to say that Josie and Trenton had finally made it to town. We were on our way down to see them. Elijah had become proficient in driving the snowmobiles, but the way down the foot of the mountain was far different than being up in the saddle where we lived. Which was why he was riding with me instead of on his own.

We were meeting at Jack's store and then would be guiding them up to Tommy's land, where Corbin and Walter would be meeting us later. Corbin would bring Elijah back up to his cabin, I would take Trenton to mine for the night, and Josie would be heading up with Walter to his land.

I hadn't been down to town since before Thanksgiving. Celebrating holidays and birthdays was another change in my life since Elijah and his kids had entered it. I had had my first birthday party in a decade last fall. Belle had asked when my birthday was and that was that. Same with Christmas, Thanksgiving, and even Halloween. Since Belle couldn't go Trick or Treating like other kids in town, Corbin had made a scavenger hunt on his land where he hid candy and treats for Belle and Lucas to find. Elijah and I had spent Valentine's Day in front of the fireplace in my living room last week.

It was interesting how much the presence of children on the mountain had changed us. Dalton, Corbin, and I had always looked out for each other and pitched in to aid Tommy too, especially after Tommy's hip fracture. But now we weren't just neighbors. We were *friends*.

I'm not even sure I had such an active social life when I was married and living in the city with my family as I do now.

Being winter, it was entirely reasonable for Elijah's face to be completely covered. Mine was too. As we entered town, we got several curious glances. It was extremely rare for the notorious 'mountain men' who lived up Big Mountain to journey down into town—and even rarer during the winter.

The ski resort was in full swing and the town was flooded with tourists. The resort rented out snowmobiles for guests to use like a rental car. As a snow town, it was not unusual to see more snowmobiles than cars on the road during the winter months. We headed down the road towards Jack's store.

I saw the curious looks from the locals. Over the years, I had heard all sorts of rumors about the 'mountain men'. Most of them believed I was one of their wives or some sort of mountain man hooker that they shared. There was talk about cannibalism and how we hunted missing tourists for sport. We did nothing to stop any of these rumors. Hell, no one would believe us even if we tried. Truthfully, none of us cared enough about anyone in town for us to correct their opinion of us. Jack didn't bother to defend our reputations either, because he knew that the ridiculous legends kept locals and tourists from journeying up our mountain.

After I parked, we dismounted but did not remove our snow gear. We left our faces covered until we entered the front door of Jack's store.

A young man I didn't recognize was sitting behind the counter. He had sandy brown hair and a unique shade of amber eyes. I placed him in his early twenties, which was why I didn't guess who he was right away.

"They're in the back with Jack," he told us.

This was Owen? This kid had rescued Trenton and Josie? And he'd faced down how many of Gunther's goons to do it? I was a bit grateful for the flannel face mask and goggles covering my face and what was no doubt an astonished expression.

"Thanks," I said, my voice muffled by the mask. I took Elijah's hand and led him towards the storage room. He had removed his goggles, so I could see his eyes taking in everything about Jack's store. I doubted he even noticed Owen or his youth.

I guided Elijah through to the large door that hid Jack's real business. He was waiting for us, closing us into the secret room. Once there, we started to unbundle our snow gear.

I had only been in Jack's computer room a handful of times. There was never a need for me to be back here, other than following Jack's initial pitch to become a Mutineer and then two other times when I'd happened to be in his store when a situation had arisen. The room had more television screens mounted around the walls than a NASA command center. He had a single desk with a keyboard and a picture of a schoolgirl I had never had the guts to inquire about. I suspected she was his daughter, but Jack had never mentioned having or having had a family. Based on the age of the picture, she was either dead or Jack was long estranged from her.

Never before had I seen bed cots set up along the left wall.

They were likely pulled from Jack's camping supply products in his store. Most of the computer screens were now turned off, giving the room a dark and dreary look to it. I'd never noticed how little overhead lighting was here before because the screens gave off so much glow.

On the cots were two very bruised and battered people I had never met before but now claimed as part of my mountain family.

Trenton was passed out. He had a cast over one hand and a splint on the other. His head was tipped away from us on the camping pillow. He had as blonde of hair as Belle and me with natural highlights. I wondered if his eyes matched Belle's too. Unconscious, with his jaw swollen and what looked like cotton hanging out over his lip, he looked far younger than his twenty-three years. A thin blanket covered him from the chest down, hiding any other obvious injuries.

On the other cot was the woman I could only assume to be Josie. She too had a cast on her hand, though hers went further up to her elbow than Trenton's did. Her left eye was puffy and colorful, but she was able to blink and move the eyelid. She had two butterfly bandages on her left cheek. Her split lip looked almost healed. She was sitting up on the cot with her back against the wall and her knees raised before her. I recognized the hardened look on her face: it was one I saw too often in the mirror myself. It was the look of a woman who had hit rock bottom but refused to stay down.

Her long black hair was up in a simple ponytail. From the gun in her left hand, I realized why she wasn't sleeping. She was still trying to protect Trenton. Jack might have told her we were coming, but she wasn't taking any chances. Most likely, she blamed herself for Trenton's condition and was taking care of him more than she was herself.

Due to that realization, I was grateful Walter was coming

down to take Josie up to his cabin. It would give her a chance to heal and rest instead of being hyper-focused on still protecting Trenton. The mountain and I would protect her charge until she was ready to take him back into her protection.

Jack was sitting at his desk, but he wasn't working his computer magic. Instead, it looked like he was counting medication bottles and various first aid supplies. That would make sense. It wasn't like we had a pharmacy up on the mountain. Anything they needed medical-wise needed to be brought with us. Including antibiotics, painkillers, anti-inflammatories... Most of us used home remedies, but there was no reason for Josie or Trenton to be in undue pain just because the other mountain dwellers and I did not want to rely on medications from town.

"Oh good, you're here," Jack said as he stood up. He walked up to Elijah and held out his hand. "Good to finally meet you, son."

Elijah shook his offered hand. "You too. I'm sorry it's taken these circumstances to get me to come off of the mountain."

Jack waved off Elijah's words. "I am the last person you need to explain staying on that mountain to. I understand its allure probably better than you do."

I thought his wording odd. As far as I knew, Jack did not and never had lived on the mountain. He lived in an apartment above his store here.

Jack turned towards me and held out his arms. "Kitten, you look good."

I smiled and accepted the hug from my old friend. I never asked why he always called me 'Kitten' and I probably never would. I loved the pet name. It gave a fatherly feel to our relationship, which is something I sorely lacked in my life since my own father's betrayal. "Jack, you're looking old."

He chuckled, stepping back to chuck me on the chin.

Then he rolled his desk chair over towards the cots and

gestured for me to take a seat. Since it was the only chair in the room, I glared at him and held my ground until he sat down himself. I didn't know Jack's exact age or even his birthday, but I placed him in his mid-sixties. Like hell I was sitting down while he was forced to stand, even if chivalry demanded it of him.

"Josie, I'd like you to meet Brooke and Elijah."

Her eyes passed me over and landed on Elijah. Jealousy was a new emotion for me. As the only woman not related to Elijah in some way, I hadn't experienced it before in our relationship. I'm not even sure I had during my marriage to Tyler and wondered if that was because I'd been secure in our relationship or blind.

It took me a second to realize that Josie's appraisal of Elijah wasn't sexual. It was calculating and assessing. Like she was trying to determine if he was a good guy or a bad guy.

"Wasted a lot of time and money looking for you, Mr. Greene."

Out of the corner of my eye, I saw Elijah's wince. "I don't go by that name anymore."

Josie nodded once. "For good reason. Even if Jack gets you cleared of all charges, you're still going to have a bounty on your head. A lot of people blame you for Gunther's downfall."

"I hear that trophy belongs to you," Elijah parried back. "Took a lot of guts to take Gunther on like that."

"Yeah," Josie scoffed, and then winced in pain. She put a hand to her ribs, making me think she either had a fractured or bruised rib or ribs. "Guts aren't something I've ever lacked." She lifted her casted hand up slightly. "Two working hands, though, seem to be in short supply around these parts."

My eyes landed on Trenton, who was still slumbering, as I'm sure Elijah's did. "How is he?" I asked, my voice low and full of concern. Even in sleep, I could see he was in pain.

I recalled seeing pictures of Sebastian Gunther from my

time on the force. The man was short and stalky. Trenton, though, was tall and lanky. Like someone had taken a younger version on Gunther and stretched him like a *Gumby*. I couldn't see his eyes as he slept, but he had the same obsidian hair as his father.

"The doc Owen took us to was able to reattach all but the one finger we couldn't find." There was a detachment to Josie's voice that made me believe she was trying not to think about how much the kid was suffering. From what little I knew about Josie, and how I knew I would react, she was likely blaming herself for his condition. "Jack was able to get a dentist to come to the clinic too. He was only able to reattach two of his teeth. In time, he'll be able to get partial dentures if he wants. After everything else, his broken nose almost seems anticlimactic."

Elijah approached the cot where the young man lay. He knelt down, gently running his hand through the man's blonde hair. "He's braver than I ever gave him credit for. He took a bullet for me the night we escaped."

I saw Josie's brows furrow. "I never knew that," she said softly.

Trenton muttered something in his sleep but did not wake.

I turned to Josie. "How are *you*?"

Her face hardened, as did her voice. "I'm fine."

I didn't believe her. Neither, apparently, did Jack. "You have a fractured hand that required reconstructive surgery, Josie. You are not *fine*."

"I am *fine*," she snapped back at him. "My hand is nothing in comparison to what those bastards were going to do to me. If I had my way, they'd still be alive so I could teach them a lesson."

The venom in her voice was palpable.

Jack's own face darkened. "While I agree with you, and I wish I could provide them to you to seek your own justice when you're mentally and physically ready, you know that Owen had no choice but to dispose of them as quietly and as quickly as he could."

Josie turned her face away, looking like a petulant child who had just had her favorite toy taken away. It was hard to tell in the low lighting and with her bruises, but I guessed her to be a few years older than Elijah and me.

"I understand your anger," Jack told her softly. "All I can offer you is a piece of Gunther when I finally find him."

Josie glanced over her shoulder at him. "Just a piece?"

"He owes a lot of people blood, Josie." Jack's chuckle had a hint of malice to it I had never heard before. "You have to share, but you'll have your turn."

That answer seemed to satisfy Josie. She even grinned as widely as her split lip would allow.

"Do you have any news on Gunther?" Elijah asked from behind me. "Anything at all."

"I have a few leads some of my men are checking out," Jack said cryptically. "With the loss of his men, he needs to find others. He's low on cash but has assets he could sell to get what he needs. I'm looking into a black-market art auction that looks promising. He's been known to frequent it before."

I walked over to where Elijah was still kneeling by Trenton's cot. I put my hands on his shoulders and leaned down to press a kiss into his hair. "Once we get back up the mountain, Gunther will no longer be our problem."

"Weather's supposed to turn tomorrow," he reminded me. "We need to get back up before dawn."

He still didn't like our current sleeping arrangement. I wasn't too thrilled about being separated from him either, but it wasn't like we were next door neighbors where he could walk across the street to check on his kids. Until the weather was better and we could get all of the kids' supplies down to my cabin, it just wasn't feasible to swap sleeping arrangements yet.

"I'll have Owen carry Trenton out to the *Jeep*," Jack said, standing. "The sooner we get them up the mountain, the better."

"What medications are needed?" I asked him.

"I'll get Trenton," Elijah offered. "I just need to know where to go."

As Elijah started to get bundled up, Jack gave me instructions for each patient and separated the necessary pills into two different zippered baggies. I assisted Josie into a heavier coat and snow boots. She wouldn't be exposed long, but in this weather, it wasn't worth the risk. She was already injured and did not need to complicate her health further.

Once Elijah was bundled up, he lifted Trenton under his knees and behind his back. Jack went out first to ensure the coast was clear. He held the backdoor open for us. I guided Josie to the front seat of the *Jeep* while Elijah laid Trenton down. I wondered if he'd been given a sedative since he'd barely moved during the transfer.

Then Jack went to switch places with Owen. Since Jack didn't have any regular employees, it was noticed when he closed down and locked his doors. Everyone in town knew when Jack had a doctor's appointment or such because those were the rare times when the store was closed or he had a townie watching the register.

Once Owen was ready, Elijah and I headed for my snowmobile. Jack would send the signal up to Corbin and Walter that we were headed to Tommy's.

Looking up at the heavy clouds rolling in, I hoped we made it back to our respective homes in time.

Chapter Thirty-Two

Elijah

We barely made it through Corbin's cabin door before the snowstorm came in full force. When Corbin had met us at Tommy's, he'd told me that Belle had begged to come with him. I was so thankful that he was able to resist the power of her Bambi eyes and told her 'no'. Corbin had no issue spoiling my daughter and letting her have her way in everything—except when it came to her safety. He knew these mountains and these winters better than I did and I was grateful he'd trusted his instincts over her desire to tag along.

Brooke and Trenton had a shorter ride than Corbin and me. As soon as we were through the door, Gertie informed us that Brooke had radioed to say she and Trenton were safe inside her cabin. I knew that Brooke was capable, but I still felt a sense of relief at the knowledge she was safe from the storm.

Trenton had woken up part way up the mountain to Tommy's. Owen and Josie explained to him where they were and what was going on. He apparently did not handle painkillers well; they tended to make him loopy and drowsy. This was unfortunate for him because that meant he couldn't take another until after he was at Brooke's. Even so, Brooke had strapped Trenton to her to ensure he didn't fall off if he passed out again.

Tommy had grumbled and groaned about us meeting up on his land. Even through his cursing, though, I saw the appreciation in his eyes when Owen and I brought more firewood onto his porch for him and Brooke checked over his stores and supplies while we were waiting for Corbin and Walter to arrive.

After giving a quick kiss and hug to each of my kids, I ran over to the radio to inform Jack and Brooke that Corbin and I had arrived safely.

Unfortunately, Walter never checked in. He and Josie should have arrived at his cabin about two hours after Corbin and I did. Even with the heavy snowfall, Corbin did not seem concerned. Walter knew how to shelter in place to wait out the storm if needed. There was also a high possibility that he wasn't able to get a signal out due to the storm.

I was on edge the next two days, thinking up all of the worst case scenarios as to why Walter was not answering the radio. What if we'd been followed up the mountain? What if the ride made Josie's injuries worse and she was hurt more but there was no medical assistance? What if they had run out of gas and were stuck with no way up or down?

Corbin tried to calm my fears, but damn I did not like not knowing where Josie and Walter were.

Finally, Walter hailed through. He said they did not make it to his cabin the first night and had sheltered from the storm. Then they were able to journey the rest of the way on foot. Per Walter, the snowmobile was buried too deep to have dug it out by hand.

Walter also reported that Josie was grouchy and was being very vocal about 'insane mountain men'.

Later that afternoon, Brooke called over that Trenton

wanted to speak with Belle. I hadn't had a chance to say much to Trenton the day we brought them up the mountain but understood that Belle was his priority.

Belle used the HAM radio often and knew how to work it as well as any child did their parent's cellphone. She was also careful about what she said over the transmission. Generally, she used it to talk to Super Jack or to Gertie if we were spending a few days at Brooke's.

Sitting on her knees in Corbin's chair, she leaned over to key the microphone. "This is Omega-Delta-Four-Six-Two-Two-Tango calling Foxtrot-Niner-Niner-Charlie-Eight-Seven. Over."

"Lyd—Belle! Hi, sweetie. How are you?"

"You're supposed to say 'over', TT," Belle informed her brother with a giggle, using his nickname from when she'd been learning to talk. She had a hard time saying 'Trenton' and had ended up with a version of *Tat*, which had eventually been shortened to 'TT'. "Brooke, did you teach him *nothing*? Over."

Brooke's laughter came over the speaker, which was like music to my ears. *"I'm sorry, Belle. He was so excited to talk to you that I didn't get a chance. Over."*

Belle preened like a damn peacock at those words. She smiled over her shoulder at her adoring audience of her grammy, uncle, father, and brother—though the latter wasn't actually paying attention to her. Lucas was babbling to himself as he doodled at the coffee table. I had a placemat down so the crayon wax didn't ruin Corbin's custom built table, but Corbin always waved it off whenever the subject of 'child damage' came up.

Belle turned back to the microphone. "TT, are you okay? Daddy says you got hurt and that I have to be careful hugging you when I finally see you again. Over."

"I'm fine, sweet girl. Or I will be. I'll look a bit scary for a

little while, but I promise I'm still me." There was a pause before Trenton added, *"Over."*

"I'm glad you're okay. You're going to love it up here. I climb trees and hang out with Uncle Corbin in his shop. I even help him paint! I am learning about different plants and Grammy is teaching me to cook. My birthday's coming up! Last year, she made me a spaghetti cake. This year, I think I want a mashed potato cake with gravy icing. Over."

I looked at Gertie, who just shrugged. By Belle's birthday, we would be living at Brooke's, but that didn't mean we would not be celebrating with Gertie and Corbin too. I had no doubt that Belle would get her cake.

"That sounds... Um, delicious," Trenton stumbled. I could hear Brooke's muffled laughter in the background. *"I am looking forward to meeting your uncle and grammy. Will you tell me about them? Over."*

Trenton had briefly met Corbin the day he'd arrived in Whitefish and was likely trying to make conversation with his eight-year-old sister.

"Uncle Corbin is *huge!* He's the biggest giant there ever was! And Grammy is his mom but she's little. She helps me with my studies when Daddy's busy kissing Brooke."—I had just taken a sip of my coffee when Belle spoke and ended up choking on hot liquid and spurting some out my nose. It burned as I tried to catch my breath but Belle continued talking without even noticing.—"Uncle Corbin is teaching me to hunt too. I'm really good with a bow and arrow. He says I'm a natural. Over."

"That's great to hear, sweetheart. What about Lucas? How's he doing? Over." I could hear the humor in Trenton's voice too.

"He's getting big! He's able to run now and I'm helping to teach him his ABCs and his numbers. He doesn't really get it, but Daddy says he will. Do you want to say 'hi' to him? Over."

"I would love to. Over."

Belle hopped off the chair. She walked to Lucas and picked him up around his waist. He giggled and squirmed, but she held on. After helping Lucas onto the chair, she keyed the microphone again. "TT, say 'hi' to Lucas. Over."

"Hi, Lucas. Over."

Belle encouraged my son to talk into the microphone. Lucas put his mouth right up to the pop shield and said, "Hi!"

Belle was still holding the microphone key down as she said, "Lucas, you're talking to TT. He's our brother. Say 'hi, TT'."

Lucas spoke again, "Hi, TT!"

"Over," Belle added.

"It's so great to hear your voice, Lucas. I can't wait to meet you. Over."

Lucas nodded and said in the adorable way he does, "Yeah!" Then he scooted down and waggled his way back over to the coffee table.

Belle retook her seat. "He left. He's coloring. Over."

"Thank you for helping him, Belle. You're a great big sister. Over."

Belle puffed out her chest and said confidently, "I know," before continuing her conversation.

Chapter Thirty-Three

Brooke

It was finally moving day. The snow had finally relented enough for Corbin to hook a trailer up to the ATV and get it down to my cabin safely. A lot had happened in the five weeks since Josie and Trenton had come to the mountain.

Both were healing exceptionally well, considering. Trenton needed a lot of help with both hands injured. It had been awkward the first few days before the two of us had figured out a routine and how I could help Trenton while still offering him a sense of modesty and pride. Having to be fed like a baby was not exactly dignifying. Eventually, things got easier as Trenton got stronger and his hands healed up more. His right hand would remain casted for another couple of weeks, but he had been experimenting with removing the brace from his left for short periods of time.

Right after Josie and Trenton came up to the mountain, Jack had fallen sick with pneumonia. In all my time here and knowing Jack, I couldn't recall a time when he'd ever been sick. Thankfully, the town pitched in to help Jack as well as keep his store open. Even with the Mutineers he had planted all over, no one could do what Jack did with a computer. He tried to keep up, but his health had faltered and eventually Jack had to concede that he lost track of Gunther. The last anyone had seen of him, he was headed overseas to visit with Trenton's mother and his in-laws—though I couldn't imagine what sort of terms he was on with them.

That was about three weeks ago.

While Elijah did not blame Jack and expressed only for him to take his time to get himself healthy, I knew that he was worried. The times the weather had cleared enough for Elijah, Corbin, and/or Dalton to make it down so we could start working on the construction, I could tell from the bags under Elijah's eyes that he was not sleeping well. I wished that I could be there for him, to help soothe his fears, but he was not willing to be separated from his kids while Gunther's whereabouts were still unknown.

I wished Elijah would trust my mountain as I did. Even if by some fluke of a miracle Gunther did learn that Adam Greene and all three of his children were on this mountain, there was no way he could get to us. The roads were still not passable. Additionally, Owen and several other Mutineers were remaining in town to keep an eye on things while Jack was in the hospital.

Construction on my cabin was not completed. We still needed some supplies from town to finish. However, we were able to install a temporary wall against the loft's banister, move the couch from upstairs to down, take my bedroom door off that room and place it at the top of the stairs, and replace the kids' new room with a farmhouse dutch door. We had to install a real wall at the top of the stairs for the bedroom door, which is mainly what Corbin and Dalton had been doing while Elijah and I worked on getting my clothes and bedroom items organized.

Now that it was moving day, my queen bed would need to

be moved out first so the kids' bunk bed could be brought inside. Corbin had it in sections that he could install together once they were through the door frames. Since we did not have any kid-size mattresses yet, Belle and Lucas were going to be sleeping on camping pads and sleeping bags for a bit. I also had a tent in case they wanted to sleep in that rather than their bunkbeds.

With the dutch door, we didn't need a monitor system or baby locks throughout the cabin. Their bedroom would also be their playroom.

Elijah and I would be sleeping up in the loft or out in the living room until our king bed was ready. As long as we remembered to get dressed after any adult fun time, I was looking forward to many fire-lit nights with him on the living room floor.

Trenton would be going with Corbin when he left and moving into Elijah's old room. I heard the engines long before I saw them. I grabbed a shawl and walked out onto my covered porch in my wool socks to watch them approach. My heart was beating fiercely in my chest—but only in anticipation. Due to the nature of our relationship, the time separated, our time together, and the construction needed, I had spent a lot of hours contemplating if this was the right decision for me and for us as a family.

I knew it was. No hesitation. No second thoughts. I *wanted* a life here on this mountain with Elijah and his kids.

We never discussed marriage. If I was being honest, I wasn't sure I wanted to get married again. Marriage meant little in the long run. Vows could easily be broken with or without that piece of paper. What was the point? What I cared about was our relationship, our *partnership*. We were a team with or without a set of rings.

Calling Elijah 'my husband' was not a necessity on the mountain.

I didn't care about titles. Husband, boyfriend, lover, friend...

It didn't matter. At the end of the day, he was *mine*. That claim trumped all the rest.

Elijah drove a snowmobile. He had Lucas strapped to his chest and bundled up in his adorable snowsuit that made him look like a red miniature *Michelin Man*.

Belle was sitting behind Corbin on his ATV. The wheels on the trailer had been removed and replaced with skis.

Lucas had not been back to my cabin since last fall. The winter weather was not conducive for him to travel in. Belle, however, had recently started traveling down with Elijah or Corbin to 'help' with the construction. Mostly, though, she visited with her big brother. It was admirable to see the two of them together. Even though Trenton was sixteen years older than her, they had a great relationship.

Trenton hadn't seen Lucas since he was six months old. I stood back, not wanting to interfere as I watched how timid Lucas was with Trenton. It wasn't until Belle hugged Trenton that Lucas followed suit. Eventually, Lucas was letting Trenton pick him up or seat him on his lap.

It took some time to get the kids settled with Trenton and then to get all of the furniture moved around. Corbin and Elijah were working on getting the bunkbeds put together while I was making everyone lunch.

I couldn't place the sound at first. The way the mountain echoed the thunder almost made it sound like an avalanche, but I knew immediately that that couldn't be right. While avalanches were certainly a possibility, the likelihood of one happening this late in the year or starting at our elevation was slim.

As the noise got louder, my hackles started to rise. I had not gotten word of any missing hikers or tourists from the ski lodge. The local SAR team had a helicopter, but they had no reason to be bringing it so close to my cabin.

Snow tornados twirled outside my kitchen window the closer it got.

That was when I saw what looked like a special ops team propelling down. All dressed in black like this was some B-rated action movie. The fools were wearing black in a white terrain.

I moved out of pure instinct.

I leapt into my pantry where my guns were stored on the top shelf. I grabbed as many as I could while calling out for Corbin and Elijah. No doubt they had heard the propellers too. It was too loud to possibly miss.

Corbin appeared in the pantry doorway. He started collecting ammunition.

"The kids?" I demanded.

"Bedroom fireplace," Corbin answered shortly. His face was alight with a fury I had never seen before.

I had let the fire in my bedroom go out in anticipation of cleaning it before building a protector around it for the kids. The room would certainly be colder but the brick was the best place to protect the kids from bullets. I didn't exactly have Kevlar in my arsenal.

"Do we know how many?" Corbin asked.

"I counted at least half a dozen." I checked my long range rifle I used for large game.

We exited the pantry just as Elijah came bursting into the kitchen. "How did they find us?" he demanded. "Is there a possibility this is the police?"

Both Corbin and I shook our heads. "Police would announce themselves," I told him. "They have to."

"Owen or one of the others would have heard something on the police scanners and warned us," Corbin added.

Elijah accepted the gun from me. "So this is Gunther?"

"Without a doubt," I answered.

The two of us paused for a moment. There was so much I wanted to say to him, but I also knew we didn't have time.

Quickly, I leaned forward and pressed a kiss to his lips. "Stay safe."

"You too," he muttered.

"Brooke, take the loft." Corbin barked out orders. "Call the others. They might not get here in time, but they also might. Elijah, you're here in the kitchen. Take position in the pantry and guard that back door," he said pointing to it. "I've got the living room."

"Trenton's got the kids," Elijah said. I could hear the slight tremor in his voice, but also the determination. "He needs a gun too."

"I'll get it to him," Corbin said. "Get to your positions and call out if you need help. If we need to fall back, we fall back to the bedroom."

I gave Elijah one last look before I ran off to the loft. The large scenic windows were both an advantage and a disadvantage. I could see everything going on at the back of the cabin—including the half dozen men circling around back through the trees—but they also provided me with no cover.

Careful to not lose track of my guns or ammo, I rushed over to my desk. I keyed the microphone, "Foxtrot-Niner-Niner-Charlie-Eight-Seven SOS. Foxtrot-Niner-Niner-Charlie-Eight-Seven SOS. Helicopter, unknown number of tangos. The kids are here! I repeat, the kids are here!" I was just barely able to keep the panic out of my voice at the last statement.

The kids...

As the first bullets began to fly downstairs destroying the home I had so painstakingly built over the past decade, I knew none of it mattered. I knocked everything off of my desk and tipped it onto its side. Using it as a barrier, I lifted my rifle and took aim.

My cabin could fall to pieces. Every item and memento I owned could be destroyed and I wouldn't care. My only priority was protecting those kids.

I fired my first shot, knowing it was far from my last.

Chapter Thirty-Four

Elijah

What movies don't tell you is how loud gunfights are. There's very little that can be heard over the piercing echoes and the sounds of destruction. Glass shattered, wood splintered, metal groaned on top of the constant *pop, pop, pop* of the gunfire.

The bad part about the noise was that I couldn't easily call out to check on Corbin, Brooke, or to Trenton with my kids. There was no calling out for an ammo refill or to know if the scream I'd just heard was one of my people or one of theirs.

The overwhelming noise did help to hone my vision. Through all my shooting lessons Dalton, Corbin, and Brooke had put me through, I never got the tunnel vision they always talked about. I saw my target, but it wasn't all I saw.

It was all I saw now.

The back kitchen door came bursting open seconds after I heard gunfire coming from the living room and upstairs in the loft. It was completely and utterly terrifying to know that my best friend and the love of my life were both engaged in battle to protect me and my kids. However, the moment that door came crashing off of its hinges, it was like my eyes and ears created blinders. All I saw and heard were the men trying to enter the cabin.

I had the kitchen table tipped onto its side to help shield me as I crouched low against the pantry doorframe. I had three semi-automatic handguns with only one spare clip each. Brooke had seen a half-dozen coming off of the helicopter, but that didn't mean there weren't more. I had to be careful with my ammo.

Both men who entered were dressed in military fatigues and carrying automatic rifles. Unlike Brooke, I did not know the names of the different types of weapons, but they looked like what movies called an AK-47 with the long clips hanging down. They had on black boots and helmets.

I knew from Corbin's hunting lessons to aim for the arteries. Hitting the stomach was definitely easier, but it would not bring down a larger animal. With the men's armor, it was useless to aim for their torsos anyway. I didn't know a lot about guns but I knew I did not have armor-piercing bullets.

I was also not a good enough shot to aim for their head and hit my target without wasting bullets.

I went for their thighs and knees. As soon as I fired, the two of them scattered. My shot went wide and ended up hitting the metal of the stove. I ducked down as the table immediately took fire. I had no idea how long it would hold.

With the continuous array of bullets coming at me, I couldn't lift my head to shoot. I knew I could wait for them to reload, but that wouldn't stop them from approaching me and slaughtering me where I crouched.

I blindly lifted my gun over the top of the table and pulled the trigger. Their gunshots paused. I took a chance to peek around the side of the table.

One was down on a knee by the backdoor while the other was running for the living room.

I didn't hesitate. I stood, revealing myself as a target, and shot directly at the second man's back. Just as he fell, I felt a piercing pain in my left shoulder.

Crying out, I fell back down behind the table.

Fuck.

The realization that I had been shot, despite the last fifteen months of my life, was so heady that I felt dizzy.

However, I couldn't let it stop me. I had shot the one man, but I didn't know if he was dead or hurt or had only been knocked off balance by the bullet hitting his bulletproof vest. The one who had shot me wasn't injured.

A glance down at my shoulder showed a large red blotch but nothing to indicate how serious the injury was. Regardless, I had to keep fighting. I had to protect my kids.

With a show of force this large, was Gunther even trying to get his children back alive or had he sentenced all of us to death? Was Gunther even here? Or had he sent these men— paid mercenaries no doubt—to slaughter us all while he sat safe in a penthouse hotel room halfway around the world?

A glint of silver caught my eye and I noticed a kitchen knife on the floor of the pantry. I wondered if Brooke had been using it before the helicopter had alerted her to the mercenaries' inbound attack.

I knew I couldn't throw it with any sense of accuracy, but it might provide me with a distraction. I was still able to use my left arm—it just hurt like a bitch.

Hearing footsteps on the hardwood floor, I grabbed the knife, stood, and slammed it forward.

I honestly have no idea which one of us was more surprised when the blade pierced—me or the guy I had just stabbed in the throat. He garbled and spluttered blood out of his mouth before falling to his knees with the knife still embedded in his neck.

Movement out of the corner of my eye showed the man I

had shot in the back was trying to stand. I raised my gun and shot three more times at his back.

My heart was pounding, my entire arm was throbbing, but silence fell in the kitchen as I stared down at the two dead bodies. Brooke's table was completely ruined and her meticulously kept pantry was in ruins.

A child's scream broke through my haze. *Belle!*

I leapt over the kitchen table, sliding on the blood beneath my boots. I didn't know whose it was and I didn't care. I jumped over the two dead bodies of the men I had just killed and into the hallway.

The front door was littered with bullet holes and lay flat on the floor like it had been kicked inward.

Corbin was in a fist fight that looked far too choreographed to be real, and yet it was. My giant best friend was battling three mercenaries who had been stripped of their guns. The living room furniture was in disarray and various pieces. A body, presumably dead, was lying face down in the fireplace. Another was dangling halfway through the living room window. Based on the blood, he had been disemboweled by the jagged glass.

Corbin fought like a rabid berserker. As he spun around to grab hold of one man by the throat, I saw the hilt of a knife sticking out of his back. My eyes widened, but I couldn't stop to help him. I had to get to my kids!

I heard the continuous *pow, pow!* from the loft and at least had an auditory confirmation that Brooke was still alive.

Blood trailed down my left arm, dropping to the floor. I clutched my gun tightly in my right hand.

I skittered to a halt just inside the bedroom door.

The past and the present blurred in my mind's eye as I saw the man who fathered my daughter jump at my sudden presence. He slammed her up against his chest and put her gun to her head.

Belle's throat was held so tightly in his fist that she struggled to breathe. Tears streaked down her cheeks and filled her eyes. She was trying to stand as tall as she could on her tippy toes to get herself a little more oxygen.

Belle was tall for her age, lean, but she was still a child in a grown man's grip. Gunther's head, chest, and shoulders were completely exposed. I had a gun too. But I wasn't so good a shot that I could risk firing in my daughter's direction.

"Drop the gun, Adam."

I flinched at my former name. I didn't know why. It was just a name. It shouldn't affect me so badly. But I knew deep in my soul that I was no longer Adam Greene.

Adam Greene was a teacher, a plain man. Though he was not a coward, he was not strong.

I was strong now. I had muscles from working hard in my new mountain life. I had a son and a daughter who were my entire world. I had *Brooke*.

I was *not* Adam Greene. Adam Greene had run from a fight. I was no longer running.

As I tossed the gun onto the hardwood floor of what was supposed to be my kids' new bedroom, I saw Trenton curled in the corner of the room. He was balled into a fetal position with his back to me, wrapped entirely around something.

Then I realized... It wasn't something, but some*one*. Trenton was not moving and I could not see signs of life from him or my son in his arms.

Something shattered within me. A rage unlike anything I had ever felt before. My nose burned with unshed tears as my eyes lifted to the man who had fathered my three children. Because it didn't matter if Trenton was an adult. He was mine, *had been* mine, from the time I walked into his life when he was fifteen years old. I just hadn't known it until this moment.

And now he and my son were gone. It was obvious from

Trenton's position that he'd tried to shield Lucas. My boy. My precious, precious boy.

My *son*.

My sons.

Innocent. Both so innocent and too good for this world to take from me so cruelly.

I thought I hated Sebastian Gunther.

I had not known hatred until this very second.

Adam, Elijah, my name no longer mattered. I was Rage, I was Vengeance. This man had taken too much from me. I would not allow him to take my daughter too.

Gunther opened his mouth as if to give me another command, but I moved before he could. I leapt across the room like a rabid dog. No weapon, I used my fists to take the man down. Belle got knocked down in the struggle too, and some small part of me noticed that she managed to crawl away.

The gun went flying, skidding across the room.

My fists flew through the air like battering rams. I connected with any part of him that I could, though mostly his face. Gunther tried to bring his hands up to defend himself, but I straddled his chest and locked his arms under my knees.

I had never noticed before that Gunther and I were about the same height. He had always seemed so large to me. But that was his power, authority, and money. He had none of that now. At this very moment, he was nothing more than a man who had cost me nothing but pain, suffering, anxiety... And my sons.

He threatened my daughter.

He *hurt* Belle.

He took Lucas, my baby, from me.

He had robbed me of the chance to claim Trenton as my own.

I howled out my agony. I forgot what was happening outside this room. I forgot about my bullet wound, the pain of which was nothing compared to the anguish coursing through my heart at the loss of my sons.

I was more beast than man.

I was Vengeance.

Long after life left Sebastian Gunther's body, I continued to pelt him. His teeth cut my fists, his nose caved in, and his blood bathed my skin.

It did not even bring me comfort to know that Sebastian Gunther's last minutes on this earth were spent in pain.

Epilogue

Corbin

We had various graveyards spread throughout the mountain known only to those of us who lived upon it. These were not gravesites that were visited or well maintained. They were nothing more than locations to dump bodies of those who tried to harm those who we protected.

The fourteen mercenaries and Sebastian Gunther claimed such graves.

By the time the others had arrived, the battle had been over. Beyond scrapes and bruises, I had a knife wound in my back. In fact, I literally had a *knife* in my back until Brooke had removed it for me. Her face was cut up pretty good from her glass window exploding too close to her. Thankfully none of the glass got in her eyes, though she did have a good piece embedded in her cheek. I got it out for her using a pair of tweezers.

Elijah was... Well, it was difficult to determine his injuries at first. Then again, not all wounds were physical.

Dalton and Tommy arrived long before Walter and Josie did. Despite still healing from her injuries, Josie insisted on coming down with Walter. We were all shocked at Tommy's appearance, but the man just stood there with a scowl and his shotgun muttering about Brooke's SOS saying the kids were in danger. I always knew the old coot had a soft heart. Not that he would ever admit it.

Other than some bruising to her neck, Belle was fine. None of the blood splatter on her had been hers. Brooke tried to shield Belle's eyes as much as possible through the living room to get her out of the cabin.

I had to physically drag Elijah off of Gunther's mangled corpse. In fact, none of us even knew it was Gunther until Belle had said something. Elijah had been so enraged that he'd kicked and hit at me to continue getting at the body on the bedroom floor. I passed Elijah off to Brooke to help calm him down.

Then I had to check the bodies of Trenton and little Lucas.

There wasn't much in this world that made me cry. My father had beaten that ability out of me a long time ago—or so I thought. As I knelt down by those two unmoving forms, tears had flowed freely down into my unkempt beard.

I didn't know Trenton well, but he'd seemed like a good kid. But Lucas? My little buddy and nephew? I couldn't imagine a world without him in it. What was I going to tell my mother, who loved him like a grandson?

Slowly, I reached for Trenton. He had such a tight hold on Lucas's little form that they both rolled together as I placed Trenton onto his back. I saw then the blood that coated the side of Trenton's face that had been pressed into the floor. So much blood...

And Lucas. He could have been sleeping, he looked so peaceful.

Tears fogged my vision so much that it took me far too long to realize that Trenton's chest was moving up and down. It wasn't much, but it was there! I quickly moved into action.

Careful of his cast and splint, I pried Trenton's hands off of

Lucas. Praying more than I ever had in my life, I checked my nephew over. He was so still, I still feared the worst, but then I felt his pulse and was able to catch his shallow breath. He was *alive!* I didn't know why he wasn't waking but he was fucking alive!

I shouted out for Elijah and Brooke to come back. They came running in. It looked like Brooke had been trying to wash the blood off of Elijah's face and hands. The crimson splatters now looked like warrior paint smeared across his face.

"He's alive!"

For a moment, I thought Elijah was going to faint.

Brooke rushed forward before Elijah could, which was probably a good idea given the amount of blood still on my best friend. "What's wrong with him?"

"I don't know, but we need to get them to a doctor!" As soon as Brooke had Lucas, I turned my attention to Trenton. "It looks like he was shot in the temple. I don't think the bullet went in though. I don't see an entry wound."

"He must have taken a bullet to the head and went down on top of Lucas," Brooke supplied. "Lucas might have hit his head from the fall."

Even after taking a bullet to the temple, Trenton had somehow kept his grip on Lucas. I couldn't imagine how.

Knowing we needed a doctor but also knowing we couldn't get down the mountain fast enough, our options looked limited. Until Dalton fired up the helicopter now abandoned on the front of Brooke's lawn. It seemed our only option to get down as fast as we needed.

Walter offered to take Belle up to my cabin and my mom, but Belle threw a fit and demanded to come with us. It was a good thing the helicopter was so massive. I didn't know a lot about helicopters or their capacities, but this one had carried the fourteen men plus Gunther up into the mountains.

Which was how we ended up leaving Brooke's broken cabin and the massacred mercenaries for Tommy, Josie, and Walter to deal with as we flew down into town. I knew Dalton didn't come down off of the mountain often, so this was a huge sacrifice on his part.

Brooke and Elijah kept hold of Lucas, continuing to try and wake him, while I was applying pressure to Trenton's head wound. I knew head wounds tended to bleed a lot but damn the kid had lost a lot of blood.

Arriving at the hospital and dealing with all of the people there was nearly too much for me, but I gritted it out to stay with Trenton so Elijah and Brooke could remain with Lucas. Dalton had dropped us off and then immediately flew away. I had no idea what he was planning on doing with the helicopter. Though there was a good chance Dalton was claiming it as the spoils of war.

Even with how often I went to town to drop off my furniture to Jack to sell, I still wasn't used to *people*. I was a big guy with unkempt hair and a perpetual scowl when not around my family. People didn't approach me or talk to me unless they had to. I was fine with that. But now I had to talk to people, the nurses and doctors, and I was not okay with it.

Trenton had been taken back for tests. I had no idea what to say if or when the police showed up. I didn't have a good history with police. Not a single one of them that had handled my arrest stopped to ask if my father deserved his death. No one had looked at my malnourished body and had asked if I'd even eaten that day. None had looked at my bruised and battered mother and wondered if she had older injuries hidden beneath the new ones.

I wanted to leave before the cops came to investigate, but Dalton had already left and I didn't know where Elijah or Brooke were.

Thank God Jack showed up. He looked awful, but I was glad to see him.

"How did they find us?" I asked him.

"Dr. Souleiman was attacked in her home two nights ago. I can only assume she overheard something of use from when Owen brought Trenton and Josie there for treatment. I'm not sure how they located Dr. Souleiman." He coughed, working to catch his breath. Walking pneumonia was no joke. "We might never know now that Gunther is dead."

"Good riddance," I muttered.

"You'll find no argument with me. Any news on Lucas?"

I shook my head. "They're in with the doctor now." I wiped a blood crusted hand down my face. "Christ, Jack, we were supposed to protect them. What if Lucas doesn't make it? What if Trenton has brain damage?"

"Speculating does no one any good." Jack indicated towards the men's room across the way. "Go get cleaned up. I'll wait for the doctors."

Epilogue

Elijah

Five Years Later

They say as you get older, all you think about are the regrets you have in life. I have regrets. Some major ones. But I will *never* regret accepting a job from a billionaire to tutor his son nor will I *ever* regret turning right at a fork in the road on a snowy mountain.

As I stood at the altar looking around at the friends and family, both new and old, gathered to celebrate this special day, I can only see the good things.

My children, for instance. Belle, who was now fourteen years old, was becoming so much like her Uncle Corbin that she'd even started to curse like him. On her lap was Lucas, who was now almost seven. Though it had been a long and arduous journey to get us to where we are, Lucas was determined to not allow his epileptic diagnosis slow him down. It was something he would be living with for the remainder of his life. Chase, his service Chocolate Lab, sat at attention next to my little family. Beast, Belle's fully trained-protection Belgian Malinois, sat on the other side.

Corbin and Gertie were two others in my life I was eternally grateful for. Corbin had his arm around his woman with their young son on his lap. Their daughter sat next to her grammy in a beautiful, pastel pink-lace dress.

Jack sat on the other side of Gertie. He was another presence I would forever be grateful to in my life. From that first phone call when he'd calmly talked me through what to do to get my kids and me to the mountain, to getting all of the charges against me dropped, to taking me under his wing and making me an official Mountain Mutineer... Jack had been there. My first assignment had been one I shared with Brooke, taking in a young, battered mother and her baby. We were never told details as to who they were or why Jack was aiding them. We did happen to know that the woman and her son were special to Owen, so we were surprised when the woman decided to leave the mountain after two years to go live in a small town in Pennsylvania.

Most of our cases ended up keeping us on the mountain, though we accepted the occasional one if we were traveling to visit my parents or when Trenton had been in rehab.

Next to me at the altar was Trenton. Though he did not call me 'Dad', I had taken on that role for him. Especially during *his* recovery. The damage done by the bullet was irreversible, but it was so much better than death. I was constantly reminding him that I would rather have to help him every day to the bathroom for the rest of our lives than bury him in a cold grave.

The brain damage Trenton had endured resulted in a speech impediment and he temporarily lost the use of the entire left side of his body. He couldn't even blink for a time and had to rely on manual eyedrops to keep his eyeball moist. He had to learn everything over again, from speech to walking to eating to going to the bathroom.

During this time, Trenton had signed everything over to me.

With his father gone, everything belonged to him. I had accepted becoming his medical power of attorney but refused to accept financial responsibility for all of his inherited assets. Trenton had not lost the ability to write and had transcribed an argument that he wanted to make sure Belle and Lucas were taken care of if he did not make it. I had reluctantly accepted.

Since then, trusts had been set up for Lucas and Belle to receive when they turn eighteen and again at twenty-five. It was enough to set both of them up for life.

Trenton had insisted on building Brooke and me a new cabin. The old one had been torn down, completely in ruins after the gunfight. The new cabin had four bedrooms and three full baths. Along with a massive kitchen, pantry, and met all of Brooke's requirements for her stores and utilities.

Trenton had fought long and hard to regain his independence and strength back. He still walked with a brace on his right leg and a cane, but that was beyond amazing progress. One doctor had told Trenton he would never walk again. Trenton had shown him, and the world, just how strong he truly was.

Though certain details were fabricated, we had controlled the narrative of what the world knew about Sebastian Gunther's death and the attack on his own children. Thankfully, Trenton had had the funds to hire private security as well as go to the best rehab facilities that would keep the public eye off of him during his recovery.

The music started up and I couldn't help the smile that crossed my face at the sight of Brooke walking down the aisle toward us. She wore boots, jeans, and a flannel top. My mountain woman, true to form.

Her long blonde braid now had some gray hairs in it. The bouquet of flowers she held were handpicked from our own land. She was just as beautiful as the day we'd met over six years ago. Just like then, she lit up my world and added so much fire to my blood I was surprised I didn't start self-combusting.

Brooke finally reached me at the end of the aisle. I offered her my arm, which she accepted with a smile. Not wanting to steal the spotlight, I gently kissed her on the cheek before leading her off to the side.

Then we stood back and watched as Trenton's future bride walked down the aisle on the arm of her disapproving, but thankfully silent, father.

As Brooke had once said, our lives on the mountain might not be conventional, but they were our own. We were safe, free, and most importantly, together.

I had found my refuge.

More Books by Elise

Books in the VDMC Series

1. Lucky
2. Bear
3. Bulldog
4. Jumper
5. Angel
6. Demo (January 10, 2025)

VDMC Novellas

- Carlos-Part 1
- Carlos-Part 2
- Carlos-Part 3
- Scotty's Halloween Adventure
- A VDMC Holiday Special (Release Date: December 1, 2024)

Books in Mountain Mutineers Series

1. Mountain Refuge
2. Mountain Revenge (2025)